M000036378

STEPHEN RUSSELL

CONTROL GROUP

A COOPER McKAY NOVEL

VISIT STEPHEN ONLINE

Website: www.AuthorStephenRussell.com
Facebook: http://www.facebook.com/stephen.russell.5855
Twitter: https://twitter.com/RussellAuthor

BOOKS BY STEPHEN RUSSELL
Blood Money
Command and Control
Control Group

Copyright ©2017 by Stephen Russell
Published in the United States by Blue Jay Media Group
Print ISBN-13: 978-1-936724-39-0
ebook ISBN-13: 978-1-936724-48-2

All rights reserved. No portion of this book, whether in print or electronic format, may be duplicated or transmitted without written permission of the publisher, except where permitted by law.

This is a work of fiction. Names, characters, businesses, places, events and incidents are either the products of the author's imagination or used in a fictitious manner. Any resemblance to actual persons, living or dead, or actual events is purely coincidental.

ACKNOWLEDGEMENTS

*L*et's start by acknowledging that kids have many talents. Intelligence. Charm. Creativity. Even larceny.

Of course, the fun of parenting is to see how those talents emerge. Like many parents, we watched our newborns sleep even when we should have been napping. Pretty soon, their cuteness crept into our conversations. Their altered sleep patterns became our own. In those early days of parenthood, *Control Group* occupied my time when sleep eluded me.

The idea emerged one crisp Labor Day weekend when visiting grandparents. While shouldering diapers bags and expectations, I realized I could spend my dawns daydreaming, writing as I waited for either her first cries or my alarm. Early drafts lacked imagination and fluency, clearly drenched in fatigue. Subsequent drafts required merciless massacres of characters and scenes. A team of specialists at the Santa Barbara Writers Conference identified issues and suggested solutions. Without the faith of the publishing team at Blue Jay, the story would have remained a daydream. The incomparable Jean Jenkins provided polish to help it shine. Copy editors Carolyn Neiman and Marla Cain saved me from dozens of mistakes destined to stop the story. And Gretel…there the whole way.

It's been twelve years since those daydreams morphed into drafts. One baby became four. And each one has contributed, one nap at a time, into stories. Now, I can add one more talent to the list of those lovable larcenists: a gift for stealing hearts.

For Molly, Denton, Ashby and Caroline

While you were sleeping…

CHAPTER ONE

Spring 1993

ON A SUNNY Saturday afternoon in Maryland, Dolores Gonzales didn't expect to go to the National Institutes of Health to die, and Dr. Scott Hoffman didn't know that he would kill her. He waited in his office, tapping his foot to the island music in his head while he scanned her chart. His mind wandered from the drug study to thoughts of retirement.

One last clinical trial.

One final weekend of work.

Hoffman picked up his dictaphone to complete the final entry for her chart. "This next dictation is for study subject number one-three-six-two. Name is Dolores Gonzales. She is a forty-two-year old, Hispanic female here for the final safety evaluation. Ms. Gonzales began the trial nine months ago, and presently she is..."

A loud metallic crash interrupted Hoffman, followed by the thud of footsteps racing down the hall. He straightened. His office door slammed open against the wall. Framed diplomas rattled.

"Jesus, Jason! What the hell's going on out there?"

The tall research assistant stumbled in, shirt untucked, dark-rimmed glasses askew. Jason gripped the door frame for balance. "Dr. Hoffman, I need you. Ms. Gonzales can't breathe."

Hoffman grabbed his lab coat from the back of his chair. "She was fine last week."

He stepped into the hallway and froze.

Dolores Gonzales leaned against the wall, gasping for breath. This could not be the same woman he had seen only one week ago. Sweat glistened on her bloated face. Hoffman heard her drowning in her own phlegm. When she looked at him, he saw terror in her eyes. She crumpled to the floor.

Hoffman kneeled beside her to find her pulse. "Hold still, Ms. Gonzales. We'll take care of you." He glanced up at Jason. "Grab the crash cart. Now!"

In the brief time it took for the research assistant to return with the resuscitation equipment, Dolores Gonzales' heart slowed. The frantic pounding of her carotid pulse eased to an irregular tap against Hoffman's fingers. He attempted chest compressions, but his hands slipped on her sweaty body, causing him to put pressure on her stomach. Frothy sputum splattered his cheeks.

"Call a code!" Hoffman yelled.

He grabbed a central line kit from the crash cart. Swiping an alcohol pad over her chest, he plunged a needle in. Purple blood dribbled onto the floor, a visible reminder that her heart possessed neither the oxygen nor the intensity to keep her alive. Hoffman threaded the guide-wire through the needle and slipped the long IV cannula over it. He pushed a syringe full of epinephrine into the IV and then resumed chest compressions.

What would happen if the FDA found out she died while taking the study drug?

As Hoffman worked, the code team, an army of blue scrubs and stethoscopes, raced toward him. He pumped harder on her chest. Red secretions gurgled up from her lungs, indelibly staining his white coat.

Oh, my God, he thought. What have I done?

Six hours later, with unprecedented cooperation from the coroner, Hoffman stood over his dead patient. The scent of death and formaldehyde permeated the room. He usually let others oversee autopsies. Tonight, he forced himself to get involved. Too much was at stake.

He locked his knees and concentrated on the open abdomen that glistened before him. Anything to avoid the face of the deceased woman. Sweat soaked his scrubs. His face mask pressed against his goatee. The spotlight above the metal table warmed his shaved scalp as it illuminated the body in front of him. Hoffman placed a gloved hand on the table but avoided touching the corpse.

"Would you look at that?" The pathologist looked up from across the table. Chest hair sprouted over the top of his scrubs like grass around a sidewalk and spread up his neck. The surgical mask muffled his voice when he spoke. "Something destroyed her liver. Check out all these divots and pits." He pointed to a purple mass of flesh that looked more like a sea sponge than a smooth organ.

Hoffman nodded. "What do you think that's from?"

"Any number of things. You say she's a diabetic?"

"For years."

"We don't see this kind of destruction from diabetes. Look at her, though." He slapped the side of the body, shaking the corpse. "A woman this fat is going to have fat in her liver, too, but this looks drug-induced. Remind me what meds she was taking?"

Hoffman carefully chose his words. "She was on insulin for a long time…"

"That wouldn't do it."

"And on some oral meds recently for diabetes." He became dizzy, and gripped the table for support.

"Careful. I don't want you puking all over my morgue. If you want to sit down or pull up a chair, that's okay with me."

"I'm fine."

"Suit yourself." The pathologist pointed to another area on the mangled liver. "It's supposed to be smooth and shiny, but all this blood indicates ongoing hemorrhage. There's blood pooled in the abdominal cavity, too. That's unexpected."

Hoffman nodded. To get the results he wanted, he needed to stay engaged. And focused.

"Which group was she in?"

"Excuse me?"

"Was she in your study-drug group or the control group?"

"Control group," Hoffman lied. "I checked before I came down here."

The pathologist shook his head. "You don't see this from a sugar pill, I can tell you that."

Hoffman straightened, emboldened by his lie. "Her chart said she'd been taking other prescription meds outside of the study protocol."

"Like what?"

"Pain meds. Aspirin. Surely that contributes to what we're seeing."

The pathologist nodded. "Could be, but it'll be weeks before the toxicology report comes back." He removed additional slices of the liver and placed them in a specimen tray. "I'm just about done down here. You want to stay while I examine her brain?"

Hoffman felt his insides lurch. "No, thanks. I've seen all I need in order to finish my report. I'm heading back to the office to update her family."

When he reached his office, Hoffman saw a janitor cleaning the hallway. The crash cart rested against the wall and the floor sparkled under the mop. As far as he could tell, no evidence remained of the afternoon's grisly events.

He walked into his office and closed the door. The stench of the morgue lingered on his hands. Hoffman glanced at the rows of charts lining the floor and at the small stack of manila folders on his desk. We should have finished by Monday, he thought. Hundreds of patients had sailed through the trial without any problems. Now this. There was still a chance that her death had come from something else. As long as the pathologist believed her to be a member of the control group, the autopsy report shouldn't implicate the study drug.

Hoffman sat down at his desk in front of the open chart of Dolores Gonzales. Calling her family would have to wait. First, he would complete her chart. He pressed the *rewind* button on the dictaphone. "This next dictation is for study subject number one-three-six-two. Name is Dolores Gonzales. She is a forty-two year old female enrolled in the phase three study..."

He stopped the tape. Hoffman massaged his temples.

This was the right thing to do, he told himself. The medicine had potential. Thousands of patients would benefit from the drug. He enjoyed an impeccable record as an NIH researcher, which was why the company had hired him to steer this drug through its clinical trials. He tried not to think about his six-figure payoff once the drug received FDA approval.

He pressed *record*. "The patient missed her last appointment, and she has been lost to follow-up."

*C*HAPTER TWO

Present Day

*D*R. COOPER "MACKIE" McKay's blood swirled in the sink basin outside the operating room. Antiseptic sizzled the wound. Outsized pain for a cut so small. He knew he had nothing to fear from a surgical breach. Not with this patient. But he dared not forget what he'd seen last year. He knew what could happen with a sliced glove. He washed again.

The hallway door behind him burst open for the second time. "Doctor McKay?"

"Ma'am?"

"That man is still standing outside the O.R."

"And I'm still standing in it. He can wait."

His nurse, Joyce, persisted. "He said it's important."

"Always is."

"I'll tell him, but he's not gonna like it." She returned to the hallway.

Warm water cascaded over Mackie's wound. He squinted through the observation glass at his case. His orthopedic resident, blue head bowed in concentration, plunged her hands into the surgical field. Lights winked off metal retractors. Mackie knew she could finish the case. She was almost as good at her level of training as he had been at a similar age.

Almost. Back before family and circumstances pulled him in a different direction. Before for better became or worse.

The door behind him opened. A shadow shifted. Footsteps approached.

"Joyce, I've already told you—"

A man's voice interrupted him. "Good to be back at work?"

Mackie's hands jerked for the second time that morning. Damn that unmistakable voice. Mackie bumped the faucet off with his leg. With sterile fingers, he groped for a towel. A trail of water dripped from the elbows of his gown. He turned.

A suited man gave Dr. McKay a tight grin. He extended his FBI badge. Same red hair. Same young features, even on a fifty-something's face. "Special Agent Brian Aiken."

Mackie didn't bother to look at the ID. He knew him well enough. He also knew he owed nothing to the FBI. They'd gotten what they wanted from him two decades ago. "You didn't honestly think I'd forget you?"

"Some people do."

"That was in ninety-three."

"Not that long ago for an old man like me."

Which makes me even older. With raised hands still dripping, Mackie made no effort to greet the FBI agent. "I'm in the middle of a case."

Aiken stuffed his identification inside his suit jacket. "This won't take long. We need your help."

"Not sure how a teaching surgeon fresh off retirement can help the FBI."

Aiken relaxed his smile. "Don't sell yourself short, doc. From what I've read, you've helped in quite a few criminal cases recently. First with the Nashville Police Department. Then with the Centers for Disease Control at Fort Detrick."

Mackie glanced back into the operating room. Bent blue heads continued their work. "I was in the wrong place at the right time."

Aiken pressed on. "A lot has changed since then, doc. Medicare is a cash cow for doctors and hospitals now. You've seen it. The cost of the hip replacement you're performing this morning could purchase a high-end sports car with money left over."

"This is not news, Agent Aiken. And frankly, not your concern."

"It is when doctors bilk Medicare for millions."

"Are you suggesting—"

Aiken held up his palms and retreated back a step. "Easy, doc. No one's blaming you. But you are in a unique position to help us."

"Because of what I do?"

"Actually," Aiken said, "because of what you've done."

Mackie tossed the towel in the sink. The white edges of the wound on his finger curled back. He'd have the scrub nurse tape it before he gloved up. He stepped toward the operating room. The door opened when he backed into it. "I've retired from that line of work, Special Agent Aiken. Thanks anyway."

Even as the door closed, he saw Aiken holding a thin envelope. "Call me if you change your—"

The door swung shut.

* * *

Three hours later, Mackie finished his case. He slumped in his office chair, cradling his head. He glanced again at his desk. The open envelope still stared up at him. Mocked him. Why couldn't the FBI leave him alone? For more than twenty years he'd hardly thought about it. Now this afternoon, the memories wouldn't stop.

The promising drug. The tainted trials. The dead patients.

Mackie fingered the edge of the obituary Special Agent Aiken had left. The actual clipping looked fresh, as if it were from yesterday's paper. The date on the page told a different story. He re-read it. He remembered Bill Baldwin, of course. Anyone who followed politics could tell you something about the famous reporter. He wondered if Baldwin would have remembered him, though. Judging by the other contents of the envelope, Mackie guessed the answer would have been yes.

Beneath the clipping, Mackie lifted the floppy disc. A misnomer for the firm plastic square, he thought. And a relic. It deserved an obituary of its own. Buried by Wi-Fi and flash drives. His current lap top didn't even have a slot for a CD, much less a diskette. How long had the FBI had this? And what information was still on it? If it was the same disk he had given Aiken back then, Mackie had nothing to worry about. But if it was the disk Mackie had left for Bill Baldwin on that frigid winter morning in D.C., Mackie had more problems than a chance encounter with an old acquaintance. Many more.

He flipped the disk over and tried to remember...

*C*HAPTER THREE

Spring 1993

*D*R. COOPER MCKAY sat on the edge of the hotel bed, trying to avoid an argument. He picked at the frayed hem on the jacket of his only suit. If he studied a rogue thread on the sleeve, he wouldn't have to make eye contact with her when she stormed out of the bathroom.

Too much was at stake to leave the room in a bad mood. Billion dollar drugs. Boundless potential. And a new beginning. At least for him. Whether she would sign on was another matter. He turned toward the bathroom when he heard the shower turn off.

"Dinner's at seven," he called.

Sarah Collins-McKay opened the bathroom door, speaking out of the steam. "Don't rush me, Mackie."

He chewed on the inside of his lip and began to lace his shoes. Friends told him to be patient. She would thaw. The death of a child did crazy things to people. Crazy things to couples, too. After a year of mourning, though, Mackie needed a change.

Not that he would ever forget his three year old son. He'd suffered through the first Father's Day without him.

Through his birthday. Through expected milestones of grief, but the pain still stabbed at him in unexpected ways. Certain commercials did it. And songs. Once, halfway through a knee replacement surgery, he broke scrub and stepped out of the operating room, leaving the circulating nurse scrambling to find one of Mackie's partners to finish the case. That's when his chief of surgery had first mentioned the term: *sabbatical*.

Sarah emerged from the bathroom wrapped in a towel and wearing a scowl. "Here's what I don't get. BioloGen Pharmaceuticals is looking to take this new drug to market next year, and they're filling a marketing position with a burned-out orthopedic surgeon?"

Mackie refused to take the bait. "Hell of a gamble, huh?"

"For us or them?"

Mackie exhaled through pursed lips, trying to be patient. He stood and placed his palm on the damp towel around her back. A gentle peace offering. Sarah shrugged his hand away, brushing past him toward the closet. Mackie wiped his palm on his slacks, then stepped in front of the foggy mirror to knot his tie.

"If there had been a drug like Anginex two years ago..." He paused. Adjusted his tie several different ways before ripping out the knot and starting over. "We've been through this, Sarah."

She pinched herself into the closet, shielding her body from him as she dressed. Her voice sounded muffled against the hanging clothes, but her tone was unmistakable. "So you're willing to disrupt life for the one-year-old daughter you already have so that you can honor the son you can't bring back?"

"Sarah, please."

"Please, what? Please don't make you examine your impulsive desire to take a year off from medicine? Please don't ask you to consider not moving to a new city while you work out your grief? Please, what, Mackie? Help me understand what we're doing in Cincinnati, Ohio in the first place."

Mackie held back. They'd been through this circular argument before. Countless times over the last few months. Nothing he'd said so far could make her understand his reaction to their shared sadness. God knows he'd tried wrapping his words in cotton to blunt the sharp edges of her grief. Just for today, though, he wanted to think about himself. Wanted to pour himself into this job interview without having to soothe her anger. Wanted to try and break free from death's undertow that threatened to drown them both.

His tie looked crooked, even when he loosened the knot. He swabbed the mirror with a towel but it didn't help. He jerked the tie free once more and turned to his wife. "It's a mid-level marketing position for a breakthrough cancer drug that might, if handled properly, keep one more family from going through the same shit we've experienced this past year. Can't you see the sense in that?"

He faced the mirror once again and in his anger threw a perfect Windsor knot before he even knew he had done it. Muscle memory. The same kind of repetitive excellence he had called upon for three years in the OR before his concentration and confidence had shattered last year. Would a year away from his chosen profession bring back those skills? His chief of surgery thought so. At this point, Mackie wasn't so sure. He stole a look at his watch. "Tom's meeting us downstairs now."

Clothed but still turned away, Sarah responded, "Dinner's not for another hour. Call me when you're done with cocktails."

Mackie reached for his jacket on the bed, frayed sleeves and all, and walked out.

* * *

Tom Phillips sat at the hotel bar with his tie loosened, face glistening with sweat. He picked at the bowl of mixed nuts, not really enjoying them but not letting them go to waste.

Condensation trickled down the side of his beer mug. He didn't seem to hear Mackie until he sat down next to him. Tom glanced at his old friend. "You're here doing what?" he asked, dispensing with all the small talk.

"I'm interviewing with BioloGen Pharmaceuticals tomorrow." Mackie ordered a draft and pulled his stool up to the bar.

"That's the NuCor company, right?"

Mackie took a long pull from his beer. "Among others. Orthopods don't prescribe that kind of medicine much."

"Right. You push pain pills."

"It hurts to have surgery on your bones."

Tom smiled. "NuCor's the next best thing in cholesterol management. I probably write a scrip a dozen times a week or more." He picked through the nuts in the bowl before finding an almond. "So this is a temporary assignment for you?"

"Sabbatical."

Tom took a sip of beer, not responding.

"I thought you'd know all about BioloGen," Mackie said, "since it's a family-owned Cincinnati company."

"You sound like a walking advertisement for them."

"I read the packet they mailed me. Don't their drug reps call on the doctors at University?"

"I only know one guy at the company. Not a rep, though," Tom said. "A researcher named Douglas Schofield."

"Name's familiar. I think he's driving me to the office tomorrow for the interview."

"Big guy with a big mouth from west Texas. He's an engineer of some type for them. I know their cholesterol drug makes almost a billion dollars a year." Tom finished his drink and set aside the glass. "I think you're probably making a big mistake by being here."

Mackie nodded. He had come for due diligence, not defense of his decision. "It's a one year assignment with an option for more. I think I told you about an idea for a blood substitute I'm working on. Could be the next best thing in surgery some day. Getting a pharmaceutical perspective could only benefit that project."

"I know you, Mackie. That's not the only reason."

Mackie took another pull of his beer. He squinted back a tear that stung the corner of his eye. Another pull. "I needed to step away from medicine for a while. Clear my head." He stared at the muted television over the bar as he spoke. "After Grant's death last year, I haven't been able to get back on track. I think this'll help."

"I can't begin to imagine what it must feel like to lose your three-year-old to leukemia," Tom said. "But do you really think going to work for a pharmaceutical company will ease the pain?"

"They're working on a cancer drug," Mackie said, grateful to shift the focus to the future. Had Sarah been present, she would have taken Tom's position. "I think this is the right choice."

"Do think you'll go back to Orthopedics after this?"

"God willing." He took one last pull of his beer, emptying it.

Tom made eye contact with the bartender, motioning for the check. "Watch your back, Mackie. From what I've seen, that company's too slick for its own good."

CHAPTER FOUR

SCOTT HOFFMAN'S PHONE echoed off the hardwoods of his suburban townhouse. At first it seemed a part of his dreams, distant and purposeless. Subsequent rings, though, startled him awake. He rubbed his eyes and blinked twice. Bed still made. Shoes still on. His crumpled slacks and untucked shirt reminded him of the day's events.

In the moments it took him to become oriented, a dull dread spread through him as he recalled the disaster at his office. So who the hell was calling now? His secretary usually had the courtesy to leave him alone after sunset. The digital clock cast a red glow on the phone. 9:34 p.m.

Still supine, he reached for the phone, clearing his throat and coughing away the fatigue. "Hello?"

"Good evening, Dr. Hoffman. Good of you to take my call."

Hoffman scratched the stubble of his chin. He knew that voice.

"We have one final drug trial we need help with," said the man he'd never met but knew all too well.

"No," Hoffman almost whispered as he sat up. "No more. You said Hepatazyme would be the last one, and we finished today. That was our deal."

Although he had yet to meet the person on the other end

of the line, Hoffman knew his voice represented trouble. The man had sounded soothing, like an avuncular priest at confession, when they'd first spoken several years ago. But Hoffman now knew better.

The man ignored him. "We need your help."

Hoffman braced himself on the side of the bed. "I put my reputation on the line during this last trial," he said through clenched teeth. "Once the FDA approves Hepatazyme, I'm done. That was our deal."

"And you'll get your money."

He bit back a further response. The less this man knew about the afternoon's events, the better.

"Don't worry about the FDA, Doctor. We can handle that end, and this next assignment is worth your while. I left instructions for you at the post office. Call once you've read them."

The line went dead.

Hoffman knew better than to climb back in bed.

Ten minutes later, he guided his red Ford Probe out of the driveway and headed south on the Capitol Beltway. He glanced at the empty street in the rearview mirror. This was ridiculous, he thought.

A flash of lightning illuminated the sleeping neighborhood. As he drove the deserted, rain-wet streets, he recalled his early days as a consultant for Big Pharma. Five thousand dollars for a company-sponsored lecture. Double that for publishing favorable editorials about a company's drug. Being a respected governmental researcher had benefits. Academic perks, Hoffman joked to colleagues, but he firmly believed he'd earned the right to take advantage of them. Besides, if he'd turned down those offers, someone else with less clout would have taken the jobs.

And the money.

He glanced at his watch. 10:21 p.m.

Hoffman pulled into the post office parking lot. He studied the building. Lights on. Lobby empty. A row of deserted mail trucks crowded the loading dock. He checked the rearview mirror then glanced over his shoulder. A single street lamp illuminated the parking lot. Satisfied that he was alone, he ran through the rain and into the building.

His shoes squeaked as he walked toward his corner mailbox and removed a thin manila envelope. No return address. No stamp. Hoffman unsealed it to find a single sheet of paper inside. He flipped the page. Nothing but a phone number followed by a one sentence instruction: Go outside and call me back.

Hoffman nervously looked behind him. He saw no one. Examining the envelope and the sheet of paper, he noticed no other instructions or identifying marks. He looked through the lobby window, spotting a pay phone beneath the hazy light of the lone lamppost.

"Damn it!" Hoffman headed back out into the rain.

He shuddered as rain soaked his back. He shoved a quarter into the phone and dialed the number. The handset smelled like an ashtray and wet plastic stuck to his ear. The cost of caution, he thought, even as he doubted anyone would trace a call on his home phone. Rain cascaded down his body, trickling its way into his socks.

The anonymous man answered on the first ring. "You'll be working with a drug that's been found to have some unexpected side effects." The man spoke as if the last hour had been a brief pause in the conversation.

"You could have told me that when you called earlier." Hoffman squinted through the rain. "Where are you?"

"You will erase any mention of those side effects from the medical record. Once you access the NIH database, you can make specific changes—"

"Bullshit!" Hoffman's rain-soaked pants added to his foul

mood. "You call me late at night, send me on some damn scavenger hunt across town, and now you expect me to break into an electronic medical record with iron-clad security?" He paused to steady his resolve. "Forget it."

"What would the Gonzales family think about this afternoon's events?"

Hoffman nearly dropped the phone. How could he know?

"Your cooperation is expected. Soon, another envelope will be in your post office box. It will contain the names of several people enrolled in the study. You will access their records in the database and delete the listed side effects. Specifically you're looking to erase any mention of chest pains, memory problems, or arthritis."

Hoffman mentally riffled through the hours following his study patient's death. The pathologist's preliminary report attributed Ms. Gonzales's death to fulminant liver failure, and he suspected the final report would not mention the drug Hepatazyme. This man should have known that.

"Of course, you'll be compensated for your cooperation," the man continued. "Five million dollars will be deposited into your account once the FDA approves this new drug. The company's trade name for it is Anginex."

Five million? Hoffman's pulse hammered. He had delayed retirement for the promise of one million dollars when he shepherded Hepatazyme through its landmark clinical trial. That work was done. He'd also made sure no one would discover the connection between Hepatazyme and Gonzales's death. So why was this guy bringing it up? How could he have found out?

Money wasn't an issue at this point in Hoffman's career. But it had been. Ten years ago, on the eve of his own financial stability, his mother filed for medical bankruptcy after her diagnosis of Lou Gehrig's disease. Helping her out had nearly ruined them both. Now with her estate finally settled and his divorce finalized, Hoffman saw the allure of a five million dollar payout as a way to turn a possible early retirement into a certainty. A win-win for everyone if he participated once more. And maybe even some cover, albeit under the cloak of blackmail, if he played the good soldier. Follow orders. Ignore the casualties. Press ahead. It might take another year, but he could leave the NIH with his reputation intact. And this new company would get a sterling stamp of approval from the NIH for their new drug.

How hard could this be? Change a few charts. Erase the trail of side effects. Pretend to know nothing. Who better to grease the wheels of a clinical trial than a respected researcher and seasoned consultant? In return for his cooperation, he would receive a small fortune.

The company that sold Anginex must be sitting on a blockbuster.

He heard the man breathing on the other end of the line. Without saying another word, Dr. Scott Hoffman hung up the receiver and hustled through the rain back to his car.

$\mathscr{C}$HAPTER FIVE

$\mathscr{T}$HE NEXT MORNING, Douglas Schofield arrived at the hotel earlier than expected. An overweight man stuffed into the front seat of a bright-yellow Mazda RX-7 rolled down the passenger window and called out to Mackie. "You ready for the grand tour, Doc?"

Mackie McKay approached the car. Wearing a fresh shirt but the same suit from last night's dinner, Mackie folded himself into the front seat of the sports car. Through the windshield, the hood sparkled in the morning sun like a metallic banana. A quick glance at Douglas's Hawaiian shirt and rumpled chinos suggested that the dress code of business causal at BioloGen Pharmaceuticals might be overstated. Still, Mackie stuck with what he knew. Either scrubs or a suit. Not much in between in his wardrobe.

Douglas noticed his glance as he pulled away from the hotel. "I used to dress up at the old job, but I left all that behind when I moved to Cincinnati. Besides, Fridays I go casual."

"Tank tops and flip flops?"

"Close. We're not in San Diego anymore, Doc."

The RX-7 zoomed into the flow of traffic toward the interstate.

"Your boss brought you over from Bolten & Ferris with

him, right?" Mackie asked, recalling Schofield's bio in the company material sent to him before the interview.

"Not exactly," Douglas said. "I was just out of grad school when Freddie Pescatelli approached me with his idea for BioloGen."

"He must've had a good sales pitch."

Douglas mashed the pedal accelerating from the on-ramp. An eighteen-wheeler swerved in the adjacent lane to avoid them. "You ever drive one of these babies? Twin-turbo Wankel engine with 255 horses?" Douglas gave an obligatory glance over his shoulder as he moved into the left-hand lane. "I was gonna teach college for a living, but Pescatelli called and asked for some creative ideas for drug development. It didn't hurt that he told me this was the best way to take my PhD in bio-medical engineering and become filthy rich. Once I heard that, I said, 'Sign me up.' "

"Sounds like your boss has a way of getting what he wants," Mackie observed.

"Like you wouldn't believe. Wait till you see the office. Forty-five acres just outside the city."

Douglas swerved in and out of northbound traffic as he spoke. He cruised most of the way in the far left lane before jetting across three lanes of traffic to reach their exit. Horns honked in their wake. He accelerated through the yellow light at the end of the exit ramp. "You'll meet Rita Martin later this afternoon," Douglas said. "Great gal, but you should have seen her in her prime."

Mackie waited for a beat. He'd researched BioloGen and knew the principal executives like he knew baseball lineups. Rita Martin was a familiar name. Doyenne of academic medicine. Retired Chief of Cardiology at University of California San Francisco School of Medicine. Universally respected in her field. "Meaning what, exactly?"

"Meaning she's getting older. Not as sharp as she used to

be," Douglas said. "But she brings her stamp of academia to the office, which is great for BioloGen."

They drove several more miles, passing strip malls and subdivisions. By the time Douglas turned onto a small tree-lined driveway, pastures surrounded them. A gated driveway offered the only visible entrance to the property. A simple metal sign nestled in a copse of boxwoods proclaimed 'BioloGen Pharmaceuticals.' Mackie couldn't see the building from the road.

Douglas rolled down the window of the RX-7 and swiped a thin plastic card through a scanner. He pressed a series of numbers on an adjacent keypad. An intercom crackled with a pleasant female voice. "Good Morning, Doctor Schofield," she said as the metal gate slowly rolled open.

Mackie craned his neck and saw two security cameras trained on the back of the car. "Nobody's sneaking in here," he said.

"Once you see ADAM, I think you'll understand why all the precautions."

"You mentioned that at dinner last night," Mackie said. "In all my reading about your company, I haven't seen any information about that."

"Because none of that information's for public consumption."

Douglas parked the Mazda in the side lot and the two men unfolded from the car. The building ahead reminded Mackie of a three-story shoebox with a tinted-glass facade. Pure twenty-first century. To one side of the building, manicured landscaping obscured a series of generators and air-conditioning units. A sign on a small post pointed toward the sliding glass door entrance.

Inside, a tall woman met them in the lobby, her sculpted calves flexing beneath her short skirt with every step. "Good afternoon, gentlemen." Turning to Mackie, she said, "I trust your commute with the Professor hasn't made you regret your decision to join us?" She flashed a smile and extended her hand. "Karen Kiley."

She looked to be in her early forties, a head taller than Mackie in her heels, with the legs of a marathon runner and the chest of a starlet. Her steady gaze exuded confidence, but a fine tremor accentuated her handshake. After their phone interview last week, Mackie had hung up with the impression that Karen Kiley had the boldness to ask for what she wanted and the charm to usually get it. But today, on her home turf, a rim of uncertainty emerged.

Mackie shook her hand and introduced himself. "I think Dr. Schofield's just reinforced that decision."

"Heaven help you."

They crossed the foyer toward the information desk and a bank of elevators along the back wall. A painted brick fountain trimmed in greenery centered the room. Sunlight streamed through the atrium and sparkled off the chrome sign which proclaimed, *Welcome to BioloGen Pharmaceuticals: Tomorrow's Medicine Today.*

Karen led Mackie to a welcome desk and walked him through the process of procuring a visitor's badge. As they proceeded to the elevators beyond, Karen commented, "Those two ladies serve as our lions at the gate. They know everyone who works here, but don't think they'll cut you slack if you forget your badge. They're under strict orders to follow a security protocol, and a photo ID tops the list. I wish I could vouch for our nighttime security detail with the same confidence."

Upon reaching the far wall, Douglas swiped his card to call the elevator. Karen adjusted her skirt in the reflection of the doors. When the elevator arrived, Douglas entered his access code on a keypad. A recorded voice prompt said, "Thank you, Dr. Schofield. Access approved." The elevator began its descent.

"Recognize that voice?" Douglas asked Mackie.

"Sounds like the one from the entrance gate," Mackie said.

Douglas gave Mackie a congratulatory clap on his shoulder. "You're not missing a thing, are you? The building developers had the original voice prompt as a computer generated voice. Every time you entered a restricted area you heard a voice like WOPR from *War Games*. Tell me how long it would take you to get annoyed with that? I updated the code at the security desk. Now we have a welcoming voice regardless of where you check in."

Mackie nodded. "Impressive security."

"Don't encourage him," Karen said. "This is the industry standard. In our line of work, innovation is money. Everybody's got million-dollar ideas, but BioloGen has the ability to take those ideas and make useful medications. Our ideas are valuable, Cooper, and we do what it takes to protect them."

"It's Mackie," he said. "You start calling me *Cooper*, and I think I'm in trouble."

The elevator stopped. They stepped out onto a linoleum hallway illuminated by fluorescent ceiling lights. As they walked, the drop ceiling muffled the click of Karen's heels. At the end of the hallway, Mackie noticed another card-swipe monitor and keypad outside a sliding glass door. A painted sign outside the door read 'A.D.A.M. — Automated Device to Acquire Molecules.'

"Here he is!" Douglas said with a *tah-dah!* in his voice. "My baby."

A magnetic lock released the door as Douglas entered his password. The three stepped forward into an anteroom the size of a small bathroom. The door behind them slid shut, enclosing them in the small space. Mackie's ears began to pop.

"What you're feeling is pressure equalization," Karen said. "The negative pressure of this anteroom helps insure a clean environment on the other side. It also decreases the likelihood that people will contaminate the system."

Moments later, the inner door unlocked and slid open with a soft *hiss*. Mackie saw a room the size of a tennis court. In the center stood a huge glass case as long and wide as a small car. Directly above the case was a ceiling trapdoor of roughly the same size. Mackie assumed that there was some way to raise and lower the glass container in and out of the room through the ceiling. Inside the glass enclosure, shelves of test tubes faced one another. A robotic arm moved in between the two rows of shelves, removing and replacing racks of test tubes. Above them, Mackie heard the low rumble of a generator.

"That's our Automated Device to Acquire Molecules," Douglas said. "Like it?"

"What is it?" Mackie asked.

"It blends molecules, of course, and those molecules help us to create drugs, which helps us treat disease and provides us with a virtually limitless source of income," Douglas said.

"Thanks, Professor, I'm sure that clears it up for him." Karen turned to Mackie. "Let me explain it to you. As I'm sure they taught you in med school, drugs used to be discovered serendipitously, like penicillin."

Mackie nodded. Finally on familiar terrain. "As I recall, Fleming stumbled upon penicillin. He went on vacation and left his culture plates in the lab exposed to the air rather than properly storing them."

"And the mold in the air contaminated the plates," Karen said. "So when Fleming returned, he noticed the mold had killed the bacteria he was growing."

"Right," Mackie said. "Most of us would have thrown away the contaminated plates, but Fleming didn't. He studied the mold that contaminated them."

Douglas waved his hands in front of him to speed along the story. "Time passes and the contaminated mold produced an antibacterial substance we now know as penicillin. Great story. From what I see, though, that was the so-called

Golden Age of Medicine and yet scientists relied on chance or painstaking trial and error to discover lifesaving therapies."

"It was the standard of care," Mackie said.

"Was," Douglas emphasized. "Now we're living in the *Golden Age of Pharmaceutical Research* where the very molecular mechanism of a disease can be understood in basic science labs across the globe."

"Like the Human Genome Project?" Mackie asked.

"Exactly. Ten years from now, scientists will have decoded the blueprint of our human DNA. Big Pharma companies can't wait to get their greedy hands on that data, because most have faltered in trying to translate molecular discoveries into meaningful treatments."

"I think you're selling your industry short," Mackie said. "Big Pharma has given doctors a cure for just about everything but cancer and the common cold."

"And heart disease. And hepatitis. And AIDS. The list goes on."

Mackie glanced at the glass-enclosed robotic arm, whirring away in spite of their conversation. "So you're saying this machine, ADAM, manufactures molecules that make these new drugs?"

Karen nosed her way back into the conversation. "Not quite. What ADAM does is mechanize the process of trial and error in matching molecules to modes of disease. This is like a library that holds every conceivable book, and you're looking for one you've never read but that matches your particular need. Of course, you could pull each book off the shelf and look at it to see if it's a match, but you'd probably go through thousands of books before you stumbled upon the right one. Libraries these days are even starting to take advantage of computerized ways to search through their card catalogs."

"Where I trained, the medical library used a system called Archie to search electronic files," Mackie said.

"That will probably change soon," Douglas said. "A couple of years ago, this guy built an interconnected network of computers to search not just the medical library at Vanderbilt but also the library at other hospitals around the country. It's called the World Wide Web, and it's being used not just for electronic file transfers but to search for information from any institution that has access to it. ADAM gives us that kind of searching power in our molecular library."

Mackie looked at the glass case. "So ADAM is your librarian, knowing the books and pulling them off the shelf one by one to see if you would like it."

"Bingo," Douglas said. "Each shelf holds molecules organized by type and held in test tubes. Some of these molecules differ by only a few amino acids, like a dozen mystery novels that only differ by their ending. ADAM is given specific search criteria to see which is the best fit."

Karen walked over to the center glass case and pointed to the mechanical arm. "Using a practical example, we have an arthritis patch that we're developing called ArthroDerm. We gave ADAM a disease map of arthritis, down to the actual molecular structure of certain receptors in the body that respond to pain medicines. ADAM searched through our library to see which molecules worked best to relieve pain."

"What if the book hasn't been written?" Mackie asked. "What if you know the molecular structure of the disease, but you don't have a molecule in your library to match it?"

Douglas clapped his hand on Mackie's shoulder. "The boy's brilliant! That's the same question I asked Pescatelli before I came to work for BioloGen. 'What are you gonna do?' I asked, 'Write a book to meet your interests?' "

"Absolutely," Karen said. "And that's what makes ADAM so special. We can search through our library of millions of molecules to find a match. If we don't find one, we can manufacture molecules that differ by only a few words, to continue the book analogy, until we find the right one."

Mackie walked around the glass structure, studying the molecular library before him. "There are lots of diseases that we don't know the molecular mechanism for."

"That's our limiting factor," Karen said. "But to be fair, that's the limiting factor for every pharmaceutical company. You've got to know what you're treating before you can find a way to treat it. BioloGen uses existing scientific knowledge about disease to make more effective medicines."

"And to make a pile of money in the process," Douglas said.

Karen *tsk-tsked* under her breath. "Of course the market will respond favorably to a product well-made and effective. We also have layers of safety built into the system. For instance, once a molecule is found that will be a promising drug, ADAM runs that molecule through a computer simulation of the disease to make sure it will work. If it does, ADAM then runs the molecule through a simulation of the body's major organ systems — heart, kidneys, liver — looking for potential side effects."

"A risk benefit profile," Mackie said.

"Exactly. When the benefit of the drug is high and the side effect profile is low, ADAM alerts the team that a seed molecule has been identified. From there, our bio-engineers amplify the molecule and begin formulating it into a drug that we can test on humans and ultimately introduce to the marketplace."

Douglas rubbed his hands along the side of the glass. "With ADAM, we don't have to use the patients as lab rats to see what kind of side effect a certain drug will have on the human body. BioloGen has taken the risk to patients out of drug development."

"But you still run clinical trials in humans," Mackie observed.

"Of course," Karen said. "Take Anginex. We're testing it

on patients around the country, and it's being independently verified by clinical trials at the National Institutes of Health. ADAM helps us streamline the initial trial and error process."

"It sounds like a leap forward in the understanding of drug manufacturing," Mackie said.

Douglas slapped him on the back yet again. A physical coda to the conversation. "It's much more than that, my friend. It's revolutionary. By the turn of the century, all of Big Pharma will be using this technology. Come look at this." He led them through the anteroom, back into the hallway, and toward the elevator. Beyond it, they approached a locked door. A generator rumbled above, muted by the low ceiling.

Douglas raised his voice to be heard. "I thought Red was crazy when he first approached me with the concept of ADAM—"

"Red?" Mackie asked.

"That's what everybody calls Freddie Pescatelli," Douglas said. "Turns out, he knew exactly what he wanted to do with drug development. He just didn't know how to get it done."

"Pescatelli has a knack for finding people to help him achieve his goals," Karen said.

Douglas continued. "I created a prototype program to show him how ADAM would work. He was so impressed, he let me name my starting salary. Red and I spent two years perfecting the machine you just saw, and over the last few years that ADAM has been fully functional, we've never had a failure."

"I find that hard to believe," Mackie said.

"Let me show you." Douglas swiped his badge in the card reader and punched in his password.

"Do I get access once I begin?" Mackie asked.

Douglas smiled. "I was reluctant to let Red have access, but he put up such a fuss I had to agree. So no, Doc, I don't anticipate you having access. This is only for the engineers."

All three walked through the door. Although it was dark, Mackie sensed the height and depth of the room. Floor lights created a path down a corridor like a darkened theater. As his eyes adjusted to the dark, Mackie estimated that this back area actually wrapped around the large room that housed ADAM. The generators sounded louder on this side of the door.

"How far back does the storage area go?" Mackie asked, his voice straining against the noise.

"The space is about twenty by thirty yards."

Mackie walked ahead, inspecting the large storage room. Several dozen metal storage units lined the corridor, each with sliding garage doors and electronic sensors on the exterior. Each one reminded him of a temporary storage facility. "These house the molecules?"

Douglas nodded. "ADAM is a working molecular library, and these units house all of the molecules we're not investigating. We've got enough storage space for millions of discrete molecules."

Mackie squatted near one of the storage room doors, inspecting the structure. "You're probably not going to fill them up anytime soon," he commented over his shoulder.

Karen came up behind him. "We're more likely to see the Second Coming of Christ than to see this storage facility fill up. We never dispose of molecules we've created, because we don't know which ones we'll need in the future."

Mackie pushed up from his squat and looked around. "So what happens with the ones you test and don't use? You put them back into storage?"

Douglas nodded. "What you're looking at is the Bone Health storage room. In there we house about three hundred thousand molecules, all stored in a large glass crate. For example, if we wanted to find a drug for osteoporosis, we remove the entire glass container and place the molecule into ADAM's working library." He pointed upward. "See that catwalk up there?"

Twenty feet above their heads, Mackie saw a crane situated

on a track. "The crane moves the molecules?"

"Yep. We call her EVE, our Electronic Vault Engineer. She picks up the molecular vault and places it into ADAM's central room through a ceiling trap door."

Mackie smiled. "Did you name her?"

"Red wanted to call it the Sliding Track Electronic Vault Engineer, but my Evangelical sensibilities couldn't stand the thought of ADAM and STEVE living together in our basement. So EVE she is," Douglas said with a glint in his eye. "Whenever a group of molecules is needed from the vault, EVE locates the proper storage room, extracts the entire molecular bank, and inserts it into a pressurized door in the ceiling of ADAM's room. The computer terminals next to ADAM have automatic programs that direct EVE to the proper storage room. Of course, you can override that and manipulate EVE by hand."

"Seems like moving those glass cases would be pretty difficult."

Douglas pointed to a circuit box with a joystick on the far wall. "It's there for emergency back up if there's a computer glitch. Even runs on auxiliary power, but I sure wouldn't want to be responsible for a two-ton molecular bank dangling overhead."

Mackie nodded. "It's an elegant system you've designed."

Karen joined the conversation. "In the years I've been with BioloGen, we've never had a failure that's resulted in a recall."

Mackie frowned. "What do you mean?"

"Once our drugs go through ADAM, we test them against computerized replicas of individual organ systems. We learn everything there is to know about how the drug will react in the body. As a result, we know everything there is to know about the side effects before testing them on humans." She turned and headed back to the entrance of the storage facility.

"Hold on," Mackie said. "You mean to tell me you've never had a drug with intolerable side effects?"

"We've had plenty of molecules with intolerable, even fatal, side effects," Douglas said. "We've just had the foresight not to develop them once ADAM discovered the glitch."

"And that's why we're able to be as aggressive as we are with our marketing," Karen said. "You'll get into all of this when you get started."

Mackie took one last look around, wondering if ADAM's foolproof methods for testing drugs might be somewhat overstated.

CHAPTER SIX

SCOTT HOFFMAN COULDN'T concentrate. Deep in the bowels of the NIH clinics the next morning, he sat in the patient exam room, sleep deprived and irritable. The sound of a pen scratching across paper filled the small space as his patient filled out a form. He knew he should be glancing at her old records to remind himself of their most recent visit, but he couldn't stop thinking about last night's phone call.

Hoffman usually spent Friday mornings seeing patients, often a highlight of the week for him. Taking a half day to eschew administrative work and delay research projects, he would focus on people instead. Any lingering joy Hoffman once felt with direct patient care had evaporated since the call, leaving behind a residue of dread. Now, every patient he saw seemed a liability.

"Are you about finished?" he asked Hazel McVey.

She put down the pen, covering it with thin fingers, and handed the page to him. "You should already have all this information in my chart, Dr. Hoffman. I've been seeing you for four years."

Hoffman smiled, humoring the woman. "We are going to take what you've filled out," he said, gesturing to the boxy, clamshell of a computer on the counter, "and enter it into our new electronic medical record."

"Damn computers." Hazel reached into her crochet bag with an arthritic hand and pulled out a paper bag translucent with grease marks. "Brought you something."

Hoffman smelled the treat and looked up from her intake form. "Cookies?"

"Snickerdoodles. I made them this morning." She handed him the bag and picked up her crochet needles.

Hoffman removed his hand from the IBM ThinkPad and accepted the bag. "The nurses will polish these off by lunchtime."

He set the cookie bag on the counter. Working his hands around the black plastic case of the notebook computer, he moved it to his lap. It was heavy. Seven and a half pounds, his secretary had bragged earlier that morning when she handed him the new device, with a battery able to last a full four hours without having to be plugged in. Hoffman scrutinized the screen for a moment, then jiggled the red rubber button in the center of the keyboard. The screen flickered awake, and he noted a large box with a pale yellow background and a blue banner bar up top. "Program manager," he mumbled to himself as he searched for the right button to push. Every time he moved his finger over the red nipple on the keyboard, a pixelated arrow moved on the screen. Assuming that the file cabinet icon was his intended target, he activated that program.

"Why can't you use my chart?" Hazel asked.

"New system," Hoffman said with his head still bent toward the screen. "I'm supposed to be trying it out today."

"I don't see the need."

Dr. Hoffman grunted assent.

A log-in box prompted him to type in a password to activated the electronic medical record. Racks of patient charts awaited him outside the room, but Hoffman tried to concentrate on getting the laptop to work. He'd interacted with the computer records before but found the process clunky and cumbersome. When his secretary greeted him earlier that day and asked him to carry the computer with him. Hoffman felt an uneasy tension in her timing. Had someone contacted her to influence her urgings? He had used this records system before on a desktop computer, but this screen looked different. His secretary assured him the only change with the portable computer was the operating system, a Windows-based look that allowed him find his files more easily. So far, all these supposed windows did was frustrate him.

Hazel spoke up. "How're you going to find me on that thing?"

"Good question," Hoffman said. "That's what I'm trying to figure out."

A horizontal blue bar paced itself in a strip across the screen, presumably indicating progress. Once the blue bar reached the other side, it disappeared, replaced by a box entitled 'CPR—Computer-based Patient Record.' Best he could tell by studying the screen, there were two options for patient searches. One box prompted him to enter a patient's medical record number. Another box prompted him to enter a patient's name, beginning with the surname. Hoffman toggled the pixelated arrow between the two search fields, deciding which one to use. While he considered the search boxes on the screen, Mrs. McVey droned on in the background about her bowel habits. Dr. Hoffman occasionally nodded, absorbed in the inscrutable screen before him. He finally decided to type her name in the search box. A prompt then asked for her date of birth.

"Remind me of your birthday?"

"How many times have I seen you, Doctor Hoffman?" she asked. "You know all that information is in my chart."

"Humor me, Hazel. We're learning this system together."

When she gave him the information, he entered it into the box below her name. Her records instantly appeared on the screen. Not that they looked anything like Hoffman knew as a medical record. Tabs waiting to be clicked on by the arrow cursor indicated a section for labs, a section for reports, and a section for patient visits. Activating each tab with a click, he found a spreadsheet with data organized according to dates. When he activated the 'Patient Encounter' icon, he noticed that someone had loaded her last visit into the spread sheet. One column for patient concerns. Another for vital signs. A third for exam findings. Interesting, he thought. And useful.

Enamored with the new device, and mindful of the nefarious task ahead, Hoffman decided to try a test search. He repositioned the bulky plastic case on his lap and opened another search box. He entered in his mother's name. Three years earlier, in the final stages of her disease, she had come to the NIH for a treatment study. A desperation move, he soon realized. After her intake visit, she'd dropped out due to side effects. He'd never seen her as a physician, of course, but the CPR data base should recognize her as an established patient through the division of cardiology. When the prompt for her birthday appeared, he entered it.

Nothing happened on the screen.

The box for the date of birth sat empty, having erased the data as soon as he pressed *enter.*

Hoffman leaned forward. He check the spelling of his mother's name. No problem. He re-entered the date of birth. How could he forget it? In a cruel irony, his mother and his ex-wife shared the same birthdays, as well as the same gift for nagging.

Again, nothing happened on the screen.

The arrow waited for him.

Hoffman tried a third time. This time, a new text box appeared: 'Unauthorized patient access. Please contact the

CPR administrator.'

Hoffman's hammering heart nearly choked off his airway. With his patient Hazel still waiting on him to continue, a prickle of sweat emerged on his neck. He felt short of breath as a balloon of anxiety welled-up inside his chest. In his mind, he heard the deep voice on the phone. The threat of exposure.

His inability to access restricted electronic records left him with an inescapable conclusion. A conclusion that would only complicate matters for him. In order to execute the required records changes, he would have to expand his deceptive circle to include someone else.

Dr. Scott Hoffman needed help.

$\mathscr{C}$HAPTER SEVEN

$\mathscr{K}$AREN AND MACKIE left Douglas in the basement and called the elevator for the third floor. Mackie grasped the process of drug development, but mostly from the prescriber's perspective. Ever since the start of his residency, his primary pharmaceutical education had come from drug reps, seemingly the only smartly-dressed, well-rested young people in the hospital. The free lunches they provided for the residents gave the drug reps unfettered access to the next wave of prescribers. Mackie, like his fellow trainees, willingly wrote for the drugs du jour. Only after he joined the orthopedic faculty did he begin to question the process of drug development, and mostly for self-serving reasons. Seeing ADAM up close exposed him to a scientific process he was just beginning to understand. He wanted to learn more.

"Our boss wants to meet you upstairs," Karen said over the din of the basement generator. "Don't let his abrasiveness distract you. Intimidation for him is mostly theater. And don't stare."

Mackie smiled. "I'm not easily offended."

The elevators opened. Karen entered her access code. The doors eased shut. Karen fidgeted with her blouse, staring ahead in a nervous silence. By the time the car stopped and opened onto the third floor, she became animated once again. She stepped into the hallway and gestured to the expanse of carpet and cubicles before her. "Welcome home, Mackie."

She pressed him forward, one hand on his shoulder and the other leading the way. "Here's where we work. The third floor is all ours. Marketing rules! Once you begin, you'll have your own space."

The floor plan before them occupied a vast space divided by cubicles and conference tables. In the center of the room, Mackie noted a glass-enclosed meeting room with a long wooden table and a projector screen at one end. The bustle of activity, like a busy news room, produced a constant hum. Few people looked up or even noticed them as Mackie followed Karen to the center conference room.

"From here you can see the layout of the entire floor. It fits well with the traditional marketing model of the pharmaceutical industry."

"You mean the maxim that a mediocre drug marketed well is better than a cure no one knows about?" Mackie asked.

"You're catching on." Karen took a seat at the table, running her finger tips across the lacquered gloss. "Our boss wanted to do things differently than the competition. He knew that when marketers were placed in a position of having to sell a substandard drug, their company was not doing a good enough job of pharmaceutical research and development. BioloGen takes a different approach, which is where ADAM fits in."

A bearded man with a bald head hustled from a corner office toward them, looking more like a well-groomed rafting guide than a pharmaceutical executive. He walked with his shoulders thrust forward, as if catching a tail wind, and carried a leather satchel pinched between his arm and chest. Bursting into the room, he thrust his hand toward Mackie. "Good to see you, Doc. I'm Red Pescatelli."

He turned to gesture to a row of empty chairs at the table. When he did, Mackie noticed the stain of a dark red, nearly purple, birth mark on the back of his head. Almost the size of a fist, it looked as if someone had smacked the back of his skull with an ink pad. What's more, it looked as if he had lost most of his hair around the stain, leaving no chance to cover it up. Mackie had to avert his gaze when Red turned and said, "Let's have a seat and get you oriented."

Mackie took the first available chair, which happened to be at the head of the table. Across from him, a pitcher of water beaded with sweat sat atop a linen napkin. Mackie poured himself a glass.

Pescatelli paused a beat. He glanced at Mackie's glass, and then he sat down at another seat along the side of the table. He poured himself a glass of water as well before removing a glossy folder from his satchel. He slid it toward Mackie. "This is the sketch of the marketing plan for our newest cancer drug, Anginex."

"Anginex?" Mackie asked. "Cool name, but it sounds like what you might name a cardiac drug."

Pescatelli looked annoyed. "Cancer, not cardiac. In fact, we expect this drug to be one of the hottest selling pharmaceuticals on the market a year from now."

"You think it will unseat one of Bolten & Ferris's blockbusters to become a top ten prescribed drug?" Mackie asked.

"That's our plan," Karen piped in. "But from a company with a sterling reputation."

Mackie absorbed this. "So the rumors about them are true?"

Pescatelli shifted in his chair. "You'll hear rumors of corporate corruption in any industry. It comes with the money. We don't worry about that. Instead, we focus on the kind of drugs that can rescue men and women from their worst medical nightmares."

"A drug like that would almost sell itself," Mackie said.

"Exactly." Pescatelli drained his glass of water and began to crunch on the ice. "BioloGen is a young company, comparatively. We're still plowing our profits back into research and development to cure diseases." He winked at Mackie with an awkward and humorless gesture. "To be sure, the executives skim their share off the top before fertilizing R&D. You'll get yours, too, Doc. The point is, with aggressive marketing to the right patients, our drug will revolutionize cancer treatments. That's where you come in."

Almost as if on cue, an elderly woman with a serious demeanor rapped on the conference room door and extended a cordless phone. The modern device, no bigger than a sleeve of saltine crackers, included a black rubber antenna that extended from its top. Her no-nonsense expression punctured the enthusiasm in the room.

Pescatelli pushed back from the lacquered table. Ice clinked against the side of his water glass as he picked it up. "One moment, please. I obviously have to take this." He snatched the cordless receiver from his assistant's hand and stepped out onto the carpeted hallway.

"Tough place for a birth mark," Mackie said once Red left the room.

"You don't know the half of it," Karen said. "He had leukemia as a kid and lost his hair during chemo."

Mackie's stomach clenched. "He survived."

"With a nickname and a complex."

Mackie's son wasn't old enough to be in school after his diagnosis and attempted treatment. Losing a child to cancer was bad enough. He could hardly imagine the anguish a parent must feel during the teasing that went along with survival. "Kids can be cruel."

"So can male-pattern baldness." Karen scooted toward Mackie, flipping pages in the glossy folder to a new section.

"Everyone in the industry, from Big Pharma to baby biotechs, wants to sell the next big drug."

"Clearly, what you guys are doing is working," Mackie tried to refocus. "You already have two blockbusters on the market."

"And it all started with good marketing." She pointed to a graph in the folder. "Of course, pharmaceutical companies need clear plans for testing their drugs in humans, pathways for proving they work, and a priority of procuring FDA approval."

"Provided they are safe," Mackie said.

"That's a given. What I'm telling you is, you can design trials that show your drug works better than the competition, but if people don't know about it, it's not gonna sell. At BioloGen, we have an advantage, not just because of ADAM, but because of our marketing department."

The sound of shattering glass interrupted her, immediately followed by Pescatelli yelling into his phone. A hush fell over the third floor as the other employees looked toward the noise. Past the glass walls, Mackie saw Pescatelli grit his teeth, leaning on a small table with both hands. The cordless phone lay at his feet.

Trying to ignore the noise, Karen took a sip of water before speaking again. "We'll submit our new drug application for Anginex to the FDA early next year, and expect their stamp of approval shortly after that. When you join us, you'll be my deputy on this project. After a year on the job—"

Pescatelli strode back into the conference room and took his seat at the table. Beads of sweat glistened on his beard. He gripped a wad of white napkins. Fresh blood from his palm saturated the napkins.

"Everything okay?" Karen asked.

"Bureaucratic bullshit," Pescatelli said. "It's nothing."

Mackie leaned forward. No stranger to trauma and

comfortable around blood, he allowed his years of surgical practice to kick in. "Let me take a look. You may need stitches."

Pescatelli flinched and withdrew his hand. "I said it's nothing."

Mackie sat back, his gaze on Pescatelli's palm. Blood soaked through the paper napkins and pooled in his palm. Mackie tried to make light of the situation. "Blood on the interview trail? Not the usual fair."

Karen stood. "I'll get the first aid kit."

"Sit, sit." Pescatelli grabbed the linen cloth from under the water pitcher and wrapped it over the napkins. "Those damn water glasses..." Switching gears, he said, "So, what else did Karen tell you about Anginex?"

"We left off talking about its status as a future blockbuster."

Pescatelli sat back and crossed his legs, seemingly unfazed by his injury and his outburst. "Karen already knows we have a butt-load of work to do before FDA approval. As soon as they say 'yes,' I want Anginex to be so well known that patients are lining up at the pharmacy to get their prescriptions. The marketing starts now. As far as I'm concerned, we're already behind schedule."

Mackie glanced at Pescatelli's palm once more. Odd behavior for sure, but not a deal breaker, he decided. The job was right. The reasons for taking it compelling. "Then what are we waiting for, Red?" he said. "Let's get started."

CHAPTER EIGHT

MACKIE CURBED HIS enthusiasm during his final interview. He sank into the leather chair in Dr. Rita Martin's corner office, listening for any hints of caution. For any hesitation in her voice. For any reason to abandon his plans for a year-long sabbatical away from the hospital and away from his grief. He said to her, "Red Pescatelli told me you would be the best person to introduce me to Anginex."

She smiled. "One physician to another?"

"Honestly, Dr. Martin, I'm not convinced."

She folded her hands at her desk, her reading glasses still perched atop her head. Her frosted hair and white lab coat accentuated her café au lait skin. She adjusted in her seat before settling back, each movement appearing to Mackie more mechanical and uncomfortable than seemed natural.

"I'm not sure the expected success of Anginex is the best place to start," she said. "To understand that, it serves us first to understand clinical trials and drug testing."

"I'm fairly well versed in that," Mackie said.

"Humor me, then. What do you know about drug testing so far?"

"That it's lengthy and expensive."

Dr. Martin nodded, her reading glasses slipping from their

perch. She repositioned them with arthritic hands. "Tim money. Excellent places to start. The average time to brii drug to the market is ten to fifteen years."

"That's from concept to consumer, though," Mackie said. "Not just the trials themselves."

"True. You've got to run the concept through many phases before the drug is even tested in patients who need it. The average cost in 1990 for all that—from discovery of the molecule to approval by the FDA—is almost 230 million dollars."

Mackie let out a slow whistle. "For one drug?"

"For one drug. And that data's three years old. The costs are climbing. Across the industry, pharmaceutical companies collectively spend almost ten billion dollars in research and development. As you might guess, it's getting more expensive each year."

"Start up companies can't afford that kind of cash," Mackie said.

"BioloGen can."

She gripped and released her fists, popping her joints with a crackling sound Mackie could hear from across her desk. "Before I joined the company in their clinical trial division, BioloGen Pharmaceuticals concentrated solely on manufacturing new molecules."

"Potential drugs."

"Right. But rather than testing those potential drugs in patients, BioloGen sold the licensing rights to a larger company like Bolten & Ferris Pharmaceuticals. This was right after Red left their company."

Mackie scooted forward in his chair. He slipped a finger under his scratchy shirt collar to loosen his tie. It has been years since he'd spent two consecutive days in a suit. "So he was previously employed at Bolten & Ferris? That never came up this morning."

"Ask him about it. I'm sure he has nothing to hide. He

his time with the competition much, but
's while working for Bolten & Ferris that
eated the concept of ADAM."

ᵤs help."

ₐgain, although Douglas was in academia at that
. ᵣed ultimately patented the prototype for ADAM and
ᵢeft to start his own company. With the help of a few angel
investors, he formed BioloGen. His business plan consisted
of creating and selling newly discovered molecules to larger
pharmaceutical companies." She reached into the top drawer
of her desk and pulled out a medical journal. She flipped
the magazine over, showing him an advertisement on the
back from a pharmaceutical company whose name Mackie
instantly recognized. Against a background of blue skies and
green grass, the ad proclaimed the release of a non-drowsy
allergy medicine. "Recognize this drug?"

"Obviously. We've been flooded at the hospital with drug
reps telling us about it."

"It's a BioloGen molecule."

Mackie paused a beat, digesting this. "But it's been in
development for ten years. That would mean...." He let his
words trail off considering the timing.

"One of the first molecules that ADAM created, back when
the computer terminals alone could fill up this room. Red said
the discovery demonstrated ADAM's potential. Personally, I
think it was serendipity. Either way," she said as she waved
the journal ad above her desk, "Red sold the molecule for
that drug outright for twenty-five million dollars. If he had
retained only one percent of the expected future sales, we'd
have a revenue stream of probably ten million dollars a year.
But the sale price of that molecule, and others like that, was
what he needed at the time to finance the BioloGen start-up."

"That changed, though. BioloGen is now in development
and distribution," Mackie said. "Which seems like a gamble.

Not every drug will end up on the back cover of magazines."

"For Red, those gambles usually pay off." Dr. Martin's knee popped when she stood to stretch. "This old body and mind aren't as spry as they used to be. I've got to move around some. Walk with me, uh...."

"Mackie," he said.

Dr. Martin blushed. "Forgive me. Back in the day, I never forgot a name." She moved beyond the desk. "Let me show you how all of this fits together in our department."

They walked down a hallway, away from the elevator and toward the center of the building. "This is the NDA war room." She pointed to a nondescript door.

"The what?"

"NDA. New Drug Application."

"For the FDA?"

"Right." Dr. Martin placed her hand on the door. "We gather all of the pre-clinical and clinical trial data in this room, and we organize it for the FDA advisory committee to review. Even on the cusp of the twenty-first century, we're still asked to submit paper copies of our data. We keep all of that information under lock and key." She removed a keychain from her pocket and jingled it. "And I'm the keeper of the keys."

They walked farther down the hallway, turning a corner that offered a view of the expansive second floor. In a nearby glass-enclosed conference room, analogous to the one from the third-floor meeting with Red, Mackie saw a team of four employees at work. Three men with open-collar shirts and rolled-up sleeves sat around a table, watching a slide-show presentation. Next to the projector, a woman appearing in her twenties and not much younger than Mackie sat at the table with one leg tucked underneath her, pointing to something on the projector screen.

"What are they working on?" Mackie asked.

"That's our ArthroDerm team. They are submitting a

publication from a recently completed clinical trial that evaluated our arthritis pain patch."

"BioloGen sponsored trial?"

"Of course. But rest assured, Dr. McKay, you won't question the quality or integrity of industry-sponsored trials from BioloGen as long as I'm at the helm. I planted those academic roots as soon as I joined the company."

From everything that Mackie had seen so far, he had no reason to doubt the sincerity or the validity of Dr. Martin's claims. "Karen Kiley mentioned the ArthroDerm team earlier today."

"I should hope so. In three weeks, we are expecting FDA approval for the drug." She walked to the center of the floor, peered at a few cubicles before finding what she wanted, and then motioned for Mackie to join her. "I'm sure you've seen something like this before. It details the three phases of drug research and development."

Mackie glanced at the chart. "Sure. Phase One deals with healthy volunteers."

"Probably the shortest part of the R&D pathway. Ours usually take just over a year to complete. By the end of the Phase One study, we typically have a full understanding of a drug's expected side effects and the expected pharmacokinetics of the medication. Levels of the drug in the blood stream, for instance."

Mackie acknowledged her comment with a laugh. "Karen said ADAM identifies *all* of the possible side effects before the drug even enters clinical trials."

"A bit optimistic, but I see her point. From a clinical perspective, though, I can reassure you that we only develop drugs that have not had any unexpected side effects in the early round of testing." She adjusted her reading glasses and studied the chart. "Of course, next comes Phase Two."

"Testing the same drug in a group of people with the

disease," Mackie said.

"Or in the case of a preventative drug, Phase Two trials study patients with a high risk for the disease and evaluates the drug's performance. That takes another two to three years," she said.

"And if all goes well, the drug is tested in Phase Three trials," Mackie concluded.

"Right again. Those trials are usually made up of hundreds or thousands of patients enrolled in test sites around the country. For instance, we have an NIH-sponsored trial for Anginex ongoing right now that will be completed later this year, before we send the data to the FDA for drug approval. The Phase Three results confirm the earlier conclusions of the drug safety and effectiveness and also screens for any other side effects. Most Phase Three trials take about four years to complete."

Mackie studied the chart once more, then turned toward Dr. Martin. "You're talking about seven or eight years for clinical drug testing. Earlier, you mentioned that it takes ten to fifteen years to develop a drug."

She took off her glasses and smiled at Mackie. "You're paying attention, Dr. McKay. Other pharmaceutical companies take more than a decade to bring a drug to market. Because of ADAM, BioloGen has shaved off years of pre-clinical testing. While it takes other companies five or more years to test compounds in animal models, we can do it in less than a year."

Mackie gestured to the conference room behind them. "So ArthroDerm is the final product in that eight-year process?"

"Seven years, actually. We already knew the molecular structure of the intended pain receptor so it didn't take ADAM more than a few weeks of testing compounds before we found a perfect match. Since the medicine is delivered through a patch on the skin, we don't have to worry about side effects of the stomach and heart that have plagued other arthritis medications. The journal article about ArthroDerm should be published the week the FDA gives its approval." She rubbed a hand over the arm of her lab coat, as if feeling for something underneath. "I can tell you from first-hand experience, though, that this drug works."

The implication wasn't lost on Mackie. Dr. Martin had enough confidence in the drug to start using it even before the FDA gave its permission to sell it. "Sounds like you have a winner."

Dr. Martin stopped rubbing her arm, appearing somewhat embarrassed at her enthusiasm. She met Mackie's gaze, now one physician talking to another about scientific facts. "ArthroDerm is expected to reach the one billion mark within two years of approval."

"Billion?"

"Dollars. In revenue. Per year. It should be our next blockbuster." She straightened her lab coat. "The reason Karen Kiley wanted you to see this part of the company today is because the marketing of a medicine begins with the first publication of a clinical trial. Everything is tightly coordinated to spread the name of the drug to the public. One day, we may even be able to advertise drugs on television. Until that time comes, though, we want our print and personal marketing to allow patients to know to ask their doctor for it."

Mackie looked at the hive of activity on the second floor, impressed with the clinical trial process he knew a little about but had never fully understood until now. "So I'll learn the ropes with the ArthroDerm marketing?"

Dr. Martin paused a beat, then slowly dropped her gaze. A smile spread across her elderly face. "You won't have time to worry about other drugs. You'll be much too busy with the marketing of Anginex."

"Whatever you guys need," Mackie said.

Dr. Martin placed her hand atop Mackie's right forearm.

"BioloGen has invested considerable resources into the development of Anginex." She tightened her grip, as if to emphasize the importance of her words. "Your entire professional focus will be to make sure that, by the time it is approved, Anginex is already a household name."

$\mathcal{C}$HAPTER NINE

Summer 1993

$\mathcal{J}$ANICE O'REILLY FOUND a note on her desk at the National Institutes of Health on Monday morning, a note unlike any she had received in her two years of employment in the medical records department. She turned the yellow Post-It note over with her acrylic nails and inspected the back. Nothing else.

Oh my God, she thought, smiling. It's about damn time.

He had not communicated with her in the last two months. Not unusual. What frustrated her, though, was that the one time that she had seen him during that period, he walked right past her in a petrified stupor, not even noticing her in the hallway. One part of her had vowed to ignore Scott Hoffman when he next contacted her, knowing that he would reach out again. In his view, their relationship was placed on hold, like so many times before. But the other part of her knew that her frustration would crumble when she talked to him. She always did, with a quiver of anticipation and a lump of self-loathing. Confusion turned to questions as she wondered why was he contacting her now? At nine o'clock on a Monday? With a sticky note? The other times he'd picked up the phone and called when he wanted to see her.

She looked at her watch. She needed to leave now if she wanted to make it to his office in time. She checked her teeth in the pocket mirror stashed in her desk drawer then popped a breath mint into her mouth. Satisfied, she headed toward the elevator.

Her last visit to the ninth floor two months ago had resulted in knocking over piles of research folders during their passionate, almost primal, lovemaking. He went out of town the next day, and she hadn't heard from him since. She figured he would eventually change his mind. But why now?

The *ping* of the arriving elevator brought her mind back to the present. She took her auburn hair out of its ponytail and ran her fingers through it, then smoothed the wrinkles in her blouse with the palm of her hand. When the elevator stopped, she took a deep breath and checked her watch. 9:01 a.m.

"Hey, good-lookin'," Dr. Scott Hoffman said when she walked up. He hugged her. "Thanks for coming."

He smells delicious, she thought, then said, "I've been waiting to hear from you." She walked over to the leather sofa near the back wall of his office as he shut the door behind her.

Hoffman moved to the chair by the sofa and picked up his coffee mug. "I've done a terrible job of keeping in touch," he said with what appeared to be strained nonchalance. "But look at you. Don't you look great?"

Even as she questioned his sincerity, she fluttered under the compliment. "I'm still working out."

"It shows." He looked at her body and grinned. "Listen, I need a favor."

You probably need a quickie, she thought. "With what?"

"Another work project. We're trying to improve recruitment for drug trials." He took a sip of his coffee.

"Like you did with the Hepatazyme trial?" she asked.

"Uh-huh."

A bubble of self-respect ballooned inside her mind. She wanted to at least say *That's gonna cost you*, but all that came out was, "Not sure how I can help."

Hoffman rubbed his goatee and laughed awkwardly. "There're any number of things you can do to help." Standing from the chair, he walked over to the couch.

"I mean with your project." Janice smiled as he sat beside her and stroked her arm.

"Would you look up some patient information from medical records for me? I want to know, uh, which of my patients are seeing other doctors."

She crossed her arms. "Why don't you call the patients and ask them yourself?"

"We could do that, but it would involve calling thousands of people." Hoffman reached for her arm.

His touch electrified her. Damn it.

He continued. "By accessing that information through the Computer-based Record—"

"—CPR?"

"Right. By scrolling through CPR, we can easily identify who to call and which questions to ask them."

"Sounds more like snooping in patient charts to me. If that's the case, I don't think I can help you."

Hoffman rubbed his thumb over the back of her hand. Then, he kissed her. She pushed back at first, but only slightly. He moved closer and caressed her cheek. Relenting, she leaned into his kiss, feeling the heat rising within her.

"Just scan CPR once," he said between kisses. "When we find out which patients participated in multiple trials, we get their addresses and mail out a questionnaire. It's that simple."

She placed her hand on his thigh, feeling his anticipation. "I can probably get you a list."

"That's my girl." He nudged her back on the sofa.

She giggled. "Very romantic."

Hoffman didn't bother with foreplay. After two months, neither of them needed it. She wondered if he'd locked the door when he'd shut it. Soon, she didn't care. Dating a fellow employee had been risky enough for both of them. The prospect of getting caught on his sofa increased the risk.

And the thrill.

* * *

Janice stood and adjusted her blouse. "If we search the entire CPR database, it could take up to half an hour, and I have to be downstairs for a meeting by ten."

"Tell you what," Hoffman said as he zipped up his pants. "Let me log onto my terminal here in the office. I already have a list of endocrinology patients whom we've enrolled in clinical trials. If you access the CPR database, you can take the spreadsheet of my list to help initiate the search. Then, just log off."

"A 'V-Lookup'."

"If you say so." He walked over to his desk. "Once the search is complete, you can send me an electronic message of the results."

She cast a skeptical glance toward him. "*You're* using e-mail?"

"Why not? I'll get my secretary to help me. As soon as I identify the crossover patients, I can get my project underway. What d'you say?"

She scraped her hair back in a ponytail then glanced at her watch. "Hurry up. I've got to get back to the office." She sat down at his desk.

Hoffman leaned over his office chair to kiss her neck, then he typed in his screensaver password. "The spreadsheet of our study patients is right here," he said, moving a pixilated arrow over a boxy icon marked *Patient Survey*. "I'm going to walk down the hall to get some more coffee while you work. You want some?"

"I'm okay."

Hoffman kissed the top of her head and then stepped out, leaving her alone in the office.

She hummed a Stevie Wonder song as she connected to the Computer-based Patient Record system. After two months, the good doctor still knew all the right moves to get her started. But maybe she was just horny. Either way, Scott Hoffman was one surprise after another. She entered her password and initiated the patient search. Her mind wandered to her schedule, thinking about when she could find time to return to his office for an encore.

With her work completed, she logged off the computer and stood up right as Hoffman came back into his office. She walked over to greet him, caressing his chest with her palm. "All done."

"Uh-huh." He avoided eye contact.

"Should I e-mail the results to your secretary this afternoon, or do you want me to bring them to you myself?"

"Just get them to my secretary," Hoffman said, brushing past her touch. "I'm booked solid for the rest of the day."

* * *

Hoffman paced in front of his window for almost ten minutes before logging on to his computer. He wanted to be sure she didn't come back. His leather chair had been pushed back from the desk, and the subtle scent of her perfume lingered. It'll fade, he thought, just like the last time. He wondered why it had taken him almost two months to come up with this plan. Janice was the most obvious person to help him with his records changes. But his own delay in thinking of her and the pause in their so-called relationship seemed to have served him well.

He sat down at his desk to type in the screensaver password. A grey message box appeared, indicating that Janice had logged off the CPR database.

Let's see if this works, he thought.

Last week, he had picked up a manilla envelope from his post office box, presumably delivered by the same deep-voiced contact he had yet to meet. Inside that thin package, Hoffman found a single sheet of paper and a blue 3½-inch floppy disk. The first line of the letter listed three discrete pieces of information: *Betty Jacobs*; 04-13-71; and the letters *D-S-E*, which Hoffman knew meant *delete side effects*. Nothing else.

Accompanying the letter was the 3½-inch floppy disk with the words 'KeyTracker' written in black marker on the outside. On the phone call advising him to check his P.O. box, his contact instructed him to insert this disk into his computer as a way to record the keystrokes of anyone using the terminal. Those same keystrokes could be obtained later from the high-density data storage of the floppy disk.

Now sitting at his desk after Janice left, Hoffman clicked on the KeyTracker icon and selected the option for *Most Recent Data Entry: 1 hour*. With a low whir, his computer retrieved the data from the floppy disk. Another grey box appeared on his screen: To activate KeyTracker, please enter password.

Scott Hoffman typed in his screensaver password and pressed *enter*. The message in the grey box reset:

```
Password  Incorrect.  To  activate  KeyTracker,
please enter password.
```

He stared at the screen then shook his head. Of course the password is incorrect, he thought. He had already entered his screensaver password.

Then, he became concerned.

Had he seen another password on the letter before he

shredded it? He searched his mind for a clue to the password. Nothing. Could it have been on the back of the paper? He hadn't looked. Was it written on the inside of the envelope? He didn't know, because he hadn't looked there, either.

Hoffman rubbed his goatee, stirring up Janice's scent. He tried to refocus. Without a password, the information on KeyTracker would remain inaccessible.

"C'mon, c'mon," he mumbled.

Perhaps the password was as simple as the name of the product. He carefully typed *K-e-y-T-r-a-c-k-e-r* into the computer, pressing *enter* afterwards.

```
Password Incorrect. Failure to enter correct
password will result in deletion of data.
```

Hoffman's tongue stuck to the back of his dry throat as a swell of panic crested inside of him. Without the password, how would he correct the mistakes of this new drug? What would happen to his reputation? To his money? Would he be exposed for what had happened to Delores Gonzales?

What the hell was the password? He wracked his brain as he reviewed the text he'd memorized almost a week ago.

Betty Jacobs.

04-13-71.

DSE.

Plus, the verbal KeyTracker instructions he'd been given. Could it be that simple? he wondered.

Knowing this was his last opportunity, Hoffman carefully entered the six numbers lodged in his memory:

```
0-4-1-3-7-1.
```

With a trembling finger, he pushed *enter*. And then held his breath.

One second.

Two seconds.

```
Welcome to KeyTracker!
```

The screen flashed.

```
Please review your data below.
```

Hoffman slumped back into his chair. Before him, a long list of numbers and letters filled the center of the screen.

Below his three attempts at finding the password, he read the keystrokes Janice had used for the V-lookup of the patient survey spreadsheet. Immediately below that, he read:

```
[Enter] x-R-8-g-3-M-*-s
```

He had it! Hoffman jump up from his seat and pumped his fist in the air like Michael Jordan after an NBA Championship.

Walking to the door to regain his composure, Hoffman checked the locked doorknob before sitting back down at his desk. He clicked on the CPR medical records icon. Moistening his lips, he typed in the stolen password:

```
x-R-8-g-3-M-*-s
```

His stomach fluttered as he waited for access to the entire patient database for the National Institutes of Health. Then, a grey box popped up on the screen before him:

```
Welcome, Janice O'Reilly!
```

$\mathcal{C}$HAPTER TEN

$\mathcal{W}$HEN MACKIE WALKED into his new office that summer for the first time, he saw an elderly woman seated at his desk, arranging office supplies. The woman looked up when he cleared his throat. She swabbed a handkerchief across the desktop, then pushed back in his chair.

"Dr. McKay, I assume." She stood to extend her hand. "I'm Ms. Franks."

Mackie was surprised by the strength of her grip. He introduced himself.

"I know who you are," she said. "Mr. Pescatelli's been talking about you for two months. You're a bit younger than I imagined, but you'll fit in okay."

He peered over her shoulder. "You were getting my desk ready?"

She shook her head. "I guess Ms. Kiley forgot to tell you. I'm responsible for orienting all new employees on their first—"

A cheerful voice interrupted her. "There you are." Karen Kiley burst into the small office. As before, she wore her trademark short skirt and heels. "I missed you earlier when you checked in downstairs. I see you've met Ms. Franks, one of BioloGen's living legends."

Ms. Franks harrumphed at the compliment.

"She used to be Red's administrative assistant when BioloGen was just a good idea," Karen said. "She's worked in about every department since then. For the last two years, we've had her to ourselves in the marketing department. She'll be working closely with you to keep you on schedule and help with any administrative tasks that need to be done."

Ms. Franks stepped around Mackie, then Karen, leaving a trail of words behind her. "I'll get his orientation materials together."

Karen perched atop the front edge of Mackie's new desk.

"That was unexpected," Mackie said. "I walked in and there's my grandmother, cleaning my desk."

"She's everyone's grandmother, but don't let her hear you say that. She's an indispensable resource. You just have to get used to her quirks." Karen rubbed her hand across the slick lacquer of the desk. "I hear your wife's still in Nashville?"

Mackie paused. "We're not ready to sell the house, yet. Young daughter and all."

"I'm sure we'll keep you plenty busy at the office. Plus, you've got lots of privacy up here. No one can hear a thing when the doors are shut." She winked as she pressed her skirt flat with the palm of her hands. "My office is down the hall. Ms. Franks is within shouting distance." When Mackie didn't respond, Karen said, "So...let's talk drugs."

"I'm all ears."

Karen met his gaze with a confident, and almost conspiratorial, look of her own. "I'm afraid we may have misled you a bit about Anginex. Strictly speaking, it's not exactly a cure for cancer."

"Not *exactly*?"

She leaned forward. "It's even better."

"Explain."

Karen slipped off the desk to close the open door, then sat back down. "Red plans to share the news about Anginex with you during his presentation at lunch. He lives for the drama that comes with talking about new drugs, so act surprised when you hear. The short version is when ADAM discovered Anginex, it discovered a molecule that is designed to change the face of preventative medicine."

"That's a big statement, even for a marketing guru."

"It's a big discovery." Karen folded her arms across her chest. "By now, you know that Douglas and Red designed ADAM to find targeted drug therapies based on specific causes of disease."

"Like with ArthroDerm. You cut a key that fit the lock of a specific receptor for pain," he said. "Cool name, by the way."

Karen grinned. "Glad you're impressed."

"That doesn't answer my question about Anginex, though. It sounds like ADAM works great if you know the cause of a disease. I don't understand how it works to prevent something, though, that hasn't even happened yet?"

"It's the same general concept. Red will explain the details. Suffice it to say, we expect this novel discovery by ADAM to become the fastest selling FDA approved drug of all time."

Mackie laughed in spite of Karen's serious expression. "Sounds like you're describing a drug to *prevent* cancer."

Karen took a deep breath and fixed her gaze on Mackie. "We are."

He didn't know what to say.

Neither one of them spoke for a minute or more. The clock on the wall ticked while the reality of her claims sank in.

Mackie crossed his own arms. "A prevention for cancer. That's eluded scientists for years."

"The *cure* for cancer has eluded scientists, that's true."

"Because cancer is not one thing. It's a thousand different ways that cells grow unchecked."

"But different types of cancer stem from the same fundamental starting point. ADAM helped us define a way to stop cancer from ever developing. Can you guess how it might work?"

Mackie felt like a medical student being pumped with questions by a professor. The tables were turned on him for the first time in years. Still, he humored her, allowing a cocky grin to spread across his face. "Simple. The drug stops renegade cell growth." Judging by the look on Karen's face, he knew he'd been set up.

"Wrong." She reveled in the moment. "The most common way to prevent cancer from growing is to cut off its food supply."

Mackie's pride and confidence took a hit. "By stopping new blood vessel growth?"

"You got it."

He stared at the wall for a moment, processing the information. "It makes sense," he finally said. "Cancer cells can only grow as fast as their blood supply will let them."

"Red loves to use the military analogy," Karen said, "explaining that an invading army can't march ahead of the supply line until it learns to live off the land. Cut off the food chain, and cancer cells wither like Napoleon's troops in Russia."

"Napoleon *did* march all the way to Moscow," Mackie said.

"Okay, hot shot. The historical analogy's not perfect, but the military one's damn close. Once an army learns to live off the land, it can march wherever it wants."

"Like Sherman through Atlanta."

"If you say so. The point is, for cancer cells to grow and metastasize, they have to learn to live off the surrounding environment."

"Angiogenesis," Mackie said.

"Aren't you full of surprises today? Do you know how it works?"

Mackie relaxed a bit, back on familiar territory. "Cancer

cells actually grow new blood vessels to meet their nutritional needs. I remember hearing about success in mice with therapies like this. You block the new blood vessel growth and the cancers melt away. I've never heard of success in humans with these compounds, though."

"No one has succeeded in treating humans with it. Until now. Do you get the name? Anginex...ex-out angiogenesis." She slipped off the desk and brushed a piece of lint from her skirt before heading to the door.

"Hold on," Mackie said. "You're gonna stroll in here, announce that BioloGen has discovered the Holy Grail of medical research, and then walk out?"

Karen winked again at Mackie. "Remember to act surprised at lunch."

* * *

With his office door left open, Mackie had a clear view of the center conference room on the third floor. Red Pescatelli strode into the conference room exactly fifteen minutes before the start of the lunch meeting, a slide carousel tucked beneath his arm. Mackie returned his attention to his orientation manual. He found himself re-reading the same sentence as one question marched through his mind. How had a small company in Cincinnati, Ohio found a drug to prevent cancer and then kept that discovery a secret?

Noise from the hallway distracted him again. Douglas Schofield sauntered into the conference room with a doughnut in hand, licking his fingers. Dr. Rita Martin followed with stately composure, reserved but purposeful in her movements. A moment later, two members of the initial ArthroDerm team sat at the conference table. Closing his white binder, Mackie grabbed a notepad and hustled across the third floor to the conference room.

Pescatelli smiled broadly when Mackie arrived. "Now that

our newest employee is here, I think we have a quorum. Why don't we go ahead and get started?"

Mackie took a chair near Dr. Martin at the back of the conference table.

Pescatelli's beard appeared trimmed. He looked as rested and tan as if he had just returned from a beach vacation. He stood near the end of the table, hands resting on the slide projector. With a nod toward Ms. Franks, the lights dimmed. "Let's begin by reviewing my ASCO presentation," he said.

Mackie looked around the room at his colleagues. Dr. Martin sat with her hands folded on the table, listening intently. The two ArthroDerm team members, now part of the Anginex crew, took notes as Red spoke. Douglas Schofield munched on his doughnut, seeming to stare through the glass walls of the conference room. Everyone appeared to understand Pescatelli's presentation except Mackie. Not ready to ask for clarification, he wrote *ASCO?* on his notepad and turned it toward Karen.

She smiled, writing *American Society of Clinical Oncologists* on the pad. She underlined it, and then wrote, *Hank's a keynote speaker for them next week.*

Mackie retrieved his pad and turned his attention to the presentation. On the screen, he saw a black and white picture of a young man with a crewcut wearing dark-rimmed glasses and a lab coat. The picture looked like it had been taken before Mackie's birth, but it was as recognizable to him as if it had been a photograph of his own father.

"Does anyone recognize this man?" Pescatelli asked.

No one said a word. Mackie looked on either side of him, waiting for someone to answer the question. When no one did, he broke the silence. "That's Judah Folkman, former surgeon at Boston Children's Hospital. An all-star in the surgical world. Pretty bright guy."

Pescatelli paused, clearly not expecting Mackie to provide

an answer. "Good guess." Turning to the rest of the Anginex team, Pescatelli said, "In his prime, Dr. Folkman was the Leonardo da Vinci of medicine, because he was so damn good at so many things." He changed the slide, now showing a picture of several antiquated medical devices. "When he was still a medical student, Dr. Folkman invented one of the first cardiac pacemakers. Later, he invented an implantable drug delivery system that's now used as a contraceptive implant by more than two and a half million women worldwide."

"Future customers," Douglas said in a stage whisper to no one in particular.

Pescatelli changed the slide and continued. Now the screen showed an artist's rendition of a molecule, its sticks and knobs resembling an Erector Set creation. "The molecular structure you see here is another discovery credited to Dr. Folkman. It's called *endostatin*, and it's a naturally occurring angiogenesis inhibitor."

Mackie piped in. "Folkman was a surgical oncologist when most general surgeons didn't specialize in cancer surgery. His discovery of endostatin was pure serendipity, if I remember correctly."

Pescatelli inhaled and held his breath, as if this disruption of his presentation would simply go away if he only waited it out. Silence gripped the room.

Dr. Martin leaned forward. "Dr. McKay is correct. Cancer surgery is a bloody business. Dr. Folkman must have wondered what would happen if he could somehow cut off a cancer's blood supply. Would the cancer continue to grow if its blood supply were interrupted, or would it shrivel up and die like an uprooted weed?"

Pescatelli exhaled. "As I was saying, Dr. Folkman's research focused on tumors and their blood supply. He wanted to understand how the body tried to stop unregulated cell growth. The body makes a chemical Folkman named *endostatin*, and as you can see on the screen, the molecular structure is similar to another chemical he called *angiostatin*. These two naturally occurring compounds are nature's way of choking off a cancer's blood supply. Starving the troops, as it were. Sometimes the body wins, and cancer is cured before we can even diagnose it. Other times, the cancer is too aggressive for the body's own angiogenesis inhibitors."

When Pescatelli paused to take a sip of his water, Mackie said, "That's when the cancer hijacks the body's blood supply for its own purposes—"

"Thank you, Dr. McKay, but if you'll let me finish, we can take comments at the end." Pescatelli stared at Mackie for a long moment, then addressed the rest of the group. "So what we have is a naturally occurring compound that can treat, or even prevent, cancer." He advanced the slide projector, now showing the image of a newspaper headline.

Pescatelli continued. "When Dr. Folkman published his initial research, headlines in the popular press proclaimed the cure for cancer was here. The National Cancer Institute went on to sponsor almost two dozen trials to study the effects of angiogenesis inhibitors in humans."

Mackie asked the obvious question when no one else around the table spoke up. "So why haven't we heard more about these compounds?"

"That is the question." Pescatelli advanced the slide carousel again. "That's the fundamental issue, Dr. McKay. The reason you have not heard more about these molecules is because, in all of the clinical trials, none of them really worked as well as expected. Until now."

The molecular structure represented on the screen looked similar to the sticks and knobs of the previous slide. Now it formed a series of rings like interconnected rims of stop signs. Printed in bold type across the bottom of the screen was the word *Anginex*.

Pescatelli extended his arms like the master of ceremonies at a circus. "This little molecule is going to revolutionize preventative medicine. Next week at the ASCO meeting, I will present the clinical trial data from our Phase Three studies on Anginex. What we are selling, friends, is cancer prevention at the cost of one pill a day."

Douglas, having finished his doughnut, gave a loud and exaggerated clap. "The money from this baby will be enormous."

"True," said Pescatelli, "but the impact we will make on patients's lives will be priceless."

Mackie looked around the table. The information was exciting, seemingly transformational for doctors and patients alike. But it didn't add up for him. He raised his hand like a school boy. "One question, Red."

Pescatelli breathed through his nostrils. "Yes, Dr. McKay."

"New blood vessels are not inherently bad. We use them all the time. A skinned knee heals with a strong supply of new blood vessels. A pregnant female relies on new blood vessels for her baby to grow. Can you comment on the side effects of Anginex, or at least the precautions?"

Dr. Martin leaned toward the table and placed a gentle hand on Mackie's arm. "We've not seen any side effects like that in our clinical trials."

"And by now you should know why." Pescatelli interrupted Dr. Martin's explanation. "ADAM tested this molecule against computer models of the human body before we even started our human trials. We've long known that pregnant women cannot take this medicine, Dr. McKay, and when you begin marketing Anginex, you will reinforce that fact to every prescriber you see. But other than occasional nausea and a rare rash, there are no side effects to Anginex."

Pescatelli fielded a few softball questions from around the room, then concluded the meeting. The executive team gathered their notepads and pens and trickled out of the conference room. As Mackie prepared to leave, Red approached him.

"With your medical background, I expect you to be an integral part of the team," Red began. "If this drug is marketed properly, it has potential to be the best selling drug of all time. You'll have a fat year-end bonus to come home to."

"It's not about the money for me," Mackie said.

Pescatelli snorted disbelief. "I'm not worried about your marketing inexperience. We have a team to help you. Once we receive FDA approval, you won't be able to open up a magazine or newspaper without reading about Anginex. Until then, I expect you to make it your life's mission to know more about this drug than anyone else."

He leaned toward Mackie and lowered his voice, staring at him like a drill sergeant eyeing a private at basic training. Mackie stared right back.

Pescatelli's voice vibrated with intensity. "Every time you shower, shave, and shit, I want you thinking about Anginex. Every time you see an old lady, I want you to come up with new ways to market the drug to her. When you close your eyes at night, you'd better be dreaming about my drug. There is nothing more important for you right now."

"Show me where to start and I'll be ready, but I need to know all there is about Anginex. Any articles you've published. Any trial data you've collected. And unfavorable data. I want access to it all."

"We'll show you what you need to know to sell the drug," Pescatelli said. "As far as your education goes, I'm flying down to the Aruba conference on Saturday with Douglas. He's giving a small presentation on the biostatistics from the Anginex clinical trials." He continued to stare unblinkingly at Mackie. "I'd like you to join us."

*C*HAPTER ELEVEN

*S*COTT HOFFMAN ARRIVED at work an hour earlier than usual that morning. For the last week, he had followed the same routine for making changes in the Computer-based Patient Record. Seated in his office on the ninth floor, the door locked and the sun breaking free of the tree line, he knew he could count on less than one hour to himself. Plenty of time, though, to make that day's record changes. He aimed to finish before 7:30 a.m. so that he could unlock his door, grab some coffee, and begin work before other members of his division arrived.

Nonchalance is the key, he reminded himself.

Turning his attention to the computer monitor, he typed in the now-familiar CPR password for Janice O'Reilly. A box appeared on the screen, prompting him to enter in a patient's identifying information. He typed it from memory.

Within moments, the medical record appeared.

Hoffman grinned. He clicked through the boxes representing aspects of Rebecca Hightower's chart. At the section marked *Clinic Visits*, Hoffman moved his cursor over a sentence which read, 'Patient reported chest pain after taking the study drug.' Hoffman deleted the text. Next, he clicked through several more boxes to reach a section of her chart entitled *Labs*. He removed three offending entries. Satisfied with the results, he saved his work and closed the chart.

Once Hoffman had sanitized five charts in the CPR database, he logged out of Janice's account. This week alone he had completed more than two dozen chart changes. Each morning he arrived at the office with newly memorized patient information, his post office box yielding him specific instructions for changing patient complaints or deleting concerns altogether.

He stood up and stretched, the tail end of his shirt coming untucked, then walked to the window to watch the morning sun. He had tried to identify a pattern to the specific data deletions, but none emerged. The instructions for chart changes seemed random and inconsistent, only unified by the patients common participation in the NIH trial for Anginex.

Over the last week, he deleted complaints of chest pain and shortness of breath, scrubbed clean any documentation of blood in the urine, and expunged an entire patient chart. The deleted patient had complained of confusion within months of taking Anginex. When the guilt of his actions needled his conscious, as it often did at some points during the week, Hoffman had to remind himself of the greater good this drug could bring. Besides, he doubted anyone would ever discern that the information was missing, because thousands of patients nationwide had enrolled in the NIH-sponsored study for Anginex.

Fatigue began to beat back his early morning enthusiasm. He needed a cup of coffee. These early starts, on the heels of late nights at the post office, had begun to wear him down.

A knock at the door shattered his tranquility. His keys rested on the edge of the desk. No other signs of his early morning activities. He glanced at his clock. 7:23 a.m.

"Hey, Scottie. Open up!" called a jovial voice from the other side of the door.

Hoffman peeled back his office door.

Yolanda Steele stepped inside. "You're here early." She sauntered past him carrying a three-ring binder in one hand and a yellow Post-It note waving from an outstretched finger.

Hoffman stepped back out of her way.

She smacked her gum with a grin. "Did you sleep in that shirt last night?"

"I wasn't expecting you yet."

Yolanda's smile widened. "Surprise."

Yolanda Steele, an employee of the National Institutes of Health for five years, had spent most of that time in the Endocrinology Department as Dr. Hoffman's secretary. The woman remained a study in contrasts. She anchored her coat-hanger frame and pulled-back hair with thick-soled shoes, giving her the appearance of an old-school librarian. She also wore the smell of cigarettes and coffee like some women wore Chanel No. 5, joking with people that her blue-collar smells suited her harsh Jersey accent. Before joining the NIH, she had worked for ten years as an administrative assistant at the New York Stock Exchange. After Reagan left office, she selected the stability of government-funded medicine as her refuge, bringing a librarian's efficiency and a northerner's steely edge to her current position.

Hoffman glanced at the binder and the sticky note. "What's all that?"

"Stuff for you to read before your afternoon conference call." She slapped the binder on his desk. "And the number of some guy named Dirk."

Hoffman straightened. "When did he call?"

"You know who I'm talking about?"

"He's an old friend—"

"He sounds like an idiot."

"*When* did he *call*?"

"Last night shortly after you left." She held out the yellow square of paper. "On your schedule this morning you have a research conference call at ten..."

Hoffman snatched the paper from her hand. He collected his car keys. Already twelve hours late returning Dirk's call, he knew he couldn't contact him from this office. He would go downstairs to the bank of pay phones in the lobby. If Dirk could meet him now, he would leave immediately.

"Where are you going all of the sudden?" Yolanda asked.

"You could have called me last night to tell me about this message." Hoffman hustled past her, not bothering to tuck in the tail of his shirt.

* * *

Dirk Waters sat in the front seat of Hoffman's red Ford Probe with his tremendous knees jammed up against the dashboard. At six foot six and one sandwich shy of four hundred pounds, Dr. Hoffman saw the former NFL lineman turned private investigator as a health risk—to others as well as to himself. The two men stared out of the windshield, observing the early morning activity at Hoffman's post office. Finally, Dirk said, "It's gotta be an inside job."

"So you didn't see anyone go into the post office overnight?"

"Not a soul." Dirk tried to adjust himself in the front seat. Apparently realizing there was no room to rotate his girth, he settled back into the position of least resistance. "I could see your mailbox from my car the whole night, and ain't nobody come near it."

Hoffman grimaced, as much at the assault on the English language as the lack of leads in his case. He should have known from their first encounter that Dirk was not the right man for the job.

One month before, Dirk Waters had arrived at the NIH to apply for a weight loss study. While he probably qualified on body mass alone, his previous steroid use during his professional football days precluded his enrollment. The study recruiter promised to keep his name and number on file for future studies. When Hoffman later spotted the rejected application for Dirk Waters, Private Investigator, he recognized an opportunity to protect his interests by exposing his own blackmailer. Hoffman discreetly noted the man's phone number, contacting him two weeks later from a pay phone in the lobby at work.

Hoffman recalled that conversation. "I understand you used to play for the Redskins," he had said. "How'd you become a P.I.?"

"Knee injury," the former third-string nose guard responded.

"So you went to work for a PI to learn the ropes?" Hoffman asked.

"Sort of," Dirk responded.

Hoffman knew he should have hung up then.

Dirk further explained that he supplemented his income during lean years by enrolling in clinical trials. "Got five hundred bucks once just for taking an experimental drug. Lots a drug trials out there. I never said nothing when the side effects got bad, though, for fear they wouldn't pay me."

Seeing few other options, he had hired Dirk Waters. Hoffman's experience told him Big Pharma took care of their physician consultants, but something felt different to him this time. The man with the deep voice seemed more threatening and too knowledgeable about Hoffman's past. With Dirk's help, Dr. Scott Hoffman hoped to learn the identity of his blackmailer.

He now turned to Dirk. "So you're suggesting that the person who is sending these letters actually *works* for the postal service?"

"Or he's working with someone who does," Dirk reasoned. "Last night, ain't none of the people I seen went to your box." He fished a tiny notebook from his prodigious breast pocket.

"There was seven people that come by. Five women, two men. The last one I seen was just before midnight. All of them went to the *left* side of the lobby. Your mailbox is on the *right* side of the lobby. Therefore, we know ain't none of them put that envelope in your box."

This guy's a real Magnum, PI, Hoffman thought. He pulled out the most recent envelope and letter shielded in a clear plastic sleeve. Instead of shredding it as he had repeatedly been instructed, Hoffman saved both, hoping Dirk might find evidence of some kind. He handed it across the center console.

Dirk accepted the protective sleeve with a delicate touch not expected from his oven-mitt hands. "I could run some tests on the envelope."

"Like what?"

"Check it for finger-prints. Maybe do some hand writing analysis. That kind of stuff."

"*You're* trained in hand writing analysis?" Hoffman made no attempt to hide his sarcasm.

"I know a guy who owes me a favor."

Hoffman's head pulsed with anxiety. "Get me everything you can find out about the person who sent this. I'm sure I don't have to remind you, but I will: this is a confidential matter. Secrecy is a very important to me."

Dirk nodded. Then, he opened the passenger door and squeezed out of the car, taking the envelope, and Scott Hoffman's future, with him.

*C*HAPTER TWELVE

*M*ACKIE STOOD IN the foyer of the conference center at the Wyndham hotel in Aruba, waiting to register for ASCO. He had left the suite early. The door to Pescatelli's bedroom had remained quiet and closed, while wall-trembling snores had emanated from Douglas's room. No other signs of life in the suite. As a conference attendee in front of him completed her registration, Mackie heard someone call his name.

"Dr. McKay?"

He looked toward the voice. A red-headed clerk behind the registration table extended her slender hand. "You look just like the photo on your name tag." She handed him a canvas bag with the *ASCO in Aruba* embroidered on the side. "Your conference materials are in there, along with a gift certificate to the jewelry store in the lobby. We also have a binder of summaries for the clinical trials we'll be discussing during the scientific meetings."

Mackie accepted the tote bag. "Have the other BioloGen attendees checked in yet?"

"Only Mr. Pescatelli," said the conference clerk as she glanced at Mackie's name tag. "From Cincinnati, I see. What a welcoming town. I worked a conference there in ninety-one. That local ice cream shop there is divine. Gators?"

"Graeters."

"Their black raspberry chip flavor is to die for."

Throughout his surgical residency and into his early years on faculty, Mackie had attended his share of medical conferences. Each had a particular focus and feel built upon an immutable spine: fancy locations when possible, fine food, and friendly coordinators. Sometimes the scientific sessions seemed a necessary distraction to the vacation. Based on past experience, Mackie knew the drill even before the check-in clerk pointed him toward the coffee and continental breakfast. He ambled across the foyer, glancing at displays of cancer drugs being set up by various pharmaceutical reps. Beyond those colorful displays, three sets of adjacent double-doors opened into the banquet hall that doubled as the main room for the scientific session.

The room seemed half-full when Mackie entered it. Dozens of men and women in casual clothes flipped through their packets of conference materials. Mackie overheard snippets of conversations about last night's dinner and tonight's reservations. As he moved to find a seat, Mackie saw Pescatelli near the presenter's table, deep in conversation with an elderly man. Mackie placed his materials on a chair near the center of the room and approached his boss.

Pescatelli looked up from his conversation as Mackie neared. He paused a beat, narrowing his eyes before finally addressing him. "Morning, Mackie. I want you to meet a friend of mine." Placing a hand atop the elder statesman's shoulder, Pescatelli said, "This is Dr. Stanley Jenkins, chief cancer researcher in Houston at M.D. Anderson. He's also this year's moderator for the conference."

The elderly researcher had a thin face that he accented with gray curls brushed straight back and tucked behind his ears. His dark-rimmed glasses, like his slicked-back hair, appeared unchanged since the Nixon administration. Mackie shook his hand.

Pescatelli continued. "Dr. Jenkins is a seasoned researcher with angiogenesis inhibitors. Dr. Jenkins enrolled over two-hundred patients in Texas for our Phase Three Anginex trial."

Stanley Jenkins seemed to bask in the glow of the flattery. "You joined BioloGen Pharmaceuticals at the right time," he said to Mackie, seeming to bounce on the balls of his feet with excitement. "Your boss reviewed his presentation with me earlier this morning. Based on what I've seen, I expect Anginex will make a splash with this audience."

Mackie's attempts to make eye contact with Pescatelli remained largely ignored. "That's what Red keeps telling me. After the FDA approval, it's going to be all Anginex all the time."

"It'll sail through the regulatory process," Pescatelli grumbled.

"When I first started cancer research in the fifties," Dr. Jenkins said, "it took the FDA years to get drugs approved. We could hardly get the chemotherapy we needed."

"It's different now," Pescatelli said, fiddling with his wedding band. "The best thing that's happened to drug development in the last five years is the AIDS epidemic. With the gay-rights lobby throwing a tantrum with congress, the FDA finally relaxed some of their rules."

"Bit of a harsh comment," Mackie said. "If you're talking about the effect of the AIDS epidemic on the business of medicine, I'd say that Magic Johnson had more of an impact. His announcement two years ago influenced the need for better drugs and quicker approval more than anything else I've seen."

"In your *vast* experience." Pescatelli met Mackie's gaze with a steely one of his own. "The right celebrity can bring national attention to any problem. But none of these advances would have happened without billions of dollars in research from Big Pharma."

Dr. Jenkins furrowed his brow even as he maintained a strained smile. "We could have a spirited discussion about this for hours, but it's time to start this meeting."

Douglas burst through the double doors to the conference room as if running late for a plane. He had a slide carousel tucked under his arm, shoving a pastry in his mouth and licking the sugar off his fingers. "Hey, Stanley. How are ya? Sorry I'm late." Douglas breezed past his colleagues toward the audiovisual crew. Once he had turned over his slide set, he made his way to the speaker's dais.

Pescatelli and Dr. Jenkins followed Douglas to the front of the hall. Mackie made his way back to his chair.

Dr. Jenkins called the meeting to order. After brief welcoming remarks, he transitioned into prepared comments on the state of clinical oncology on the eve of the twenty-first century. "Every year we start the ASCO meeting with a keynote address that sets the scientific tone for the conference. An address that shines a light on the new insights in the fight against cancer." He paused for water.

"Those of us who've made a career battling cancer are dependent upon the artillery provided by our friends in the pharmaceutical industry. Now that we are half-way through 1993, one company stands out among the giants in the industry. In the next few months, BioloGen Pharmaceuticals expects the FDA to consider, and hopefully approve, a modified version of an old cancer-fighting drug. It is my honor to introduce two men who intend to change the face of cancer treatment and prevention as we know it. Please join me in welcoming Freddie Pescatelli, President and CEO of BioloGen Pharmaceuticals, and his chief biostatistician, Dr. Douglas Schofield."

A polite round of applause rose from the audience. Mackie looked at the attendees seated around him. When he turned around, he noticed a cadre of reporters standing near the back of the conference hall, note-pads in hand, red-lights glowing on their tape recorders.

Pescatelli approached the podium. The longer his silence, the more the murmurs in the audience dissipated. Finally, he began. His first slide appeared as he asked the same rhetorical question he had posed in Cincinnati the previous week. "Does anyone recognize this man?" As before, a black and white image of the bespectacled Judah Folkman in a white lab coat peered from the screen.

Pescatelli gave a flawless presentation. With crisp timing and an informed discussion about the development of Anginex, he had much of the early-morning audience sitting upright and eager to hear more. By the time Douglas reached the podium, nothing about his rumpled appearance and messed-up hair dampened the atmosphere. He provided an additional half hour of data from the Anginex clinical trials. Douglas's lack of personal polish did nothing to distract from the force of his presentation. Mackie saw none of the remnants of the drunken gambler with whom he'd spent the last twenty-four hours. Douglas commanded the podium like an accomplished conductor orchestrating a symphony of statistics.

The change in mood of the audience was not lost on Mackie.

Many around him looked skeptical when Pescatelli spoke of preventing cancer with a single pill a day. This crowd comprised seasoned medical veterans in the fight against cancer. Most had probably lived through the promise of certain cures, only to be disappointed at the dismal results exposed in the bright light of a clinical trial. Pescatelli's history lesson of endostatin softened up the crowd, though, because when Douglas began to speak, the faces of these embattled physicians brightened. They leaned forward to listen. Their eyes lit up with the promise of the pill. They began to believe.

Knowing the punchline of the presentation, Mackie craned his neck to see the reporters behind him. Their pens moved with frantic fury. Handheld recorders pressed toward the podium as if straining to catch each word. After Douglas's concluding remarks, audience questions began.

How long before Anginex is commercially available?

"Early next year."

Will there be an early release by the FDA for compassionate care use?

"We hope so, but no decision has been made as yet."

Can you revisit your comments about the lack of side effects?

"Nothing significant has been seen."

And so it went for ten minutes or more. The questions didn't probe or parse out nuances of the presentation. Most seemed to offer unequivocal praise of the promise of Anginex couched in a query. Near the end of the allotted time for BioloGen, a man behind Mackie stepped up to the audience microphone. "Can you comment about reports from Europe of angiogenesis inhibitors depositing abnormal proteins throughout the body?"

Pescatelli squinted into the light, trying to identify the questioner's location. He maintained a smile with his answer, but Mackie knew better. "As I mentioned moments ago, there are no clinically significant side effects with Anginex. What you describe may have been a problem with other drugs in this class, but Anginex has delivered on its promise to be both effective and safe."

Dr. Jenkins rose from his moderator's chair at the speaker's table, cutting off further discussion. "Ladies and gentlemen," he said, bouncing on his heels with excitement. "As we adjourn for a break, I encourage you to come forward to continue to ask your questions. Mr. Pescatelli and Dr. Schofield will be glad to speak to you individually about their presentation."

Several attendees surged toward the podium. Members of the press hustled forward as well, likely looking for soundbites for the evening news. As Mackie stood, the man who'd asked the last question gathered his materials. He recognized him.

Had he seen him in the casino last night?

"Impressive talk," the man said.

"It's an impressive drug," Mackie responded.

"Perhaps." The man hitched up trousers that seemed one size too big for him. With his open-collared shirt, casual slacks, and sandals, the man dressed like most everyone else in the room. What was missing, though, was a dangling lanyard with an ASCO name tag attached.

Intrigued, Mackie introduced himself.

"Jason Lampley," the man responded as he shook Mackie's hand. "I saw you with Dr. Schofield in the casino yesterday, so I figured you were part of the BioloGen team. I hope Dr. Schofield has as much luck with Anginex as he did with blackjack."

"I don't think luck will have much to do with this drug's success," Mackie said.

The tall man pushed his glasses up on his nose. "Did you know about the side effects I mentioned?"

"The pre-trial scrutiny of Anginex is extensive and complete," Mackie said. "Nausea, rash, and the risk of delayed wound healing. That's most of what you're going to see. When given to the right patients, it's relatively risk-free."

The tall man nodded his head, causing his oversized glasses to slip again. "You're a company man, aren't you?"

"What's that supposed to mean?"

"Have you ever heard of FEBS?"

"Who?"

"Not who. What. FEBS is a European journal of biochemistry. They published an article about angiogenesis inhibitors. Not Anginex, of course, but endostatin. The one Mr. Pescatelli just talked about."

"It's a different drug," Mackie said, feeling somewhat defensive.

"Of course it is, but some of the side effect profiles might be the same." Lampley looked beyond Mackie to the front of the room, as if curious about who might be watching them. He hitched his pants once more. "You've read the early clinical trials for Anginex, I'm sure. Did you pay attention to the drop-out rate, though? Seemed awfully high to me, for a drug that's so safe."

Mackie's defensiveness morphed into curiosity. He knew the published data for Anginex. Knew the benefits. Knew the risks. Pescatelli had promised him access to the preliminary trial data when they returned from Aruba. So how did Lampley know so much about it? Mackie groped for a pen in his pocket. Finding none, he turned toward the table behind him, speaking the whole time. "Give me your contact number, and I'll get back to you about your concerns."

Lampley had already taken a few steps toward the back of the room but not out of ear shot. "Don't worry about it, Cooper. I'm sure you're in the phone book. I can probably contact you at BioloGen if I find out anything more." He continued toward the exit.

Mackie froze. He hadn't introduced himself with his given name, and his ASCO identification simply displayed *Dr. McKay* on the name tag. What else did Lampley know?

*C*HAPTER THIRTEEN

*M*EREDITH BEUKELMAN SAT on the edge of her older sister's hospital bed that first summer, trying to maintain a smile. Holding her sleeping niece helped. The rhythmic rise and fall of the newborn bundle warmed her hands. Relaxed her. Almost made her want to fall asleep herself, which she knew would be a disaster. She dared not move to the bedside recliner, though, for fear of waking up either mom or baby. How long had she sat here? Fifteen minutes? Maybe twenty? For Meredith, inexperience with babies made it seem like an hour. She looked from the baby's peaceful, swaddled face to mom's sunken cheeks, draped with an oxygen tubing and topped with a scarf. Wisps of hair, ravaged by chemotherapy then partially regrown by prenatal vitamins, sprouted from beneath it. Meredith looked away from the chemo-cap, focusing on the IV pump instead. All she needed was a slight distraction.

The door opened behind her.

A heavy-set nurse rolled in a bassinet. She introduced herself with a sign-song whisper to the baby as Nurse Lydia. She eased the plastic cradle toward the head of the bed. "And you must be Aunt Mer."

Meredith smiled. Genuinely this time.

"The doctor's gonna round on all the babies in about half an hour," Nurse Lydia said, still speaking with a stage whisper. She squeezed herself between an IV pole and the head of the bed to check mom's ID bracelet. Her scrubs strained against her girth as she reached for the baby, deftly scooping the child from Meredith's arms. Nurse Lydia placed the child in the bassinet. The baby never stirred.

As quiet as Nurse Lydia was, heft and all, Frances' eyes fluttered open. When she saw the baby in the crib, her gaunt features relaxed. Meredith hadn't seen such a peaceful expression on her sister's face since before Frances' diagnosis. Certainly not since the pregnancy. "We won't be gone long, Mrs. Frances," the nurse said. "Get some sleep while you can."

Freed from the burden of the sleeping baby, and with Frances now awake, Meredith moved from her perch on the mattress to the bedside chair. "How're you feeling?"

"Scared."

"Mama would've been so proud of you."

"I thought she would've still been here this summer."

A tear trickled along her cheek as Frances pushed herself up in the bed. She winced as her IV yanked against the bed rail. As she untangled the cannula, she said, "The doctor wants me to restart chemo before I leave."

"That's efficient." Meredith felt stupid for saying it as soon as the words left her mouth.

"I can't breast feed," Frances continued, "which is fine, I guess. Not that I'd want to contaminate her from these damn things."

"Breast cancer's not contagious."

"Unless she's got the gene, too."

"That's just speculation."

"So first grandma, then mom, and now me? Speculation? Are you serious?"

Meredith knew all too well about that. Couldn't stop

thinking about it, in fact. She'd read the headlines. Heard the talk of the breast cancer gene. Listened to excited predictions that scientists were close to being able to actually test certain women for the genetic time bomb. Defuse it before it exploded and ripped apart families like it had hers. Genetic tests like that had done nothing for her sister, of course. Wouldn't bring back her mom. Probably wouldn't be available any time soon to help her.

Even with such familiarity, and maybe because of it, Meredith hated cancer talk. She assumed she'd be bitter, too, if she'd come back from her honeymoon with a breast lump. What woman wouldn't be pissed if she had to stop chemotherapy three months into treatment because her birth control failed? Frances hadn't been the same over the last year and Meredith couldn't blame her. But it was so damn exhausting talking to her sister about it all. She hoped the baby might finally give Frances something else to focus on.

Meredith reached for her purse. The pill bottle inside rattled when she picked it up. "I've got some exciting news to tell you," she began.

"I'm exhausted," Frances said. She repositioned in bed and turned her back on her sister. "The nurse said I should sleep when the baby does."

"It's a new pill," Meredith persisted, "called Anginex."

"Tell me later."

Meredith stood, stung but trying to understand. She gave her sister's leg a love-pat and left. The clatter of pills in a plastic bottle kept time with her swinging purse as she walked down the hallway.

Maybe later, she thought to herself.

CHAPTER FOURTEEN

SCOTT HOFFMAN SAT at his office desk later that week, concentrating on a patient's paper chart. Each of the clinic records looked the same to him. He studied the first page, scanning the standard demographic information before turning his attention to his computer monitor. He crosschecked the same information on the Computer-based Patient Record. While the program upgrade didn't exactly replicate the paper chart, it contained all of the key information. He flipped a page with one hand then clicked to find the corresponding second page on the computer. Again, the contents of the chart and the screen matched.

His secretary, Yolanda, stood nearby, smacking her gum and cradling a black binder while Hoffman cross-referenced two more pages. "What do ya think?"

He looked up. "Every patient encounter will be documented like this?"

"Ultimately just on the computer, but yeah, it'll look like this when you use it. Since you've been so resistant to changing your charting habits, Compton Drew has agreed—"

"The computer guy?"

"Yeah, the head of medical records." Yolanda didn't miss a beat. "Compton's agreed to let you use six months of shadow

ts to transition your research patients to CPR"
graded version."
Right."
Hoffman sat back and scratched his chin. "I want to keep
the paper charts."
"And I want a raise," Yolanda said. "C'mon, Scottie. Our
division is the last one to transition to complete computerized
charting, and frankly, the hold-up is you. I've been logging
patients into the general database for months. All of our
research at NIH is done on CPR except for your notes. As
long as we keep some charts paper and others computerized,
there's more chance for error and less security for patient
records." She paused, then said, "Hold on. That's my phone."
She marched out of his office.

Hoffman studied the paper chart once more. He preferred
to look at other doctors's notes on CPR, but he didn't want
his own research so exposed. He smiled at the irony. His
anachronistic charting system had limited his own exposure
during the Hepatazyme fiasco. Yet, since other divisions at the
NIH used CPR for their charting, he could use Janice O'Reilly's
password to access the computerized medical records of other
doctors's patients and make changes for the clinical trials of
Anginex.

Bad for them. Brilliant for him.

The dual system made his pharmaceutical consulting
easier, but he knew that would soon end. What if Janice
changed her CPR log-in code? he worried. What if I lose
unrestricted access? He felt an uncomfortable tightness in his
chest. He loosened his tie and took a deep breath.

Relax, he thought. You're in control here. Remain calm and
stick to the plan.

Hoffman leaned back in his chair and practiced his
biofeedback. He took a long, slow breath and held it. Exhaling
slowly, he counted to ten. When he did, he felt his body relax

into the chair. He thought of a Caribbean beach and a warm breeze as he tried to take his mind to a peaceful place. Much better.

"Did you forget about your lunch meeting?" Yolanda asked.

Hoffman bolted upright. "What?"

"You're supposed to be downstairs in ten minutes." She placed a binder on his desk.

Once a quarter, the directors for clinical research gathered for lunch to discuss problems and opportunities for research within each division. It was a chance for the brightest minds at the NIH to come together and discuss ways to improve medical research and share new developments.

"Here's the agenda and the reference articles," she said, not waiting for a response from her boss. "It's a list of recent Institute publications as well as entry criteria for trials still accepting patients. Happy reading." She walked out, leaving behind the familiar scent of Marlboros and Maxwell House.

Hoffman glanced at the binder and then at his watch. He needed to leave now. He grabbed his white coat and cinched up his tie.

When he arrived he saw several men and women, holding plates of sandwiches and pasta salad, engaged in cocktail party chatter. The catered lunch proved adequate, per the usual. Still, Hoffman enjoyed talking with the country's brightest researchers at the NIH to find out new developments in the world of investigational treatments. Earlier this year, Hoffman had presented to this same group his clinical trial results of Hepatazyme and had talked about the once daily treatment for diabetes. His colleagues had congratulated him on his innovative research and favorable trial results. Today, the noted oncologist, Dwight Erlanger, would discuss his cancer treatment research. Hoffman approached him.

"Hey, Scott," Erlanger said. "Congratulations on your

write-up in *The Washington Post.*"

Since the FDA approval of Hepatazyme, Hoffman had become somewhat of a medical celebrity at the NIH. His fame came, in part, because diabetes affected so many people worldwide. It also came because Hepatazyme's manufacturer, Bolten & Ferris Pharmaceuticals, decided to market Hoffman's name in selling the drug. The company recognized that American consumers respected opinions from NIH researchers, considering them unbiased guardians of the public's health. The noted *Post* reporter, Bill Baldwin, had interviewed Hoffman in his office, subsequently writing a front-page article on his life as a leading medical researcher. A framed copy still hung above his office sofa.

"Thanks," Hoffman said, "I saw your lung cancer article in *The Medical Weekly.* Nicely written."

Dr. Erlanger beamed. "I'd love to take credit for writing it, but you've consulted for Big Pharma long enough to know we don't write half the published studies funded by those companies. Fact is, I submitted all of my data to the drug company, and two months later they sent me this article that was fully written and referenced. 'Read it, edit it, and submit it,' they told me. So I read the study, made sure they spelled my name right, and submitted it to *The Medical Weekly.*" He snapped his fingers. "Easy as that. Pharmaceutical consultation has its privileges, right?"

Hoffman gave a nervous laugh. Like you wouldn't believe, he thought.

"Let me ask you something else," Dr. Erlanger said. He leaned closer and lowered his voice. "Have you been having any problems with your data on the new medical records system?"

Hoffman nearly choked on his ham and swiss sandwich. "What do you mean?"

"I found some data missing from my patients," Erlanger

said. "When our department switched to this computer-based record last year, I was forced to dictate all of my notes since I can't type. The other day, I had this patient come in for a return visit for one of the drugs I'm testing called Anginex. I swear, I remember this lady having abnormal labs and a funky chest x-ray. When I checked back on CPR, though, the lab was normal and the chest x-ray wasn't even there. Just gone." He took a bite of his sandwich, talking with his mouth full. "I used to be able to go back to my notes to see what I'd written down. Of course, now I'm dependent on what's transcribed from my dictation, and no one saves the tapes."

Hoffman swallowed, chasing the suddenly stale wheat bread with a sip of water. "I've not noticed anything like that." His palms began to sweat.

"I called medical records and spoke to some woman named O'Reilly down there," Dr. Erlanger said.

"Uh-huh."

"She told me there's nothing wrong with the medical records system. 'If it says normal, then the lab was normal,' she said. She even transferred me to the head of medical records. I spoke to some officious ass named Compton Drew. Told him the same thing, and he got all defensive about my accusations of medical record tampering. He said we've got the tightest security of any medical records system in the world. He started talking about how they password protect all terminals and crap like that."

Hoffman's plate began to slide off his sweaty palm. He placed the plate on the table and mopped his hands with a napkin.

Erlanger continued. "So Compton says, 'If it makes you feel better, we can audit your patient's medical records to see who's been looking at them.' "

Hoffman coughed.

"You okay?" Erlanger asked.

Hoffman nodded. "Sandwich got stuck," he lied. His stomach felt sour. "So what did you tell him? About the audit?"

"What do you think I told him? I said, 'Hell yeah you can audit my charts!' If someone's been messing with my data, I need to know about it. A few changes in results can mean the difference between a meaningful study and one that's a bust."

Hoffman felt the blood drain out of his face. He steadied himself against the table. "When did you talk to Compton?"

"Yesterday. He said he'd check it out and let me know by next week if someone's been changing my patient records."

CHAPTER FIFTEEN

THE BIOLOGEN CHARTER from Aruba didn't touch down in the private airstrip in Cincinnati until well after sunset, but Mackie made it to work at his usual early morning hour the next day. When he walked into his office at BioloGen's headquarters, he was not alone. Ms. Franks greeted him with her trademark abruptness. "Mr. Pescatelli's waiting for you downstairs in his office." Not even taking time to sit, Mackie placed his satchel on the desk and headed back to the elevators.

When he reached Pescatelli's second floor office, he saw the door cracked and heard his boss's booming voice on the other side. Mackie knocked twice and stepped inside. Pescatelli, the handset to his phone cradled between his ear and shoulder, motioned Mackie forward.

Mackie had visited the spacious office only once. It provided Pescatelli direct oversight of his company. Behind his desk, an enormous tinted window overlooked the lobby. On the far wall to his right, Mackie noticed a picture window that framed the view of the pastoral beauty of southwestern Ohio. On the opposite wall, floor-to-ceiling wooden bookshelves held photographs, souvenirs, and hardback books. As Mackie walked over to inspect them, he noted a prominently displayed photo of Pescatelli alongside two rail-thin African men. They stood on rocky terrain, clouds seemingly at their feet, the name *Kilimanjaro* engraved on the frame. Next to it, a photo showed a disheveled and grinning Pescatelli with three other hikers on the grassy stone steps of Machu Pichu.

Mackie heard Pescatelli say, "Let me let you go. One of my top marketing execs just walked in." He grinned at Mackie and motioned to the chair in front of his desk. Appearing even more tanned now than when they left Aruba, Pescatelli hung up and shook Mackie's hand. "It's hard coming back from paradise, but things are heating up here. The response to the ASCO presentation has been amazing."

"I heard you've got a CNN interview today," Mackie said.

"The major networks called, too. I'm trying to spread it out." Pescatelli grabbed two pages from his desk and held up an article written in a single-column strip down the center of the paper. "Galleys of a *Newsweek* cover story coming in the next issue that highlights Anginex. I've already put off the editors at *The Economist*, encouraging them to wait until FDA approval before they do a cover story. You get on the front of a magazine like that, and it's worth a month's worth of print ads." He set the pages back on his desk and picked up a glass. "Get you a drink?"

Mackie took a seat in the chair. "No, thanks."

The ice rattled in the glass as Pescatelli drained the soda, then made eye contact with Mackie. "Douglas finally told me last night about that guy who came up to you after our presentation."

Mackie's gaze never wavered. "He mentioned a trend of problems with other angiogenesis inhibitors."

Pescatelli sat on his own side of the desk and pushed back. "Total bullshit. There's never been any mention of illegal activities at BioloGen. Not one hint of impropriety."

Mackie waited for more. Hearing none, he responded, "The man never said anything about illegal activities. He mentioned side effects, like the ones that plagued other angiogenesis inhibitors."

"He's stirring up trouble."

"Are there any side effects with Anginex we've not already discussed?"

"None." He rolled his chair up to the desk, leaning forward on his arms. "You know this, Mackie. You've seen what ADAM does. You know we can screen out the bad ones before they even reach clinical trials."

"I've seen that we put a lot of faith in a mainframe computer to screen for side effects. Seems to me there's a chance ADAM could occasionally be wrong."

Pescatelli lowered his voice. The fresh smell of cologne mixed with his sour breath. "I've spent a career in the pharmaceutical industry, working the business from every conceivable angle. I've seen the biggest companies do whatever it takes to sell their drug. Stupid things, even lie, just to push one more prescription. There is no doubt in my mind that many of our competitors are still practicing unethical, even illegal, marketing practices. We don't have to do that."

Mackie leaned back in his chair and lifted his hands, palms up. A truce. "That's all I'm asking."

"I called you down here to show you something." Pescatelli reached into a lower desk drawer and pulled out a handgun. He looked up and smiled. "Not this. That's in here for some insurance against the unexpected." He reached back down and pulled out a thick file folder fastened with rubber bands. "This is what I want you to see."

The folder bulged with magazine and newspaper clippings that spilled onto the desk as Mackie removed the rubber bands. He began to thumb through the articles. Clipped and filed in chronological order, each one had its source hand-written atop the article. Most of them came from nationally circulated newspapers and magazines.

"That folder keeps me honest," Pescatelli said.

Mackie randomly read titles from the collection of articles.

Pescatelli pushed a meaty finger across his desk. "That one shocked me," he said as Mackie read several paragraphs of one article. "Paying doctors to prescribe a drug. Can you imagine that?"

Mackie turned to another article.

"And that one!" Pescatelli roared. "They hid safety data from the FDA so that the drug would receive FDA approval."

"Wasn't that drug eventually pulled from the market?"

"Yep. But not before the company earned billions. There's another one in there about the criminal charges brought against one of those companies." He sank back in his chair, enjoying Mackie's attention to the egregious fouls of the pharmaceutical industry.

"Taken together, it looks like all of Big Pharma is mentioned in this folder."

"You won't find a written word or a whisper about impropriety at BioloGen. And that's the point. You won't find it, because we've never been accused of wrong-doing, including hiding side effects. In fact, we've never had an investigation into our business practices. Never had a formal complaint about our marketing or drug development." Pescatelli stood, walked over to the wet bar next to the bookshelf, and poured a Diet Coke into a fresh glass filled with ice. Mackie made a conscious effort not to stare at the scarlet birth mark. Red asked, "You sure I can't get you something?"

"I'm fine."

"So what did Sarah say when you told her about your encounter in Aruba?"

"She doesn't know," Mackie said. Pescatelli didn't need to know that Mackie's three phone calls to Nashville remained ignored. Not a single return message on his home answering machine when he'd returned last night. "I knew she'd ask a thousand questions—"

"Lawyers tend to do that."

"—so I thought I'd talk to you first."

Pescatelli returned to the desk, soda in hand, and leaned a hip on the front side of the desk. "I wouldn't even worry her with the information. Forget you ever saw that guy. There's plenty of work to do around here without having to look over your shoulder. If you hear from him again, though, I want you to come directly to me. I'd like to know his agenda."

"Maybe it's just to find the truth."

* * *

Once Mackie left, Pescatelli returned to his desk. He gathered up the newspaper clippings and placed them in the folder, making sure to keep them in chronological order, the way he liked them. After rubber-banding the file, he tucked it into his desk drawer. He turned toward the tinted window and stared down at the lobby below.

Of all the shitty luck. He had made worldwide headlines with the most important drug in a generation, and some arrogant academic in Aruba had to come to the party and piss in the punch. He thought he had convinced Mackie not to worry about Anginex, but with so much at stake, he couldn't take any chances.

He drained the rest of his Diet Coke and chewed on the ice for several more minutes. Finally, he sat down at his desk and removed a business card from the top drawer. Then reaching into the deep middle drawer to his right, he removed a grey push-button phone, looking typical in every way except for a fold-down screen the size of a pack of index cards. Pescatelli positioned the state-of-the-art videophone on the edge of his desk, arranging the cords behind it. He unfolded the card-shaped screen with a built-in camera. An AT&T Videophone 2500. Less than a year old. Used only for urgent situations. He dialed the number from the business card and waited. On the small screen he could see a fair representation of himself, but the video feed showed slow, deliberate movements slightly distorted from reality, as if he were working under water.

Soon the line connected. An unseen woman answered and instructed Pescatelli to hold a moment. The video feed changed as soon as the line connected. He saw an empty chair behind a desk. An office setting. Pescatelli heard a door open. A man entered the camera's view, initially only capturing his suit and tie before he sat down. The kind worn by politicians and company presidents. He faced the screen with a visible scowl.

"What?" he demanded.

Pescatelli leaned toward the card-like screen and built-in camera. "I just spoke to Dr. McKay."

No response. At his best, BioloGen's boss in Manhattan was a man of few words. Stressful situations like this only caused longer, more uncomfortable pauses in conversation. The man abhorred small talk. He wanted his subordinates to supply facts without editorial comment. Pescatelli heard him grind his teeth. Hearing no other response, Pescatelli continued. "The Anginex situation is under control."

"Who else knows?"

"Douglas Schofield. And the two of us. That's it."

"His wife?"

"Not that I can tell."

"Hold on." The man reached out to the monitor as if trying to reach through the screen, then the phone went blank. Pescatelli knew he had not disconnected because he could still hear muffled scuffling on the other end. Thirty seconds later, the screen flickered back on.

"Every thing all right?" Pescatelli asked.

"There's been a screw up at the NIH. It doesn't concern you." The suited man paused, then asked, "Tell me about his wife once more?"

"She doesn't even live in Cincinnati right now. Their relationship is strained."

"That could work to our advantage."

"We've given McKay no reason to suspect a problem here."

"Don't. We can't afford bad press on this. Understood?"

Pescatelli pushed back, trying to control his anger. "I said it's under control."

"It better be, Red. And don't call me on this phone again unless it's an emergency."

The screen went blank. The audio feed clicked off.

Pescatelli sat back to consider his options. He needed someone to keep an eye on Mackie. Someone to insure that Anginex's past remained buried. Someone he trusted implicitly. He shoved the videophone back into the cavernous desk drawer and reached for the phone on his desk. This time, he dialed the number from memory. After a few rings, a man with a deep voice answered.

"Eddie."

"Mr. Pescatelli. What do you need?"

"Help with a situation in Cincinnati."

"Anginex?"

"Again."

The man gave a deep-throated laugh. "I thought we handled that."

"This is different."

Pescatelli gave Eddie the pertinent information with a promise to call back when he had a more specific plan. Once finished, he used his thumb to disconnect, never putting down the handset. Then, he dialed one more number.

Ms. Franks answered on the first ring.

"Get Karen and Douglas to my office in the next five minutes," Pescatelli instructed. "We've got a situation with Mackie."

Chapter Sixteen

*S*TACKS OF DUSTY medical journals surrounded Mackie as he scanned the bookshelves of the medical library. He ran his fingers along the bound spines, searching for a title. He walked down the aisle once more, in case the library filed the journal according to its abbreviation and not its full name. No such luck. He walked to the end of the stacks. Tom Philips, his longtime friend, sat on a wooden bench near the elevator, holding a notecard.

"Happy Anniversary," Tom said. "Four years?"

"Five tomorrow."

"Congrats on the wooden anniversary."

Mackie gave a wry smile. "That about sums up the relationship right now."

"She's still pissed?"

"She's still in Nashville," Mackie said.

"Ouch."

"I think she and Reagan are coming up next weekend."

Tom nodded. "So any luck with what you're looking for?"

"It's not here," Mackie said.

"F.E.D.S?"

"FEBS. It's a European biochemistry journal," Mackie said. "I'm not surprised they don't have it."

"If you're not surprised, then why are we here?"

"To get your help."

Mackie had left the office at lunchtime, telling Ms. Frank he'd be gone for a couple of hours to meet an old friend from medical school. He drove straight to the biomedical library at the University of Cincinnati medical school. He knew Tom Philips couldn't take much time away from his clinic hours, but he had no intention of having a long lunch. He told Tom to meet him alone in the library basement with a blank notecard. As expected, Tom showed up without asking questions. Mackie arrived early, and when he didn't find the back issues of the FEBS journal, he intended to ask Tom to help him take the next step.

Tom stood, waving the blank card. "So you want me to get it for you?"

"The librarian will want to know who I am and what journal I'm searching for. If we were in Nashville, no one would think twice about getting me an inter-library loan. But I'm an outsider here."

"And you can't call home to ask for a favor?"

"It'll be easier for everyone if I didn't."

Tom took a Bic pen from his pocket. "Tell me the name of the journal again."

Mackie gave him everything he knew, including any reference to endostatin or other angiogenesis inhibitors. Tom recorded it all, promising to speak to the librarian as soon as Mackie left. They arranged to catch up later to see what the medical library found.

He drove straight back to the office, arriving two hours from the time he had left. If Ms. Franks noticed his late arrival, she didn't say a word. Nor did she ask about his lunch. Mackie logged a couple of more hours at his desk before calling her into his office about four o'clock that afternoon. He still needed to send an anniversary gift to Sarah.

"Yes?"

"Am I done for the afternoon?" he asked.

She studied him before answering, her thin frame hardly occupying the door to his office. "Are you done with conference calls and meetings? Yes, you are. Are you done with your paperwork for the day? I cannot answer that for you, Dr. McKay. I'm not your mother."

"Do you know any good florists?"

"Is this work related?" She waited for an answer, and not getting one, walked back to her desk.

Mackie laughed to himself at Ms. Franks's single-minded focus as he finished the draft of the sales report he was reading. He grabbed a stack of papers and packed a few more hours of work into his satchel. Earlier that day, Douglas had invited Mackie to his house for dinner. With his own wife out with her friends that evening, Douglas said it would be a great time to hang out away from work.

The drive to the Schofield's house took less than half an hour from the BioloGen headquarters. For Mackie, it seemed like a world away. The Schofields lived in the affluent suburb of Indian Hill, an idyllic country-side of rolling hills, dense forests, and open pastures that probably didn't look much different than it had fifty years ago. Douglas had described it to Mackie as a midwestern refuge for the wealthy. "This is our kind of neighborhood," he had told Mackie when he called earlier for directions. "It's about the only place close to downtown that I could find enough land to keep our horse happy."

Gravel crunched under the tires as Mackie drove into the roundabout. A stone fountain matched the stone façade of the house. He parked his car right next to Douglas's yellow RX-7. He locked his doors out of habit even as he realized the wide-open spaces offered built-in protection.

A note taped to the front door instructed Mackie to come

in and head toward the backyard. He knocked anyway as he opened the heavy wooden door. The temperature seemed to drop ten degrees as he stepped into the marble-lined foyer. To his right, tall ceilings and a stone fireplace dominated the décor with a bearskin rug and a stuffed boar's head prominently displayed. Mackie walked forward. He heard muted humming from an adjacent room. "Douglas?" he called out.

"Come on back," his friend called.

Mackie followed his way through the house toward what must have been the back. As he reached the modern kitchen, he saw Douglas coming through the patio door wearing a denim apron over white Bermuda shorts. Flecks of grease glistened on the end of the spatula in his hand. "I've been meaning to get you to our humble abode long before now."

Mackie smiled. "Not so humble."

"I got a steal on this house," Douglas said as he made his way to the sink to rinse the spatula. "It was supposed to be a family homestead in the Old English tradition, which meant no air conditioning and poorly insulated windows. It'd been sitting on the market for so long that we squeezed the family into selling us the land *below* the market value *and* paying our closing costs."

"Nice rug in the front room," Mackie said. He walked to the refrigerator and helped himself to a Bud Lite long neck. Guys's night rules: make yourself at home.

"My wife won it at a Muscular Dystrophy auction in Vegas. You should've seen her trying to get that damn thing through airport security just to bring it home." He wiped the wet spatula on his apron. "Let me show you something." He grabbed his own beer from the refrigerator en route to the front of the house.

Mackie followed him.

Douglas stopped at the boar's head hanging above the stone fireplace. "Now this is my kind of decoration."

"You hunt?"

"Hell, no. I wouldn't know the ass-end of a gun if it were held to my face. But Becky," he paused to swill his beer, "she loves this stuff. I came home one day to find this head in a Federal Express box sitting in our foyer. I asked, 'Where are we gonna put that?' She looked at me and said, 'You stick to engineering and yard work, and I'll worry about the decorating.' So I get home one day and this room has changed from Martha Stewart to Crocodile Dundee."

Mackie admired the hall of taxidermy, thinking of food the whole time. In an effort to return quickly from the medical library, he had skipped lunch. "What's for dinner?"

"Steaks are on the grill. Let me show you the backyard."

Mackie retraced his steps back to the kitchen and through the patio door. "Driving in, it looked like you have six or eight acres out here."

"Ten in the back alone." Douglas beamed as they walked onto the patio. "Much of that is original Ohio forest, but we've still got plenty of space for the horse. You see her home out there?" He pointed with his spatula to a building near the edge of the property.

"The red barn?"

"Stable. That's where Pepper lives. Sometimes I think Becky loves that animal more than me." Douglas doubled back to the grill and opened the top.

Mackie immediately smelled the smoke from the sizzling meat on the flames. A feast for a half dozen people, maybe more. "Who else is joining us?"

"Just us, buddy."

"You and Becky are going to have some leftovers."

"She won't touch this. Ever since we got Pepper, she's been on a red meat strike. Some crap about cruelty to animals."

Mackie smiled as he sipped his Bud Lite. "But she bids for bear pelts and boar's heads?"

"I know, right? But what the hell am I going to do." He flipped the meat over and grease splattered on his apron. "We hosted the company picnic here last year."

"Did you have a good turn out?"

"Almost everyone came. Red rented a tent and catered the barbecue ribs. Becky and I provided the refreshments. Damn near went through four kegs and two-dozen bottles of wine before the night was done. It's amazing what people can do to a keg when you give them an afternoon off. Everyone had a buzz by the end of the evening. We even got Keg-Stand Kiley into the act."

"I haven't seen that side of her, yet," Mackie said.

"Stick around. I like to remind her every so often of that party just to watch her squirm. You folks in marketing have a reputation for being a bit stuffy at times." Douglas took a long pull on his beer. "I heard you and Red had a chat this morning."

Mackie froze. A shiver chilled his spine that he tried to hide behind another sip of his beer. "What'd you hear?"

"Not much, which is why I'm asking. I spoke to Red when we got back from Aruba about what you told me—that some crackpot was pestering you with questions about the side effects of Anginex. So, what'd Red say?"

Mackie folded his arms across his chest. "He seemed pretty defensive. Essentially said it was foolish to even suggest BioloGen had a blemish in its sterling reputation."

"Did he show you the file?"

"Of articles?"

"I love that thing," Douglas said. "The audacity. Patients collectively spend billions of dollars each year on prescription drugs, but some companies still hide data to get a piece of that pie. You'd be amazed at the stupidity of some of the competition."

Mackie uncrossed his arms, dropping his guard ever so slightly. "One article mentioned a company actually paying doctors to prescribe their medications."

"That's what I'm talking about. Do you really think a company is going to get away with stuff like that?" He didn't pause for Mackie to answer the question. "Of course, not. That file is living proof that you can't get ahead by cheating in this business."

Mackie considered this. "Almost verbatim what Pescatelli said. I went back earlier today to look at the early Anginex trials, and I can't find any mention of side effects that this guy mentioned. Unless he knows something we don't."

"Are you kidding? This is about competition. If someone can plant a seed of doubt about a drug, it gives another company the chance to sell more of their drug. It's a cutthroat business, pal, but BioloGen is in it for the long haul. We'll make more than our share of money once Anginex is approved." Douglas gulped down the rest of his beer then tossed the bottle toward the trash can next to the grill. "What'd Sarah say about the encounter?"

"Nothing. It hasn't come up yet."

"She probably doesn't care about all this shop talk, anyway." Douglas nudged Mackie with his elbow. "When's she coming up, anyway? I wanna meet that little daughter of yours."

"I'm hoping they'll fly up next weekend." That Mackie had already bought the tickets didn't guarantee his family's arrival. Sarah had changed plans on him more than once.

With the juice from the steaks no longer running red, Douglas removed them from the grill and set them on the outdoor dining table. Stacks of baked potatoes and a platter of cole slaw waited for them, along with a cooler of long necks. The conversation turned to cars, then horses, and finally vacation homes. Neighborhood hobbies, Douglas said, which Mackie interpreted to be straight from a Robin Leach script for Lifestyles of the Rich and Famous. Mackie bent the conversation to the Reds recent championship, and what that meant for their future. Two hours later, both men appeared tapped out of conversation and energy.

"It's time for me to head home," Mackie finally said. Enough leftover food for a family of four sat untouched on the table. "I'll have to get you and Becky over to our place when Sarah gets in town."

"I've got a better idea," Douglas said. "Let's find the two of you a house in our neighborhood, and then we can have a welcome party in your new backyard."

* * *

Douglas left the dishes on the outside table as he walked Mackie to his car. He waved with a beer in hand as he watched the red glow of the taillights ease down the driveway then disappear in the canopy of trees lining the road. He walked back inside and into the front room that doubled as a home office. The boxy screen of his Macintosh II vx was dark, but Douglas activated the home computer and logged in to his account. He didn't bother sitting in his plush leather chair, nor did he even turn on the desk lamp. The glow of the screen was enough for him to complete his task.

Earlier that spring, he had convinced each of the executives at BioloGen to connect to the company's electronic mail system. No one used it much at first, but Douglas knew they would warm to it. Especially in a situation like this.

His mailbox indicated that he had one message. As per protocol, little identifying information came across in messages like this. But little was needed. Douglas read the two-word message from his boss. "Damage control?"

Douglas hit the reply button and banged out any equally terse response. "None needed. He doesn't suspect. She hasn't been told."

He pressed *Send*, logged off his computer, and went back to the patio to clean up from dinner.

$\mathscr{C}$HAPTER SEVENTEEN

$\mathscr{S}$COTT HOFFMAN DIDN'T sleep at all for the next twenty-four hours. He was losing control. After learning that others suspected medical records changes, waves of nausea plagued him for the rest of the day and into the night. By midnight, cold sweats and fever. Diarrhea came next. If he had not experienced it himself, he would never have believed that mental stress could cause such a visceral reaction in the human body. It was as if his conversation with Dwight Erlanger had inflicted a violent gastrointestinal virus. Hoffman even thought of calling his primary care doctor so that he could be evaluated, but he knew that he would be asked more questions than he cared to answer.

In the early morning hours, wrapped in a wool blanket and drinking hot tea, Hoffman reviewed his options.

He could call Janice O'Reilly again and explain his predicament. He knew she'd come back to see him, even though he'd ignored her for the last several weeks. She would undoubtably ask questions. Why hadn't he told her sooner? And what was he doing deleting patient's medical records?

Or he could contact her boss, Compton Drew. "Someone's broken into my office, and I think the intruder may have been using my computer," he would explain. That would certainly lead back to Janice O'Reilly. If pressed for an explanation, Hoffman would have to defend his previous affair with her. Even if she contradicted him, Hoffman felt certain Compton would take the word of a long-time research physician over that of a records clerk.

What if I talk to Erlanger himself? Hoffman wondered. He could claim a member of his endocrinology staff had broken into his office and randomly deleted patient data from his computer. No. Erlanger might demand to speak to the fictitious employee responsible for the deletions. Worse yet, he'd probably continue the investigation.

Hoffman returned to his original conclusion. He needed to get in touch with his blackmailer. No other choice. The man with the deep voice knew too much about the workings of the NIH medical record system.

Hoffman wanted to call him, but he didn't have a number.

He would try to contact him through the post office. If Dirk Waters was right that the envelopes were hand delivered, he might leave a letter in the post office box to communicate his fears.

Leaving the letter constituted a risk, plus no guarantee the right person would receive it. Even if the man with the deep voice received the letter, Hoffman despaired that anything could be done about his predicament.

The depth of his uncertainty sent Hoffman rushing to the bathroom in a fit of colonic spasms.

Weakened but resolved, he showered and dressed for the day. He put on a pair of surgical gloves that he kept in his first-aid kit and carefully removed a blank sheet of paper from his desk drawer. He picked up a N$^{o.}$ 2 pencil and began to write in block letters. He knew the note would probably never be examined for fingerprints or hand writing analysis if the wrong person received it, but he tried to limit his exposure.

He wrote:

HEAD OF MED. REC. MAY BE AWARE OF
THE PROJECT.
CONCERN FOR COMPROMISED MISSION.
PLEASE ADVISE.

He looked again at the note, certain it sounded silly. He didn't know what else to say in order to convey the urgency and secrecy his communication demanded. He removed a blank envelope with his gloved hand, folded the note, and moistened the envelope flap with a wet wad of tissue before sealing it.

It felt unusual to drive to the post office on a Thursday morning. The pale sunrise combined with high doses of aspirin began to lighten Hoffman's mood. He would leave this letter in the post office box, and then pray it wouldn't be there when he returned the following day.

* * *

Earlier that evening, Compton Drew had audited recent computer entries for the computer-based patient record system. After six hours, he needed a break from the tedium. He logged off his computer and headed for his car. As he drove south from Bethesda, he pieced together the events of the previous week, trying to understand the unexpected spike of medical record activity from a computer on the ninth floor.

He had received a call from an obnoxious oncologist, who complained that his electronic charts has been altered. "I swear there is missing information from what I dictated," Dr. Dwight Erlanger insisted. "And some of the lab tests I ordered aren't even there!"

None of this could be verified in the absence of a paper trail, but Compton knew CPR better than anyone. "I hear your concerns, but I assure you the problem is not with our system," Compton had said. "If you give me the patient's name and date of birth, I'll trace the access to their medical record to be sure."

Compton routinely tested compliance with departmental security standards. When he began the trace on the oncologist's patient that afternoon, his system revealed a leak. Rather than showing an intra-departmental source for the leak, though, he discovered those records had been illegally accessed from the ninth floor. Why would an oncologist be in the endocrinology clinic? he wondered. Further investigation showed each patient entry came in the early mornings, usually before normal business hours.

So far, none of it made sense to him. As far back as he could remember, he had always hated problems that didn't make sense.

Friends in high school teased Compton, poking fun at his love of country music and telling him that he was the quintessential boring guy. Classmates called him UPS because his oily hair was as brown and slick as packing tape. When he smiled, crooked teeth dominated his face.

What he lacked in appearance, though, he made up for in aptitude. When affordable personal computers hit the market in the 1980s, Compton bought one of the first. He considered it a defining event in his young adulthood.

Tonight, he felt particularly troubled by the glitches in his electronic record keeping. CPR had worked flawlessly since its introduction at NIH. "This is a researcher's dream," one doctor had told him, because it enabled access to, and comparison of, patient study data. The doctors who made the whole-sale transformation from paper charts to computerized ones seemed to enjoy the most benefit from CPR. Others held out, preferring a dual system. Compton had plans to get everyone on it by the end of 1994, and his biggest fear until then was a leak of private patient information. But so far, he had not had a single breach of security with CPR.

Until now.

This new development altered Compton's comfort with his security protocols.

His own security standards hindered this present search for the culprit. Because each medical record employee had a randomly selected password, he had no way to discern who'd accessed CPR on the ninth floor, but he intended to find out.

He sent out an electronic mail to the members of each department, asking all employees to respond by entering their CPR password into a designated box attached to the electronic communication. He had designed a simple program that functioned as a lock and key. If the password matched the one used during the ninth-floor records breach, a return electronic message would automatically be sent, which read, "Please come see me next week when I get back." Compton sent off the electronic mail right before he left the office that night.

Resigned that he would not figure out the riddle of the ninth floor intruder until he returned from his trip, Compton rolled down his windows, opened the moon-roof, and turned on his car stereo, signing along with Garth Brooks at the top of his voice.

CHAPTER EIGHTEEN

KAREN KILEY SAT at the far end of the third floor conference room, taking notes on a yellow legal pad. Mackie stood by a dry-erase board near the front of the room, waiting for feedback. "That time was a little better," Karen said. "Now, I want you to use the name of the drug three times in the ninety-seconds that you have their attention."

Mackie cleared his throat. He introduced himself, then launched into his spiel. "I've brought six boxes of NuCor for you. As I'm sure you know, NuCor is the only drug in its class to lower LDL cholesterol by forty percent at the starting doses, and the only drug to lower cholesterol up to sixty-five percent at the upper doses." Mackie stuck to his lines this time. "In addition, NuCor has the lowest incidence of side effects of any statin on the market. Our three-year data shows less than one percent incidence of liver enzyme abnormalities and not a single case of hepatic failure."

Karen interrupted, playing the role of obnoxious physician. "Sounds about like the other leading brands, and I'm sure it's expensive."

"It's actually the lowest priced statin on the market, for both out of pocket expenses and insurance co-pays."

Switching back to her role as head of BioloGen marketing,

she said, "Nice touch with the out of pocket expenses comment, but that's not our market. Also, keep the name of the drug and the low cost in the same sentence so they can associate the two. Keep going."

"NuCor is also..." Mackie forgot his lines. "NuCor's the... it's, uh..."

"Cut!" Karen yelled from her seat. "You bit it at the end, doc."

"Lost my train of thought."

"Which is why you need a closing. Some of your brethren won't have time to chit chat with you. Other will get pissed with the intrusion. You must have a closing comment. Plant a seed on your first visit. Most will simply thank the doctor and leave a few boxes of samples. I had one hot-shot working with us a few years back who used a more bold closing, asking the prescriber if he would be thinking of NuCor the next time he wrote for a cholesterol lowering drug. Whatever works for you. Either way, you need a memorable closing."

Mackie ambled to the conference table and took a seat. "I felt like a medical student examining patients for the first time."

"I tell my marketers they're more like your in-laws. During your periodic visits to the doctor's office, you don't have to be liked but you do have to be tolerated." Karen pushed back from the table and gathered her note pad. "You ready for me to show you how the pros do it?"

"You're the boss."

"That's the smartest thing you've said all morning. Grab your coat. I'll drive."

It took a half hour to get to the medical school, retracing the same route Mackie had taken earlier that week. He glanced at the entrance to the biomedical library as they walked past, wondering if the journal article his friend requested had arrived. Karen led him past the lecture halls and toward the lunch room. The surroundings reminded Mackie of his own medical school. "You ever notice there's a universal smell in these academic centers?" he asked.

Karen's fluorescent smile made her eyes sparkle. "It's the smell of opportunity."

"I was thinking formaldehyde."

She stopped her long-legged pace and looked at Mackie. "This medical school has one-hundred sixty students enrolled in each of the four years of training. My goal is that when they get their diplomas, BioloGen will be a familiar name to them."

"Not specific drugs?" Mackie asked.

"Those, too, but if they associate us with the purveyor of quality pharmaceuticals, we've done our job."

"To be honest, I can't tell you a single thing about the drug reps that called on us in medical school."

"Pharmaceutical reps, not drug reps. We're not selling Ecstasy." She resumed walking, leading them deeper into the corridors of the school.

Mackie persisted. "But isn't that a problem? Spending all this money on lunches and freebies for something the med students can't prescribe and won't remember anyway?"

"You're missing the point of the investment, Mackie. Our return on investment here is for the students to know that the pharmaceutical reps are the friends who feed them and give them free stuff. Regardless of what their professors say, we want them to know they have nothing to fear from the pharmaceutical industry."

"A kinder, gentler company," Mackie said, "showing the softer side of big Pharma."

Karen pointed to the tote bag on her arm. "Look at all this stuff we give away. Notepads. Pens. Textbooks. In the academic setting, we want to be seen as a resource. It's a simple way to lay the ground work for future prescribing practices. What I really want from today is that years from now, these future doctors will open their doors when we knock."

They arrived at their destination. Moments later, the delivery man brought in stacks of cardboard boxes filled with pizzas for lunch. Mackie helped Karen set out their freebies and set up two BioloGen displays. Shortly before noon, medical students began to stream into the hallways. Some wore neck ties and short white coats. Others had on rumpled scrubs. As each one grabbed a plate, Karen would hand out a pen or a notepad with the BioloGen logo on it and the statement: 'NuCor—Highest in Safety, Lowest in Price.' Mackie greeted the students near the end of the food line, handing them a lottery ticket with the NuCor logo emblazoned on the back. He instructed them to hold onto their stubs, as once everyone had been served, there would be a drawing to win a free textbook.

The medical students could have been extras from the set of Mackie's past. Some arrived with tussled hair and untucked scrubs, showing the tell-tale signs of having spent the night in the hospital. That group looked at Mackie through drooping eyes, seeming to relish the thought of being a doctor who didn't have to take overnight call away from home. Others met Mackie's eyes with a purposeful gaze of their own, swelling with self-importance at their station in life. Those rested students had an idealism that once resonated with Mackie, valuing direct patient care above all else and likely wondering how one of their own could become a pharmaceutical mercenary. Students in this camp never envisioned a desire to be a doctor in the business world. To be fair, Mackie had not envisioned it for himself until the fatal turn of events in the last year, so he understood their confusion. Those students tended to see people like Mackie not as a partner in pharmaceutical research but as Judas in scrubs, selling knowledge to the highest bidder and then having the audacity to return to the scene of his betrayal.

As the remaining medical students picked up their pizza and filed into the large conference room, Karen gave a five-minute spiel on NuCor, ending with the raffle drawing. Afterwards, one of the medical school faculty thanked them for their time and began his own lecture for the students.

By early afternoon, the medical students had returned to the wards with new pads and pens while Karen and Mackie covered a half-dozen doctors's offices in their marketing territory. Mackie studied his boss's marketing pitch carefully, knowing that within months he would represent the company and Anginex on his own.

Leaving their fourth medical office, Karen climbed into the driver's seat and buckled her seat belt. "Now this next guy we're seeing…he's your typical obnoxious physician."

"Those last few doctors seemed quite cordial with the drug companies."

"Because we're respectful of their time and ask little in return. This next guy, though, wants medicine samples but hates having to deal with the detailers." She merged into traffic and accelerated down the two-lane road. "I think he sees Big Pharma as a bunch of ingratiating idiots who take up his office time and interrupt his pursuit of unbiased medical knowledge. What's funny about him is that he comes to all of the fancy pharmaceutical dinners."

"We've all done that at one time or another," Mackie said.

"Sure, but this guy shows up thirty minutes late, signs in under someone else's name—as if we don't know who he is. He got an invite, right? Then he leaves before the dinner lecture is even over." Karen accelerated past a car. "He's a real pharmophile."

"A what?"

She zoomed back into their lane, narrowly avoiding the oncoming traffic. "You know the type. He uses the pharmaceutical industry for his own benefit. He's promiscuous with all of the other companies, eating the free food and dispensing the samples we provide. Like a true le, he wants nothing to do with us in the light of

: smiled at the term. "Sounds like we're wasting our time caⅼⅼⅰng on him."

"He hates to admit it, but the marketing works on him. After we started calling on his office, his scripts for NuCor doubled. He's got about thirty of his patients on it, so if you crunch the numbers, he alone generated almost forty thousand dollars for BioloGen last year. Most pharmophiles don't recognize it, but Big Pharma uses them as much as they use us. The physician-pharma relationship is symbiotic. I continue to be surprised that most docs think they can get free stuff from us without having it affect their prescribing practices."

Mackie found himself at a loss for words. He'd spent three years after training being subjected to the influence of pharmaceutical reps, presumably not even realizing it.

Karen took her eyes off the road momentarily, looking at Mackie in the passenger seat. "You want to hear some unflattering commentary about your first profession?"

"Do I have a choice?"

"Not really. The radio doesn't work, an Enya cassette is stuck in the tape player, and you're too nice a guy to ignore someone who's talking to you."

"Excellent points," Mackie said. "What's your unflattering commentary?"

"Physicians are a marketer's wet dream. You know why?"

"Our influence?"

"Nope. Your arrogance."

"Ouch."

"Maybe not you, in particular, but your breed." Karen signaled to pull into the parking lot of the medical office building ahead. "Even obnoxious physicians, like this next doc, are generally pretty intelligent. You spend seven years or so after college accumulating debt, while most of your beer-drinking buddies from the fraternity are already working steady jobs with good incomes. Add to that a baseline arrogance most doctors have—no doubt built up by battles against death and disease—and you've got someone who feels impervious to marketing." She pulled into the lot and killed the engine.

Mackie kept his seatbelt clipped. "I'm listening."

"Pharmaceutical marketers know all of this, and we use it to our advantage. We'll provide food for a busy practice, and the doc thinks, 'It's only food. I'm not influenced.' Then we flatter them with comments that take their intelligence for granted, and before you know it, the doctors are talking to a colleague, not a sales rep."

She opened the driver's door and made her way to the trunk of the car. Mackie did the same. He found Karen removing samples of NuCor and placing the boxes in her tote bag. "The denouement comes in the form of free samples," she said, holding up the snappy purple NuCor box. "We provide them by the boxful, doctors give them out to their patients, and soon those same patients are demanding that scripts be written for them. It's the perfect storm for physicians, and they never even see it coming."

Mackie ducked out of the way as Karen closed the trunk. "Obviously, it works."

"To perfection. And it's not just BioloGen, although we're damn good at it. This is the industry standard, and it results in billions of dollars for us each year, eclipsing the hundreds of millions of dollars Big Pharma eats annually by passing out free stuff."

"But we don't really eat that cost," Mackie said. "Look at the drug cost to consumers."

"Added on to the price of the prescription. Every time you fill a scrip for NuCor, you're paying a percentage to fund those free samples."

Mackie pressed her point. "Don't you think the ethical thing to do would be for drug companies to write-off the cost of the samples instead of passing that cost on to the insurance companies? To not charge extra to those patients paying out of pocket for the drug."

Karen laughed at this. "We throw a bone to the poor and the terminally ill through compassionate care programs. Of course, that's a win for us, too, because it enhances our reputation as philanthropists. You're thinking too much like a doctor and not enough like a marketer, Mackie. We're simply playing by the rules of our capitalist culture."

Mackie scoffed in disgust even as he glimpsed an image of what he was becoming.

Karen hardly seemed to notice. She slung her tote bag over her shoulder and sauntered toward the lobby of the next doctor's office.

* * *

Mackie and Karen returned to BioloGen headquarters just before dark. He went straight to his office to grab his keys before heading home. As he sat down at his desk, Karen walked in, carrying a black binder. She shut the office door behind her. "Hell of a day today."

"You're a natural," Mackie said, glancing at the closed office door. "Those docs love you."

Karen took off the jacket to her suit and draped it over the back of the chair. Her sculpted arms poked out from her sleeveless blouse. "I hope you watched closely how I did my job today."

"I noticed you didn't miss a chance to say the name 'NuCor' three times in the first ninety seconds of contact." He pointed toward the binder in her arms. "Whatcha got there?"

Karen set the binder on the desk. "Half of my time, it seems, is spent tracking the progress of our pharmaceutical reps. This helps keep me organized. Lists of local doctors. Pages of their prescribing practices."

"On everyone in the community?"

"Not just our community. Everywhere BioloGen has a presence we have a record of our target market." She locked her eyes on Mackie's. "Don't be surprised, doc. We would've had one on you if surgeons prescribed our drugs." She turned the binder toward him and leaned over the book. "Look at these," she said.

Mackie studied the spreadsheet with its rows of numbers and percentages, trying to avert his gaze from her cleavage.

"Over the last month, this doctor I called on increased his prescriptions for NuCor by twenty percent. Two other doctors on my route wrote more prescriptions for our competition during that period, so they're a target for our marketing."

The closer she leaned toward him across his desk, the harder it was for Mackie to ignore her perfume. He didn't pull back, though. He just kept up his guard. "How do you nudge the reluctant ones to prescribe more of us and less of them? Do you simply ask them to write NuCor more?"

She unclipped the three rings of the binder and removed a stapled journal article. "We're a bit more nuanced than that. Next week, I'll send a different rep to his office with a copy of this medical study that demonstrates the increased side effects of our competitor's drug compared to NuCor."

Mackie recognized the article immediately. "BioloGen funded that study."

"That doesn't change the results, though. We'll hit the highlights of this paper and then track this doc's prescribing practices over the coming months. That type of marketing usually makes a difference."

Mackie flipped through the first few pages of the journal article before handing it back to Karen. He leaned back in his desk chair. "The med students seem to love seeing you."

Karen slipped off the edge of Mackie's desk and took a seat in a nearby chair. When she crossed her legs, her already short skirt slid up her thigh even more. "The University and med school have been fertile ground for us. Last year, they accepted NuCor as their preferred drug on the hospital's formulary."

Mackie knew the politics of stocking drugs in a hospital pharmacy from his years on the orthopedic faculty. "So anytime a doctor at University Hospital writes a script for a cholesterol lowering drug, the pharmacy changes it to NuCor?"

"Unless the prescriber specifically assigns another name brand drug. We gave the hospital dispensary a cut rate on the cost so that it's dirt cheap for patients who get their meds filled there."

"And they're trained to ask for it by name if they go to another pharmacy."

"You got it."

Karen sat back and stretched, causing her lifted blouse to expose her pierced navel. "Any money we lose discounting the drug at the hospital will be recouped once these medical residents graduate. Once they move on to a new community, they'll start prescribing our drug."

"So it becomes a habit to write NuCor."

Karen leaned forward, reaching across the desk to touch Mackie's hand. "Think about what you said."

Mackie forced a smile before sliding free his hand and sitting back in his own chair.

Karen kept speaking. "In three years, a medical resident might write one-hundred fifty prescriptions for a cholesterol-lowering drug. If we can get the hospital pharmacy to preferentially dispense NuCor, then we have an entire residency program training their future doctors to write for it. By the time they graduate, writing NuCor will be as comfortable as writing their own name. For that three-year inconvenience of discounting the drug to the hospital, we will probably have thirty years of prescribing from those docs."

Mackie shifted in his chair. "The amazing part of that story is how quickly NuCor became a block buster drug for BioloGen."

"One billion dollars in sales within two years of FDA approval."

"But to be perfectly honest, NuCor is simply a safer version of an old drug, so you had to know the sales would be there because people were already taking cholesterol-lowering drugs," he said. "How do you know that there will be a market for a drug that is the first of its kind like Anginex?"

"Because ADAM designed a safe molecule that gives America what it desperately wants… a chance to cure cancer." Karen placed both arms on his desk. She lowered her voice. "Can I tell you something?"

"Go for it."

She looked Mackie in the eye, then turned her head. "Never mind."

"What were you going to say?"

Karen blushed. "I probably shouldn't say this, especially after the Anita Hill allegations two years ago, so don't bust me for sexual harassment." She smiled. "Guys shorter than me turn me on."

Mackie felt a reflexive flutter of anticipation. "That's gotta be most men you meet."

Karen glanced over her shoulder at the closed door then stood up. "I want to show you something." She approached Mackie. As she reached his side of the desk, his phone rang. Both glanced at the phone, then at one another.

Mackie placed his hand on the handset.

"You don't have to answer that," Karen said.

"It's probably Sarah. She knows I'm still at the office."

Karen paused a beat as the phone kept ringing, then dropped back, reaching for her blazer. "Okay, Doc. Think about what I said." Karen winked at him as she opened the office door.

Mackie watched her walk out of his office, his hand still resting on the ringing phone.

CHAPTER NINETEEN

SCOTT HOFFMAN DROVE his car to the familiar post office parking lot. He parked near the lone security light, still amazed at how different the place looked in the daytime. He saw several customers waiting in line for the postal clerk. To the side of the building, employees loaded crates of mail onto delivery trucks. Hoffman rubbed his temples with both hands, silently cursing his alarm clock. If he'd woken up on time today, he'd already be at the office.

This was his first return trip to the post office since he'd placed the hand-written plea for help in his mail box. He had slowly recovered from the bouts of nausea and diarrhea that plagued him after he'd discovered that Dr. Erlanger suspected someone had tampered with his patients's charts. Yolanda Steele blamed the ham sandwich for Hoffman's illness.

Hoffman needed to resume his daily routine at work, but he feared he'd been compromised. He took a deep breath, exhaling slowly to steady himself. Then, he hurried from his car and into the building. With his head down, he walked to the corner of the room toward his mailbox. Spotting a postal employee, he avoided eye contact with her.

"Good morning, sir," she said.

nodded and focused on his mailbox, removing
⁊ from his pocket to open it.

....an stepped forward. "You the owner of that box?"

He nodded, struggling to fit the tiny key into the lock. Right as he inserted it, a touch on his shoulder made him jump. They key clattered to the floor. "Watch it!"

"Lemme see if I can help you." The woman stood at his side. "Name's Melvina."

Hoffman's heart beat so fast in his chest, he felt sure she could hear it.

She picked up his key. "Been working at this branch going on twenty years, and I guess I met just about everyone who comes in here. I don't recognize you, though." She deftly inserted the key into the small lock.

He reached for the key. "I've got it."

The woman stepped back. "Yes, sir. I've met more congressmen than I can remember, and almost every day I see a doctor or two from the Health Institute up the road. I guess most of them live close by, but sometimes they just come in to get stamps."

Hoffman tried to ignore her. Adrenaline flooded his mind like an overdose of speed. When he opened the mailbox, it was empty. Oh my God! he thought. No letter replaced the one he had left. His nervous stomach flutters turned into nausea. The letter was gone.

"So mama said to me—" She stopped in mid sentence. "You okay, sir?"

Hoffman looked up once more, the tiny key still gripped in his hand. He felt as hollow and lifeless as a mannequin. "Excuse me," he said in a barely audible voice as he brushed past her. He tasted bile as he hurried to the car.

He couldn't recall a single detail of the drive back to his office. If anyone spoke to him in the lobby or on the elevator, he didn't remember. He heard his secretary's voice above the din of the office chatter as he walked to his suite on the ninth floor.

"Are you serious?" Yolanda said into the phone. She stopped smacking her gum when Hoffman walked past. "Hold on a second," he heard her say. She cupped her hand over the receiver. "Scottie, you're late. You oversleep? I put some papers on your desk that need to be signed ASAP." She craned her neck to get a better look at him. "You look terrible. Are you sure you should be here?"

"I'm fine."

He walked down the hall toward his office, feeling disconnected from his surroundings. He shut his office door and put on his lab coat. Normally, he didn't wear his white coat unless he met with dignitaries in his office. Today, though, with his body giving an encore performance of last week's illness, he needed more than a Tylenol to stop the chills. The coat helped.

Yolanda had placed a stack of papers on his desk, each neatly marked with a red 'Sign Here' sticker. He signed without even looking at the content.

Yolanda walked into his office, the scent of cigarettes traveling with her. The stink made Hoffman's stomach churn.

"I'm almost done with these," he said without looking up.

"You're not going to believe this," Yolanda said. She walked over to his desk.

"Try me."

"You know that computer wiz that heads up CPR?"

Hoffman froze. "Compton Drew?"

"Right. I just got off the phone with your ex down in medical records. I could hardly understand her through the tears. Janice said that at about six this morning, a guard doing routine surveillance of the parking lot at Washington National Airport found Compton's vandalized car."

Hoffman's pen dropped from his trembling fingers. "Was he robbed?"

"Must have been. They found his license and an empty

wallet beside the car, but that's not the worst of it."

Hoffman stared at her.

"When the cop bent down to pick up his things," she said, "he looked under the car and found Compton's body."

CHAPTER TWENTY

Fall 1993

MACKIE STOOD IN front of his desk at BioloGen headquarters with his arms folded across his chest, studying an Anginex ad. The previous three months had flown by, keeping him as busy at work as any day he could remember as a doctor. Gone were the summer days of flying to conferences on the company jet or loitering in the lecture halls at the medical school. With the FDA submission of the new drug application for Anginex expected in the next few weeks, Mackie plunged into its marketing with a singular focus. He devoted his days to conference calls and strategy meetings. At night he read every published report or article he could find about angiogenesis inhibitors. All except one.

As was her custom, Karen strode into his office unannounced. She laid an envelope on his desk, then took a sip of the soda in her hand. "Fill me in on your mock ups," she said.

Mackie uncrossed his arms and pointed to the poster board displays to his right. "One of these ads will come out the week we submit to the FDA. Which do you like better?"

Karen read from the ad. "'From the makers of NuCor comes

the ultimate weapon in the fight against cancer. BioloGen Pharmaceuticals: Tomorrow's Drugs Today.' I like that," she said. "Kind of a twenty-first century feel to it. Did you come up with that?"

"The team did."

She moved over to the other poster board displayed on an adjacent easel. The BioloGen logo visually popped out against a metallic blue background. She read aloud, "'Are you ready for a revolution?'" Nodding her head, she turned to Mackie and said, "Really good."

"We have to choose one."

"Says who?"

"You, for starters."

Karen laughed. "I like the two-pronged approach. The familiar and the mysterious. But that's going to cost extra, and no sense busting the budget at this stage of the game. I think I like the NuCor one. I've already instructed my NuCor and ArthroDerm teams to simply mention to their prescribers that something big is in the pipeline at BioloGen. Of course, that's all they can say before we get the FDA stamp of approval for Anginex. Otherwise, we could be fined, or worse, asked to delay the launch. That's about the *only* kind of publicity we don't need."

Mackie glanced at the envelope Karen had placed on his desk. He didn't recognize it. "Who gave you that?"

"Ms. Franks. It came in the morning mail." She picked up the envelope and read the return address. "Do you know a T. Phillips?"

"I went to school with a Tom—" Mackie stopped himself.

Karen didn't seem to notice his hesitation. She handed over the thin package and shrugged. "Maybe from your friend. I told Ms. Franks I'd give it to you." She rapped her knuckles on his desk as she considered the ads. "Impressive proofs, Mackie. Get me a decision by the end of the day."

She breezed out of his office as quickly as she had arrived.

Mackie stepped around his desk and shut his office door. He remained standing as he slid his finger under the seal of the envelope and opened it. Inside, not much thicker than a few pages, he removed a stapled photocopy of a journal article. He looked at the citation along the top of the article but already knew what Tom Philips must have sent. The quality of the photocopy was poor. In slightly blurred lettering, Mackie read the summary on the first page from a journal called *Federation of European Biochemical Sciences*.

FEBS.

Mackie took a seat in the guest chair in front of his desk. He stopped skimming and started at the beginning of the article. As he read, he realized the article's implications. He also immediately thought of Aruba and the lanky man with large glasses who'd approached him after the big Anginex announcement. He'd mentioned the dropout rate from the earlier Anginex studies.

After Pescatelli's office discussion with him upon their return from Aruba, there was no way Mackie would trust sharing this information with him. He doubted Karen would understand the scientific implications of the article, and he wasn't yet ready to share it with Douglas. There was one person, though, that Mackie trusted implicitly in the months that he had worked at BioloGen.

He slid the journal article back inside the envelope. Mackie reached across his desk and picked up his phone. Ms. Franks answered on the first ring.

"Yes, Dr. McKay?" She made no attempt to hide the annoyance in her voice.

"Please call down to the Clinical Development department. I need to see Dr. Martin."

* * *

It took an hour before Dr. Martin could break free from her other responsibilities to see him. Still, she gave him a good-natured smile when he walked into her office, setting aside the stack of papers in front of her. Tired eyes didn't hide her enthusiastic greeting. "How's the marketing marathon going?"

"We're readying for the Anginex launch, which adds a few hours on to an already busy day."

She removed her reading glasses and perched them atop her bone-white hair. "When I retired from academic medicine, I thought a second career at BioloGen would offer me fewer hours, but that's not proven to be the case. No matter, though. We both volunteered for this assignment. When Ms. Franks called down, she indicated you had somewhat of an emergency."

"I do have some questions." Mackie slid the journal article out of its envelope. "This is a study from one of the sister drugs of Anginex. It's more of a basic science article rather than a clinical trial, but it raised the concern that angiogenesis inhibitors have a problem with amyloid deposition."

Dr. Martin repositioned her glasses, speaking as she skimmed the article. "Like Alzheimer's?"

"Same mechanism."

She flipped the page of the article. "This is news to me, Mackie."

In all of his reading about angiogenesis inhibitors, this was also the first time he'd heard of any problems like this. Most doctors knew that amyloid proteins could stain vital organs in the body like soot stains a chimney. Mackie had seen amyloid deposits cause kidney failure and arthritis. He'd seen the sticky proteins cause heart enlargement and tongue swelling. He'd also seen the ravages of amyloid on the brain causing dementia.

Mackie tried a different approach. "In looking back at the

Phase One Anginex trials, it appears there was a higher than expected drop-out rate."

Dr. Martin studied Mackie for a moment, her expression unreadable. Finally, she said, "Patients drop out of studies all the time. I don't recall the particulars of our Phase One trial, but I also don't remember patients leaving the study because of side effects. Those patients that left the study stopped coming for their follow up appointments." She peered over the top of her reading glasses. "You know we've tested Anginex in over twelve thousand patients so far. With that many people involved, some won't finish the study. Some move away and don't send us a forwarding address. Some become ill for other reasons. And as much as we don't like to admit it, some don't like taking an experimental drug every day. Data from the largest study to date of Anginex shows that patients taking the drug were more likely to complete the study than those who received the placebo."

"May I look at the raw data myself?"

Dr. Martin shifted in her seat. "There are over sixty-thousand pages of data and documents in the new drug application, some of which isn't even organized yet. I suspect you'll have a hard time finding what you need."

"The information's arranged chronologically?"

"Of course."

"Then I can find what I need."

Dr. Martin gave a resigned nod. She pushed her chair back and opened the top desk drawer. She furrowed her brow, leaning forward to inspect the contents of the drawer. Not finding what she was looking for, she opened the two drawers below it, mumbling, "I swear I left it here..." She stood up, patting her pockets. Soon, a smile spread across her face as she withdrew a key on a BioloGen key chain. "Here it is."

Mackie chose not to acknowledge her obvious embarrassment at the mental lapse. He followed her as she walked around the corner from her office and to an unmarked door, which she unlocked. She stepped into the room and turned on the light.

"Help yourself to what you need," she said. "I think our intern has the place pretty well organized. It still might take you a while to find your way around the data, but I'll be in my office if you need any help." She propped open the door when she left.

Mackie looked around the windowless room, taking in the empty walls, two office chairs, a collapsible table, and numerous cardboard boxes. Every piece of scientific and clinical trial data generated for Anginex would occupy this room by the time the new drug application was ready for submission. Most of the data already here was organized into file folders. Mackie counted fourteen boxes. Taped to the wall above each one was a piece of paper indicating the contents of each box. Stuffed into the cardboard containers were patient charts, manila file folders, and photocopied pages.

When the FDA approved the investigational new drug application for Anginex several years earlier, it had simply given BioloGen permission to test the drug in humans. This time around, the FDA required the company to submit not only published scientific papers about Anginex but also the individual patient data used to write those papers.

"Turning in a new drug application is like turning in a college term paper," Karen had told Mackie during his orientation., "except along with the paper, you would also have to turn in every book, article, and interview used to write it. The FDA wants to review everything in their new drug application. It's their way of verifying the safety and efficacy of a drug."

Mackie thought about her words as he studied the handwritten pages taped above each cardboard box. He assumed he would find what he was looking for in one of the first few boxes. He squatted next to the cardboard containers and began walking his fingers over the marked files. By the time he reached the third box, he found it. Marked in the company's designation for the first trial, he pulled out the first binder of charts marked, *B-AGX-23*.

The first folder provided a summary of the Phase One trial, detailing the types of volunteers enrolled. Behind that folder, Mackie found individual patient charts for each of the fifty two patients who'd participated in the B-AGX-23 trial. Looking at a sample chart, he found a cover page containing demographic information about the patients. Another page documented any patient complaints about the drug. A separate section of the chart included results of any blood work obtained by the study coordinators. The last page of the chart summarized all the dates that BioloGen had contacted that patient, from the first visit to the last one.

Once he had familiarized himself with the study's structure, Mackie retraced his steps to remove the chart of the first patient. *Patient #1* had sailed through the trial, showing up for each monthly visit with the study coordinator and logging no complaints about Anginex. Mackie replaced that chart and pulled the next one. He found the same unremarkable information detailing regular check ups with no concerns. This pattern continued for ten or more minutes. Then, he found the chart for Donald Sims.

When Mackie pulled Sims's file, marked as *Patient # 15*, he glanced at the biographical data. Mr. Sims was a middle aged man living with his wife in Louisville, Kentucky who described himself as healthy. Flipping through his chart, Mackie saw that Mr. Sims had no complaints one month after starting Anginex, and his blood work was completely normal. At the three-month follow up, the research coordinator wrote, 'periodic confusion noted by the patient's wife,' but Mackie again noted normal labs. No other complaints had been documented at that visit. However, no subsequent visits were listed. When Mackie turned to the summary flow sheet in the back of the chart, he read in bold letters: patient lost to follow up.

Mackie grabbed a blank sheet of paper from atop the workroom table and jotted down Donald Sims's name, address, and phone number. He then replaced the chart back inside the box.

Mackie reviewed another seven consecutive normal charts before stumbling upon the next complaint. This time, *Patient #23* documented 'some forgetfulness' since the last visit. On the study flow sheet at the back of the chart, bold letters proclaimed that this patient was also lost to follow up.

Three other patients of the fifty-two enrolled in the B-AGX-23 study could not be accounted for. The trend appeared to be similar. Mackie noted they were all middle-aged, healthy men with vague complaints at the three-month visit, and each of these patients missed their subsequent appointments. Mackie again recorded the relevant contact information from these suspicious charts.

Behind him, Mackie heard the scuffle of footsteps outside the propped open door, then a pause and an accusatory voice. "What the hell are you doing?"

So engrossed was Mackie in the B-AGX-23 charts that he startled when Pescatelli spoke, letting go of his scratch sheet of paper. It fluttered to the floor. Turning, he saw Pescatelli standing in the doorway. "What's up?" Mackie asked nonchalantly.

"I could ask you the same thing." Pescatelli loomed in the doorway, his broad shoulders and beard back-lit from the hallway lights. He stepped into the room and looked at the boxes full of data. "How'd you get in here?"

Mackie bent over to pick up the paper. He folded it in half, then folded it again, placing it in his pocket. He knew he had nothing to hide, but Pescatelli's demeanor did not invite open conversation right now. "I'm following up on some patient data in the Phase One study. Do you remember hearing about memory problems in some study patients during that trial?"

"Those kind of side effects don't exist with Anginex."

"But you knew of problems like that with endostatin? I found a report that detailed amyloid deposition, which can lead to—"

"I know what amyloid is," Pescatelli snapped. "What are you getting at?"

Mackie gestured to the rows of cardboard boxes behind him. "You brought me on board to market Anginex, so in order to do my job, I need to know if there are any rare or unreported side effects with the drug. Pharmaceutical reps have an obligation to at least be knowledgable about potential side effects of the medications they sell, especially if those side effects are going to be listed in the package insert of the drug."

Pescatelli stepped farther into the room, closing in on Mackie. "We've been through this. Those kind of side effects don't exist. Over the last seven years, BioloGen has considered this drug from every conceivable angle, first with ADAM and then with the clinical trials. Frankly, I don't need some self-righteous hotshot with a chip on his shoulder trying to drum-up side effects that don't exist."

Mackie stepped back from Pescatelli, but kept his gaze steady. "You chose to bring me on at BioloGen, Red. Now that I'm here, I have a responsibility to the patients who will be taking Anginex—"

"You have a responsibility to BioloGen Pharmaceuticals and our investors!" Pescatelli's voice echoed off the walls in the small room. "I suggest you get back upstairs and do what we hired you to do, which is to figure out the best way to market this drug." A bead of sweat trickled down Pescatelli's already slick head.

Stunned at his boss's defensiveness, Mackie didn't respond at first. Then, he said, "We're on the same team here, Red. I would have moved heaven and earth to have this drug for my son. What you've created could've saved your family years of heartache and worry, too." He turned his back on Pescatelli and filed the last patient chart back into place. Confirming that the new drug application was as he found it, he walked toward the hallway. Pescatelli remained in the doorway, blocking his path. Mackie said, "We both want this drug to succeed. If there is a problem with Anginex—"

"There are no problems."

"But would you stop the new drug application if there were?"

Pescatelli glared at him before answering. "What do you think?"

Mackie sized up his boss even as he chose his words carefully. "I think you're not going to find any problems if you don't look for them."

He brushed past Pescatelli and walked down the hall toward the elevator.

CHAPTER TWENTY-ONE

OF ALL THE SEASONS of the year, Meredith Beukelman liked autumn the best. Not just because of college football, which she followed passionately, or the irresistible Cincinnati weather, which made her want to skip afternoon classes. She also loved autumn because of Tim Styles. They shared a September birthday. They had met at the lake the previous Labor Day. And now, they could add the anniversary of their engagement to the list of autumn's highlights. She hoped to schedule their wedding for this time next year. After graduation, of course.

Tim walked beside her on this gorgeous afternoon, fingers intertwined with hers. He absentmindedly twirled her engagement ring.

"It's not like you to be so quiet," Meredith said, although she knew he had a tendency to be withdrawn at times. Still, he hadn't said much since they'd left her sister's house after lunch. "Everything okay?"

Tim looked ahead as they walked. "I'm worried about you."

"About cancer?"

"Seeing your sister struggle makes me concerned."

Meredith squeezed his fingers between hers. "You've got nothing to worry about. I'm not Frances. And I'm able to do something to prevent what she's gone through."

"The clinical trial?"

"And the frequent screening visits that come with it. She didn't have access to either."

"So how's this whole thing work for us with Anginex?" Tim asked. "Do you stop it when it's our time to start a family?"

"We've got at least a year until we're married."

"True. And three years after that before kids."

"Maybe two," Meredith teased.

This time, Tim squeezed her hand. "You said you can't take Anginex when you're pregnant."

Meredith released her grip to wipe her hands on her shorts. Talking about cancer always made her palms sweat. When she reached back for Tim's hands, they were in his pockets. Meredith pressed on, patiently without patronizing him. "We've talked about this. As long as Anginex doesn't cause problems, I keep taking it. Since I'm at high risk for cancer, I see the doctor twice a year for check ups. When we're ready to start our family, I stop the drug."

"And run the risk of getting breast cancer."

"We don't even know that I have the gene."

"Obviously a risky assumption."

She folded her arms across her chest as they walked. The edge of the diamond solitaire pinched the underside of her arm. They walked to the edge of the path, stepping onto the lawn that led to the parking lot. As Tim led them across the grass, her knee ached. Then, she stumbled. Her arms flew out to steady herself. Tim caught her before she fell. Meredith winced.

"Your knee again?" he asked.

She managed a smile. "Let's hope I don't do *that* walking down the aisle."

"You're twenty-one years old, Mer. That's not normal."

She steadied herself. Bent her knee with an exaggerated

move and declared herself ready to continue. "See. No problems. Just a stumble."

Tim looked at the beautifully manicured lawn without a defect in site. He took her hand, tightening his grip this time as they walked on. "I don't want to see you suffer like the rest of the women in your family."

Meredith grinned at him. The September sun made his blue eyes sparkle, giving her one more reason to enjoy the fall. "That's why I'm taking Anginex," she said. "To give us one less thing to worry about."

*C*HAPTER TWENTY-TWO

*E*ARLY THE NEXT Saturday morning, Mackie pulled his car into a gravel driveway in Louisville, Kentucky, hoping to find the first study patient supposedly lost to follow up. A doublewide trailer with a thick row of evergreen bushes flanked the modest front porch. A tattered 'Welcome' flag with a faded brown pineapple snapped in the morning breeze. Flaking blue paint peeled off the trailer. Mackie saw the edge of a wooden porch and a chain-link fence in the backyard. Steam rose from vents on the roof.

When he stepped out of the car, he smelled a rustic combination of pine trees and bacon. He shut the car door and walked toward the house. The porch creaked when he stepped on it.

"Just a minute!" a muffled woman's voice yelled from inside. Moments later, the front door opened and an overweight woman with gray hair greeted him. She wore a housecoat that looked handmade and hung from her shoulders like a drop-cloth. Whiskers sprouted from her chin.

"You Dr. McKay?" she asked, wiping her hands on her apron and opening the screen door.

Mackie extended his hand and introduced himself.

Earlier that week, he'd called the number for Donnie Sims

to ask why he'd dropped out of the Anginex study. His wife had answered the phone. "He ain't talking today," Loretta Sims had snapped. Mackie explained that he was a doctor following up on patients who had enrolled in a certain clinical trial. At first, Mrs. Sims sounded skeptical, but when Mackie said he was investigating whether participants in these trials had side effects from the study drug, her tone had softened. She had invited him to drop by the house when he was next in Louisville.

Mrs. Sims stood in the doorway. "Come on in, Dr. McKay. Ain't no use in letting all that morning air in." She stepped aside and let Mackie into her home.

Glancing around, he felt as if he'd stepped into a room that had not changed in thirty years. Thick shag carpet in shades of tan and brown covered the floor. The carpet in front of the sofa was worn down while the carpet under the end tables appeared to be as thick as the day it was bought. A green sofa and two matching easy chairs with threadbare seat cushions sat in front of a boxy television. Framed pictures, yellowed with age, covered nearly every available surface. Right inside the door, Mackie saw a framed wedding picture showing a much younger Loretta grinning next to her handsome groom.

"Gitcha coat?" Loretta asked.

"I'm sorry?"

"I asked if can gitcha coat?"

Mackie handed her his windbreaker. "Is it just you and your husband living here?"

"Lord, yes. You see room for anyone else? Our kids is long gone, but they come by every now and then for dinner." She hung Mackie's jacket on a hook behind the front door and headed toward the kitchen. "Gitcha some coffee?"

"Straight black, please." Mackie followed his hostess.

"I'm glad you called about Donnie. Ain't heard from nobody in over four years now." She reached around a stack of breakfast dishes in the sink to retrieve a fresh coffee mug. A cigarette butt smoldered in a nearby ashtray.

Mackie slipped into a chair at the kitchen table.

"I swear them researchers told us that pill Donnie took would prevent cancer if it worked like they hoped. I told Donnie he shouldn't be taking no medicine that was experimental, but he said he'd get paid a thousand dollars to take it for six months. Can you imagine having an extra thousand dollars?" She stared out of the fogged up kitchen window as she spoke.

After a moment passed, Mackie asked, "So what happened?"

She turned and faced him. "I thought you was gonna tell me that," Loretta said. "If *we* knew what happened I'd a sued that damn company for what that drug did to my Donnie!"

Mackie found himself slipping back into the patient interview skills he'd learned in medical school. He enjoyed gathering a patient's medical history, likening it to Sherlock Holmes with a stethoscope, solving medical mysteries with clues provided by patients. Once he transitioned to orthopedic surgery, his focus shifted to cures, not clues, but he didn't lose his skills. "Take me back to the first time you thought your husband had symptoms."

She took a sip of her own coffee and then lit a new cigarette. "It was about three months after taking that drug. I noticed that Donnie weren't as sharp as he used to be. You know, forgetting stuff like eggs at the store or where he'd put his keys. We had seen the research assistant the week before—a real tall fella, as I remember it—and he told us everything looked great on Donnie's labs and stuff. So I figured we'd wait until we go back in three months." She took a long drag off her cigarette and blew a trail of smoke over her shoulder. "He *was* getting older, so I thought he was just forgetful."

"What did the research assistant say when you went back?"

Loretta took another sip of coffee. "That's the funny thing.

They ain't never called us back for our follow up appointment once we told them what was going on."

The perplexed look on Mackie's face prompted her to continue. "I called and spoke to that research man about a month later. Told him Donnie's not thinking right, because, you know, it was getting worse. Six months into taking that pill, Donnie'd look at me some days and not even know who I was." She shook her head in disgust. "You know somebody for almost forty years and then they look at you like they ain't even met you? That ain't right."

Mackie asked, "Did you call them back to get him seen?"

"About every day for a month. Even drove to Cincinnati to see a brain specialist at the University. Once we got done, I left a message for the researcher at that company and told him what the specialist said. That got his attention. That researcher called me back that afternoon, but do you know what he said?" She didn't pause for Mackie to answer. "He said he sure was sorry about Donnie's thinking but it had nothing to do with the cancer medication. Then he said because of Donnie's new condition, he couldn't keep participating in the study no more." She punctuated her story with a sarcastic laugh. "We did get that thousand dollars they promised, but by the time we paid off them medical bills for the brain doctor, we had nothing left."

Mackie sat in stunned silence for a moment. He shifted in his chair. "What did the neurologist say?"

"The who?"

"The brain doctor. What did he say was wrong with Donnie?"

"Said he had dementia."

"Alzheimer's?"

"That's it. You know of it?"

Before Mackie could answer, he heard someone shuffle into the kitchen. Mackie turned to see a shell of the man he had seen in the photos in the den. Donnie Sims was tall and lean to begin with, but now his hollow cheeks and blank stare made him an apparition. He smiled when he finally noticed Mackie.

"Howdy. I'm Donald Sims, but you can call me Donnie."

Mackie shook his hand, which felt as lifeless as a cadaver's. Next, Donnie turned his attention to Loretta. "Howdy do, ma'am. Nice to meet you, too. I'm Donnie Sims."

Loretta smiled wearily. "Donnie, it's me. Loretta. This nice young doctor come down from Cincinnati to see how you was doing."

"I went there once," Donnie said as he shuffled into the living room and sat in one of the easy chairs.

"Some days is better than others," Loretta said to Mackie. "Some days he knows me, other days he don't. First, he was only forgetting stuff like those eggs I mentioned. Then, he started getting lost around the neighborhood. Even had to take his car keys away, because he'd go out and couldn't find his way home." Loretta made no attempt to hide her tears. She wiped her nose on her apron. "I know what I been told about this Alzheimer's. I know them doctors up there told us we could give some medicine to Donnie, but that ain't going to stop or change the forgetting. Said it may slow it down a bit."

"Did you start any of the medicine?" Mackie asked.

Her tears continued to flow. "Look around you, Dr. McKay. We ain't got a lot of money to spend. We's living on a fixed income, and ain't no way we can afford to buy something that ain't going to cure him anyways."

She walked back to the kitchen sink and began to wash dishes. Mackie finished his coffee, not sure what to say next. He heard Donnie softly humming to himself in the other room.

"I don't imagine you're coming here to give me no answers," Loretta said over her shoulder.

Mackie looked up from his seat. "I wish I could. I'm just trying to piece together what may have gone wrong with this study medication. I want to see if the medicine is responsible for what happened to your husband."

"You do what you gotta do. I'm here to tell you, though, Donnie was fine until he took that cancer-preventing drug. Them researchers can say all they want about how this was going to happen to Donnie even without the experimental medicine, but I ain't buying it. Donnie is the way he is cause he took that damn drug. And all we got for it was a thousand dollars and a stack of medical bills."

She turned off the water and looked at Mackie, raising her voice as she spoke. "You tell that company I said so, Dr. McKay. Ain't nobody took an interest in us until now, so if you know how to get in touch with them, you tell that lousy company exactly what I told you!"

Mackie set down his coffee cup and nodded, absorbing her painful gaze with his own. "Count on it, Loretta. I'll get to the bottom of this."

*C*HAPTER TWENTY-THREE

*D*IRK WATERS FIDDLED with a straw while he waited for his order to arrive. Seated across the table, Scott Hoffman glanced at Dirk's hulking frame while he considered his own predicament. The death of Compton Drew spawned a palpable fear in Hoffman. He knew that anyone who would kill a governmental employee based on a cryptic note left in a mailbox probably wouldn't hesitate to dispose of him if the Anginex approval demanded it. But over the last few months, Hoffman's fears remained unrealized. No further instructions had arrived in his mailbox. No late night phone calls came to his house. No mention at all about the medical records changes. As the weeks of silence marched on, Hoffman wondered if he had reached the endgame of his pharmaceutical consulting. But one phone call earlier that evening had changed his thinking.

Two hours ago, as Hoffman sat on his living room floor surrounded by Caribbean brochures, the man with the deep voice had called back. "It's time to finish the job," the man had said. "Meet me at the post office at midnight."

That was it. One menacing command. Hoffman must have passed out after hearing the voice, because he awakened lying among the glossy sea of blue oceans and white beaches. When his mind cleared, he called Dirk.

Now, sitting at the table of a local all-night eatery, Dirk said, "Let me get this straight. You've got somebody who wants to meet you tonight, but you can't tell me who. And this guy—who you've never met—might want to hurt you, but you don't know why. So you want me to sit in my car and take pictures of the whole thing, but you can't tell me for how long?"

"Exactly," Hoffman said, his voice tight with tension. "You'll be handsomely paid for your time."

"I'm not worried about that. I'm only trying to figure out what my role in all this is, seeing as I'm former law enforcement and all."

"I want you there for protection," he said. "But I also need to identify this guy so I can expose him."

"You want me to go in with you?" Dirk asked.

"Good God, no! He can't find out he's being watched. Sit in the shadows somewhere, close by but invisible." Hoffman looked over his shoulder before surreptitiously sliding a manila envelope across the table. "I want you to document the entire meeting. If something should happen to me, immediately take this envelope and your photos to the police."

"And if nothing happens to you?" Dirk asked as he covered the envelope with his gigantic hands.

"Then I get that back and you get your money. Of course, this all remains confidential—" Hoffman stopped talking when the waitress arrived with their food.

"There you are, sweetie," she said to Dirk as she set down a heaping plate of corned beef hash, fried eggs, and a short stack of pancakes. "Your oatmeal's on the way."

She placed a small omelet in front of Hoffman. "You want spicy or mild salsa with that?"

"Neither," he said.

"Suit yourself, sweet pea, but the Special's not the same without the salsa." She rummaged through her apron pockets to find their check and then placed it on the table.

By the time she went after the oatmeal, Dirk had eaten half of his pancakes. Hoffman tentatively took a bite of his omelet, testing the eggs and tomatoes on his sensitive stomach.

"Does any of this have to do with the envelope we tested for fingerprints?" Dirk asked around a mouthful of food.

Hoffman nodded. "Probably." He moved his omelet around his plate, then took another sip of hot tea. "The person who left me that envelope stopped leaving me letters shortly after you met me in the parking lot. While I don't think that has anything to do with you, I want to make sure you are extra careful this time. As I said, it's critically important to maintain secrecy on this project."

The waitress returned with a bowl of oatmeal and placed it in front of Dirk. "If y'all need anything else, let me know," she said.

Hoffman continued when she left. "How much?"

"For what?"

"The entire job."

"I'd say fifteen hundred now..."

"Dollars?" Hoffman asked indignantly.

Dirk held up the envelope. "If I've got to be driving all over town delivering packages and developing pictures, it's gonna cost me extra. Gas is almost a buck ten a gallon these days."

Hoffman stared at Dirk. "You don't develop them yourself?"

"Walmart does a nice job with their one-hour photo," Dirk said defensively. "I only use them if I need a quick turn around. You know, with cheating spouses, affairs, and stuff like this."

Exasperated, Hoffman said, "Do whatever the hell you need to, but I need some answers."

"So we got a deal?" Dirk asked as he wiped his mouth with his napkin and tossed it in his empty oatmeal bowl.

"Sure." Hoffman reached into his wallet and peeled off fifteen one-hundred dollar bills, feeling certain that this large investment might save his career. And his life.

* * *

Twenty minutes later, Hoffman drove to the post office in his red Ford Probe, passing Dirk's dark SUV on the side of the road. He pulled into the parking lot and parked under the familiar lamp post near the pay phone. He turned off his engine.

He closed his eyes, concentrating on his breathing. Ever since the death of Compton Drew, Hoffman tried to control his stress with biofeedback and meditation. He found that it helped calm his nerves and quiet his stomach. He began to relax. Hoffman felt himself slip into a light sleep. He could almost feel the warm Caribbean breeze of his dreams.

A clap of thunder shattered his tranquil dream. He bolted upright. Not thunder. A teenager with a wool cap pulled below his eyebrows pounded on the metal hood again.

Hoffman braced the edge of his seat as he stared out of the closed window. "What?"

"You the doctor?" the hooded youth asked.

Hoffman turned the ignition and cracked the window. "What do you want?"

"You deaf, old man? I asked if you was a doctor?"

"Yeah. Who are you?"

The teen ignored Hoffman's question. "I got a message for you from a man who said he's supposed to meet the doctor here."

Hoffman flinched when the teenager tossed a crumpled piece of paper at the window, then walked away. Hoffman held his position in the locked car until the boy disappeared from sight. Then, he unlocked the car and reached out to retrieve the paper. Once he had it, he immediately shut the car door. Hoffman smoothed out the wrinkled sheet and saw a phone number written in bold black ink. He turned the page over. Nothing else. Peering into the night, he saw no one else.

Hoffman stepped out of his car and looked around. He didn't see any movement from Dirk's car, so he jogged over to the darkened SUV. The tinted window rolled down when he approached, revealing a wide-toothy grin on Dirk's face.

"Did you see what happened?" Hoffman said, seething.

Dirk chuckled. "Probably gonna be some good shots of your face when that boy banged on your hood. You looked like you just about shit yourself."

Hoffman held up the crumpled paper. "Did you see who gave that punk this piece of paper?"

"Nope. I saw nobody until you drove up. That kid came from down the road on his bike, spotted your car, then tapped on your hood. I got some close-ups of his face, case you need those." Dirk took a sip of his coffee. "After that, he biked back down the road, same direction he come from."

Hoffman looked around again, hoping to see the person he was supposed to meet. He felt like a prisoner shackled to the demands of an unseen voice of evil. The realization momentarily paralyzed him.

"Now, what?" Dirk asked.

Hoffman resigned himself to completing this last consulting assignment. He thought he could still work this to his advantage if he could identify his blackmailers. "Follow me when I pull out of here. I've got to call and find out where we go next." Hoffman turned and walked back to his car. He studied the number on the crumpled paper beneath the light of the parking lot lamppost. Closing his eyes, he willed himself to relax. One more assignment. Finish this job, take your money, and disappear.

After two more deep breaths, he walked to the pay phone and fished a quarter from his pocket. After inserting the coin, he dialed the number.

CHAPTER TWENTY-FOUR

BY THE END of the weekend, Mackie had met with three additional families. All of their stories started with themes similar to the ones he'd heard in Loretta Sims's kitchen: healthy patients looking to make some extra money by taking an experimental drug. Two of the former patients he spoke with began to experience trouble concentrating within four months of taking Anginex. One man required hospitalization for dementia. Another developed kidney failure. Each study patient reported that once their symptoms developed, BioloGen dropped them from the trial. Each participant told of phone calls being ignored and follow-up visits being canceled.

After interviewing the last family on Sunday, Mackie doubled back for one final visit with Donnie Sims. He could not shake the image from his mind of the emaciated man who didn't recognize his own wife. Mackie wanted to confide his concerns about Anginex with Dr. Martin, but he felt he needed to solidify his evidence first. That his medical mentor at BioloGen was out of town on business bought him some time, but that didn't dampen the urgency to complete his weekend fact-finding mission.

As he drove, Mackie wrestled with the new information

about the Anginex safety profile. He felt he had indisputable evidence that Anginex was tainted, and he began to believe that BioloGen knew about it. What he didn't understand was how this could happen with a drug that had been so extensively tested. Why hadn't ADAM picked it up? And why had no one else addressed the problem before now?

Mackie reviewed the possible scenarios for documenting the Anginex side effects, and each involved participation from Loretta and Donnie. Assuming he could document Donnie Sims's condition, Mackie believed the executives at BioloGen would be forced to re-examine their potential blockbuster drug. He knew that after seven years and hundreds of millions of dollars in drug development, no one at the company would be eager to uncover new side effects. But he also suspected that, if a small fly in the Anginex ointment could be identified and removed, the new drug application to the FDA would only be delayed, not derailed.

He took the exit off the interstate and drove along darkening roads that led to the Sims's trailer. Mackie rolled down the windows, looking for familiar landmarks. The late afternoon air chilled the car, accented by the smell of chimney smoke. He tapped his brakes and pulled onto the gravel road. Mackie straightened in his seat, studying the surrounding terrain. He slowed his car even more, and pulled into the driveway.

"Holy shit!" He jerked on the emergency brake and flung open the car door. He ran toward the trailer. He knew from the stench what had happened. It was not the rustic smell of dried pine but the harsh smell of melted plastic and singed hair. The chain link fence still surrounded the wooden back porch, which now stood alone like an abandoned dock. The doublewide trailer Mackie had visited one day ago was now a pile of rubble and ash. A metal chimney stood near the back porch, defiantly keeping watch over the debris. Through the harsh glare of the car's headlights, he saw humps of charred furniture and the metal skeleton of a bookshelf. The smoldering ashes warmed his feet as he walked closer.

Mackie moved forward into the nightmare. The railing of the front porch stairs still stood, but the rest of the wooden structure had collapsed. Lying on the ground nearby, he saw a metal pole and the singed corners of the 'Welcome' flag. One thought continued to clang like a bell in his mind. He needed to call someone.

The headlights of his car cast a long shadow in front of Mackie. At first, the darkened tree line and burned-out trailer blended together. As his eyes adjusted, he saw them. His stomach heaved. No amount of orthopedic trauma could have prepared him for the sight before him. Tears stung his eyes.

Where the sofa once sat, Mackie saw the scorched remains of Donnie and Loretta Sims, their hands clasped even in death.

* * *

The sheriff said it was arson.

Mackie had climbed back into his car and driven back to the interstate, searching for a pay phone. He called the police and then returned to the remains of the trailer. The sheriff arrived first, followed by the coroner. They took their turns documenting the scene and taking notes. Mackie waited by his car, hoping for an explanation. After a walk around the property, the sheriff ambled over to Mackie.

"Looks like the person who did this was on a mission," the sheriff said.

"Meaning what?"

The sheriff shined his light across the yard toward what was left of the trailer. "Didn't you smell the petroleum when you got here? That was the first thing I noticed. Come take a look at this." He walked over to the remains of the front steps and squatted down. "If you look at the wood from the porch, you'll see this piece here has a hole in it, almost as if someone poured a flammable liquid."

"Gasoline?"

"Or kerosene. Look around to the side," he said, pushing up from his squat to lead Mackie toward the back porch. "There's a low burn pattern here. Most unintentional fires are gonna burn upward, but the scorch marks here look lower. We'll know more in the daylight, but that pattern suggests to me a liquid accelerant. If we really needed to be sure, we could send those boards to the state lab for gas chromatography."

Mackie nodded. "To look for the fingerprints of the flammable liquid."

"You a scientist?"

"Doctor."

"So here's the thing, Doc. The Sims were simple people. Donnie and I used to play softball together before he got sick. He was a hell of a second baseman, by the way. But Donnie and Loretta didn't have two quarters to rub together. I know they didn't have insurance policies. They had a handful of friends in the area, but mostly kept to themselves. Frankly, even if we get a confirmation of arson, it's not going to help catch the person who did this. If we find an empty gasoline can down the road, my boys will dust it for prints, but don't hold your breath for any breakthroughs."

Mackie had to contain his frustration when he responded. "So you're saying that's it? Maybe it's arson, maybe not, but it's out of our hands?"

"Unless you got some other leads, I'd say you about summed it up." The sheriff handed him a card. "Call me if you can think of anything else."

Mackie returned to his car. He drove toward the interstate and found a McDonald's near the southbound entrance ramp. He circled the parking lot until he spotted a pay phone, then pulled up next to it. Even on Sunday evening, he didn't doubt he could track down the information he needed. He dialed the home number of his friend from medical school. Tom Philips answered on the second ring.

"You got that article?" Tom asked.

Mackie pressed his ear to the plastic receiver and lowered his voice, even though no one else was close. "I've got a few more questions about angiogenesis inhibitors."

"I'm surprised you're still looking into that."

"When you picked up the copy of the article, did you tell the librarian anything about what you were looking for or why you needed it?"

His friend's laugh crackled through the handset. "You sound paranoid, Mackie."

"A BioloGen patient is dead, Tom. Two more are dying."

"Jesus, Mackie. Are you sure there's a BioloGen connection?"

"I'm trying to figure out what the hell is going on."

"Maybe you should try and figure out what the hell you're still doing working there."

The thought wasn't lost on Mackie. For almost six months, he had lived in a new city, working an unfamiliar job that kept him far away from his family. This was not the sabbatical he'd anticipated. But he couldn't pack up and leave, could he? If he knew that four patients had problems in a fifty-person study, how many more Anginex patients with side effects existed? And how many more would come once the FDA approved the drug? Mackie already knew the data from the published trials of Anginex, and none of what he had seen this weekend was contained in the new drug application. As far as the FDA would know, Anginex was as safe as aspirin.

A recorded voice prompted Mackie to add more money for the long distance call.

A few moments later, Tom said, "You asked me to use discretion in finding that article. There's no mention of you or BioloGen on that request. The librarian gave me one other reference to a related article, but that's the extent of her involvement."

"What article?"

"Hold on."

Mackie heard Tom set the phone down, then heard what sounded like a desk drawer opening and closing, followed by the shuffle of papers. Tom picked back up on his end.

"The citation of the article says, *The Other Endostatin: Promise and Problems of Isomers in Medicine.* Sounds thrilling, Mackie."

"Isomer?" Mackie said, more to himself than to Tom as he glanced at his hands. Could it be that simple that even ADAM had overlooked it? Did the problem lie with mirror images of molecules?

When Mackie didn't say anything else, Tom asked, "You okay?"

Mackie dodged the question. He wasn't sure himself, but he felt certain about his next steps. He thanked Tom for the lead and told him he'd be in touch. Mackie climbed back into his car and headed for the interstate.

He drove the one hundred twenty miles in just over ninety minutes. His mind sped along the possibilities of Tom's discovery. Learning about isomers was the stuff of Chemistry 101. His college chemistry professor had explained the concept by holding up two gloves as examples of molecular isomers: similar in almost every way but not interchangeable. Even if Anginex was the other-handed glove of endostatin, what difference did that make to the body?

It was almost 8:00 p.m. when Mackie pulled up to the gated entrance at BioloGen Pharmaceuticals. He doubted he would find the answer to the Anginex riddle in the new drug application, but he suspected some clue may be buried in the original patent for the molecule. If not there, it could be in the basic science research given to the FDA prior to the first clinical trials. Mackie had limited access to each of those files at the office. If he didn't find his answer, he planned to approach Douglas on Monday morning.

Mackie showed his ID card to a security guard posted at the gated entrance. He pulled into the parking lot before swiping his badge again to enter the building. In the lobby, he saw another security guard seated at the same front desk station usually occupied by the women he saw each morning.

The middle-aged cop sat up when Mackie approached. He introduced himself as Earl. "I'm not used to seeing anyone but the engineers here on Sundays."

"I'm not used to working on Sundays," Mackie replied as he showed his ID badge a second time.

The guard leaned forward to scrutinize the identification. "*Doctor* McKay?"

"Yes, sir."

The security guard pushed himself up from his chair. "Got something for you," he said as he bent over a crate of mail behind the desk. "Came in yesterday."

Mackie paused as the man handed him a flat manilla envelope addressed with his name. The thin package had a Washington, D.C. return address. Mackie's hand trembled as he read the name of the sender: Jason Lampley.

"You okay, Doc?"

Mackie took his eyes off the return address long enough to ask, "What time do you leave?"

"I'm here all night. Call me if you need anything."

Mackie walked toward the elevator, taking it to the third floor. His hands continued to shake even when he sat at his desk to open the envelope. No note or letter accompanied the stapled pages. The only item inside was a journal article. When he glanced at the title, his heart skipped a beat as he realized Tom was right. He *was* in over his head at BioloGen. Jason Lampley, the same man in Aruba who had warned Mackie about Anginex, had sent the same article Tom had mentioned a few hours ago. *The Other Endostatin: Promise and Problems of Isomers in Medicine.*

Mackie scanned the article at first, then re-read it with an investigator's eye. The difference in the pair of angiogenesis gloves, the isomers, was a difference in what was left behind in the bloodstream. The classical endostatin dissolved like sugar in tea, sweetening the blood without a trace of its presence. The isomer, though, didn't dissolve, swirling in the blood like coffee grounds. Seemingly similar in every way except its ability to dissolve.

As Mackie read further, he realized the problematic isomer was not Anginex but another cousin drug. He knew that pharmaceutical engineers should have been able to separate the right-handed from the left-handed molecules. They should be able to remove the impurities of the one that didn't dissolve while isolating the beneficial type. What this journal article suggested, though, was even a small amount of impurity in the sample could foul up the system, leaving behind a protein residue called amyloid.

The last of the stapled pages was not part of the original journal article at all. Instead, Mackie found a photocopy of an old newspaper article from *The Cincinnati Enquirer.* The headline of the small article shouted, Man Killed in Car in Downtown Neighborhood.

Mackie's stomach sank as he read, *A local man was found dead in the front seat of his car early Wednesday morning with his wallet still on him and a bullet in the back of his head...*

This cannot be happening, Mackie thought, as he read the handwritten note at the bottom of the article. Next to a local area code and phone number, someone, presumably Jason Lampley, had simply written, *Call us when you're ready to talk.*

CHAPTER TWENTY-FIVE

EDDIE FACKLER SCRATCHED his nose with his gloved hand and waited for the desktop phone to ring. As much as he loathed getting out of bed for nighttime jobs, the pay was good and the time commitment short. In less than two hours, he'd be home in bed with the problem fixed. He studied the thick envelope in his lap, marveling at how far he'd come in his profession.

The phone on the desk top rang. Right on time, he thought, because who else would be calling at this hour on this phone. "Dr. Hoffman, I'm glad you received my note," he said in a low voice flavored with cigarettes and artifice. It was the same voice he used for all his business-related calls.

"We were supposed to—" Hoffman began.

Fackler cut him off. "Plans change. We'll meet in the abandoned strip mall two miles from the post office. Come in the last door on the left, next to the sign."

"But..."

Eddie severed the connection. His heart surged with adrenaline. He loved his job.

* * *

Hoffman peered through the windshield at the dark

building before him. A large placard read *Space Available* on the nearest storefront. He didn't understand why they had to meet in this unfamiliar section of town.

He checked his watch before glancing in the rearview mirror. Aside from the passing headlights of Dirk's SUV, the street remained empty.

As instructed, he approached the front of the building and pulled open the door at the far end. A small bell announced his arrival with a metallic tinkle. A security light glowed in the back of the room.

Hoffman paused to let his eyes adjust. He saw an unfamiliar room with industrial carpeting, empty walls, and a sliding glass receptionist window. We're meeting in an abandoned doctor's office, he thought. Clever bastard. He saw the fog of his own breath when he exhaled, but he heard nothing other than the sound of his own breathing.

Walking forward, he leaned through the open receptionist's window. "Hello?" His voice echoed off the metal desk and bank of filing cabinets. "Hello?" he said again, louder this time. No response. He strained to see any sign of activity in the dark. "Anybody here?"

The bell on the front door jingled.

Hoffman jerked, cracking his head against the top of the receptionist's window and biting his tongue. "Shit!" He tasted blood, but was too frightened to care. He whirled around.

Hoffman had envisioned a tall, muscular man with a weathered face, but standing before him was a young man with a stocking cap and a mustache, hands tucked into his coat pockets and a thick envelope wedged under one arm.

"Dr. Hoffman?"

Hoffman hesitated, despite the familiar deep voice. "What do you want?"

The man tossed the thick envelope at him, which nailed his chest before it hit the floor. "Those are the final medical records changes."

Hoffman swallowed, nearly gagging on the blood in his mouth. He picked up the envelope. When he straightened, a gun was pointed at his face. "Jesus Christ!" Fear paralyzed him.

The gun never wavered as Eddie talked. "You got sloppy. We've lost valuable time on this project because of you. That ends now."

"If there had been a more reliable way to—"

"Shut the hell up!" Eddie reached inside his coat. He pulled out a much thinner envelope and tossed it at Hoffman's feet.

"What's this?" Hoffman asked, staring at the second envelope.

"Let's just call it insurance to guarantee your full cooperation."

Hoffman's eyes watered. Bending down, he grabbed the smaller envelope, fumbling as he struggled to open it. He finally withdrew two sheets of paper. "My God…"

He stared at a photocopy of Compton Drew's obituary. The next page contained a color photograph of Compton's body, blood pooling on the asphalt from a gun-shot wound to the back of his head.

When Hoffman looked up, his blackmailer had disappeared.

$\mathscr{C}$HAPTER TWENTY-SIX

$\mathscr{M}$ACKIE CALLED THE number that night from the phone in his office. He could think of multiple reasons not to call, but behind each of his excuses to procrastinate, he returned to the inevitable fact that he, and BioloGen, were being watched. Mackie assumed the same person who'd overheard his conversation with Tom Philips would also listen in on other Anginex-related conversations. If those who were listening could travel to Aruba to confront a new employee and then eavesdrop on a conversation in a medical library, how much further would they go to get the information they sought? Mackie didn't know the answers to any of this, but he could either call now and learn or wait and be caught up in the subsequent fall out.

When he called, the conversation was short. A man on the other end of the line who did not identify himself, but sounded different from Jason Lampley in Aruba, said that he had some relevant information about the upcoming new drug application for Anginex. He asked Mackie to meet him in half an hour at a restaurant off the interstate. "Go inside," the man had said. "I'll find you."

Mackie pulled into the deserted parking lot thirty minutes later. He killed the engine and peered through his windshield into the backlit restaurant, which reminded him of an Edward Hopper scene. He saw one table occupied by a young couple with a baby near the front of the diner. The man munched on his meal while the woman fed the baby a bottle. Two tables over, an elderly man read a newspaper. Outside the restaurant, a middle-aged waitress in an apron stood a few paces away from the door, smoking a cigarette. That was it. No sign of anyone else. There would be others in the kitchen and maybe out back, but no one who looked ready for a clandestine meeting.

Mackie waited a few more minutes. The waitress crushed the cigarette butt under her foot and walked back inside. The young couple traded tasks as the woman handed over the baby and then began to eat the fries. When nothing changed, Mackie stepped into the cool fall night and followed his instructions.

"Welcome to Frisch's Big Boy," the waitress said through a yawn. "You're picking up a to-go order for McKay?"

He stopped at the sound of his name. The man meeting him here must have called ahead. Mackie followed the lead set out for him. "Is it ready?"

"I'll grab it from the kitchen," she said.

The greasy smell of a short-order dive reminded Mackie of his lack of sustenance that day, but uncertainty and anxiety stole his appetite. When he casually looked around the restaurant, no one gave him more than a passing glance. The waitress returned with a grease-stained brown paper sack and rang up the ticket. Mackie paid the tab. Not knowing what else to do, he stepped outside to return to his car.

As he crossed the parking lot, a black Lincoln Town Car intercepted him as it eased into the parking space next to his car. The back window rolled down.

"Dr. McKay?"

Mackie's heart rate accelerated.

"Agent Aiken," the man said, introducing himself from the car. "FBI."

Shit. Any lingering desire to eat the contents of the bag evaporated. Images of his investigations and interviews over the past two days flooded his mind, followed by thoughts of articles and obituaries. Clues from the last six months at BioloGen coalesced in Mackie's mind. When combined, they offered a trail of evidence that apparently interested the FBI. Mackie stepped back toward his own car.

"You are the same Dr. McKay who called us tonight?" Brian Aiken made an exaggerated look over his shoulder at the near empty parking lot. "I don't see any one else carrying a to-go bag. Why don't you hop in the car for a few minutes? We've got some information about your company you may find interesting."

Mackie saw few options. "How about we get a table inside?" he suggested.

"Too exposed," the man in the backseat responded. "Get in. We'll bring you back in a few minutes."

The window of the Lincoln rolled up.

Was this a set up? Mackie wondered. Had Pescatelli orchestrated this elaborate ruse to expose Mackie for his snooping? The car and the man who identified himself as Agent Aiken appeared to fit the part of the federal agency, but what did Mackie know about any of this? He hesitated, but then decided he'd come too far to ignore what he'd seen at BioloGen. He opened the door and slid in. The car backed out of the parking space and eased onto the road that led to the interstate.

"I'm Agent Brian Aiken from the FBI," he said as he nodded his head toward the front seat. "And this is my partner from the Cincinnati Field Office, Agent Ronald Thibodaux."

The middle-aged man in the driver's seat made eye contact with Mackie through a glance in the rearview mirror.

"A pleasure," he said as he merged the Town Car onto the interstate.

Mackie sank back into his seat. Unsure of what to say or do, he set the bag of food at his feet and waited. Neither Agent spoke at first. Finally, Mackie turned to Aiken who sat across from him. "Tell me what you know about BioloGen."

"More than you might think, but not as much as we would like." Aiken tapped a thick accordion folder positioned beside him. "We've been monitoring BioloGen for over a year now—"

Mackie interrupted, "Why?"

"That's a fair question." He opened the elastic strap on the folder and lifted a sheaf of papers and photos. "You may have seen this before." He handed Mackie the same obituary that had been stapled to the back of the journal article from earlier that evening. "The newspaper sanitizes the scene. Take a look at these." Aiken dealt out three crime scene photos.

The first one was a glossy photograph of a corpse hunched over a car steering wheel. Dark blood matted the back of his head. Flecks of flesh and brain covered the dashboard. Mackie only felt comfortable in a trauma scene when time counted and he could call the shots. But seated in the back of a government-issued Town Car and looking at images of a murder scene made his uneasy stomach lurch. He lowered the back window a fraction of an inch, hoping the cool air would settle his nerves. He flipped through the other two images, each detailing a different angle of the gunshot wound.

"That case is still open," Aiken said, "but based on what we've learned from our interviews with the local police and his family, this man was the fifth patient enrolled in the Phase One trial of Anginex. I believe you identify it as the B-AGX-23 trial?"

"The *fifth* patient?" Mackie asked.

"Pretending you don't know what I'm talking about won't win you any favors with me, Dr. McKay. You talked to the other four patients this weekend that dropped out." Aiken removed several more pages from his folder. "I'm sure this will help jog your memory."

Mackie looked at six pages of medical records, almost perfect photocopies of the originals, but the name of the patient had been redacted. As he flipped though the pages under the dim dome light, he noticed a few familiar phrases written in a doctor's hurried hand. *Rapid onset. Loss of executive functioning. Most likely Alzheimer's.* An MRI report in the chart showed that the front parts of the patient's brain, as well as the memory centers tucked behind the ears, were shrinking.

"These are more of the same, but you already know that by now. Those are the last records we have on him." Aiken handed him two additional sheets of paper. "A patient by the name of Donnie Sims."

The image of the burned-out trailer still smoldered in Mackie's mind. He glanced at the final records, then handed them back. "And the others?"

"Same stuff. Different patients, but all the ones you visited this weekend."

Mackie's disbelief turned to anger. "How long have you been following me?"

"Long enough, Doc, to realize you know enough to help us."

Was he really being propositioned as an FBI informant? "I know what I've been told," Mackie said. "I wasn't even a part of the company when the B-AGX-23 trial was ongoing."

"Which makes you the perfect person to help us out," Aiken said. "Let's face it, Doc, you don't belong here. Your surgical mentor in Nashville told us you had some noble intentions in coming to BioloGen. I applaud you for that. But regardless of your motivation, you are a full time employee of a company that we believe is directly involved in a ring of interstate murders. That man right there," Aiken gestured toward the glossy crime scene photos still in Mackie's hand, "took Anginex for four months before he was murdered. When he first lost some of his memory, he hired a lawyer and gave a deposition regarding his condition."

Mackie had seen enough. He handed the photos back to Agent Aiken, who turned around and placed a bound ream of pages on the seat next to Mackie. "This is a copy of his deposition. Not your typical study patient, at least compared to the others in the trial. This guy was well-educated, upper middle class, and altruistic. Kind of like you."

That comment elicited a chuckle from Agent Thibodaux in the driver's seat.

Aiken continued. "He told his wife that he wanted to participate in a study that would find a way to cure cancer. Once he noticed his memory slipping, he called the FDA and filed an adverse drug reaction complaint with them. Of course, the FDA notified BioloGen that one of their study drugs had a possible side-effect. Two weeks later, this guy was found dead in his car."

"And you know it wasn't some random robbery?" Mackie asked.

"At first, the police said it was a random crime. But it doesn't take a smart surgeon like you, Doc, to ask what kind of robber leaves two hundred bucks in a man's wallet but ransacks his briefcase." Aiken lifted the pages of the thick deposition. "Maybe he was looking for the information contained in this. What I can tell you, though, is that the shots came from the back seat, so either this victim never heard the perp get in the car, or this was a two-man job with our guy knowing the people who killed him."

Mackie rubbed his eye with the base of his palm, as if by pushing on his forehead hard enough he could make this nightmare go away. "Did the FDA ever follow up on the complaint?"

"Not their job at that point in the process. They told BioloGen, relying on the company to make the necessary changes. The risk of not doing so is the risk of not getting a drug FDA approved."

Neither man spoke for a moment. Agent Thibodaux eased the Lincoln onto the next exit ramp before looping around and onto the interstate, heading back to the restaurant. Mackie couldn't envision this conversation ending well for him. Even though Aiken had only shared information so far, there was bound to be a catch. Exactly what he wanted from BioloGen was not clear, but Mackie could guess he would be at the center of getting it for them. Whether he could help Aiken without compromising his own future was the most uncertain part of this entire conversation.

"The Anginex studies aren't isolated to BioloGen," Mackie finally said.

"We already have several NIH experts combing their medical records to find out about other reported problems with drugs of this type."

"How'd you get all of this material?" Mackie felt naive for asking, but he also wondered what the FBI didn't have access to in building their case against BioloGen.

"We've enough information to move forward."

Mackie studied Aiken for any sign of additional information. "Someone else has come forward with concerns?"

"We have an informant," Aiken said. "A former employee."

"Who?"

"I can't tell you that."

"So what are you going to do about it?" Mackie demanded.

"Not us, Doc. The question is: what are *you* going to do about it?"

Mackie seethed. "I'd like to nail their asses to the wall."

"Here's your chance." Aiken began to refile the material he had passed out to Mackie.

"Red Pescatelli and Rita Martin deny any problems with the drug. Both have assured me it's as safe as a placebo."

Aiken snapped the elastic band around the file and set it at his feet. "The FBI thinks the problem with the B-AGX-23 trial extends beyond BioloGen Pharmaceuticals. I could give you a half a dozen examples of big pharmaceutical companies sitting on side effects so a drug's approval wouldn't be held up by the FDA. We've had our eye on some of the biggest names in the business for years. Based on what we've found, BioloGen's not alone. It's just the most egregious example of greed we've seen."

Mackie stared out the back window at the tail lights of the other cars on the interstate. He needed his wife's input right now. Even if he and Sarah could communicate about little else these days, she would have a practical legal opinion about his situation. But from where Mackie sat, he saw few options. Even before the FBI contacted him, he'd already decided to investigate the dropout rate on his own. His gut instinct told him to go to the police, but crimes in multiple cities across state lines obviously fell outside of any one department's jurisdiction. He could probably resign from BioloGen tomorrow, but that decision did not guarantee immunity for him from all that he knew. And if he left, how many more people would be harmed before someone else blew the whistle?

"What about the other informant?" Mackie finally asked.

"He doesn't work for BioloGen any longer."

"So what exactly do you need from me?"

"You've already started a parallel investigation for the type of information we need. Tracking down those who did not complete the trial is important. But even more so, we want to know what BioloGen knew of side effects and when they knew it."

"And I'm supposed to provide that?"

"You have unparalleled access to their files."

"I have access to the building, not to the locked rooms and monitored hallways."

"We can help with that." Aiken cleared his throat, adopting a more business-like tone. He leaned toward Mackie as the shoulder strap of his seatbelt strained against his suit. "Imagine a million people taking Anginex in the first year. Your own trial data from B-AGX-23 showed a ten percent drop-out rate due to side effects. Let's be conservative and say that small trial over-estimated the risks. Even if side effects happen to only one percent of patients, that's still 10,000 people who will develop dementia in the first year the drug is approved."

"With the number of people already being diagnosed with dementia a year, that'll barely be noticed," Mackie said.

"Except by the families of the victims of your company, Doctor McKay."

"I didn't sign up for this, Agent Aiken."

Aiken laughed for the first time since their encounter. "Shit happens, Doc. The jury won't care how noble your intentions were for signing up for BioloGen. What they'll want to hear is what did you do with this information once you found out."

Mackie knew Aiken was right. As the black Lincoln Town Car pulled off the interstate and into the parking lot of Frisch's Big Boy restaurant, Ronald Thibodaux parked in the empty space next to Mackie's car. He kept the engine running.

Aiken reached toward his feet once more and picked up a package the size of a shoebox. "We're already moving forward with this investigation. You called the number, so I assume you're willing to help us get a copy of those documents." He placed the box on the seat between them. "Go ahead and open it."

Mackie lifted it from the seat between them. It was heavier than expected, and as he opened the lid he found a stack of 3.5 floppy discs, a box the size of a soap bar, and a black plastic camera just larger than his outstretched hand.

"That's a Dycam Model 4," Agent Aiken said, "latest digital camera technology on the market. We've adjusted the memory so you can take up to twenty-four digital images."

"No film?"

"Digital is the next big thing, doc." Aiken reached into the box in Mackie's lap and removed a small circular lens. "When you attach this lens, it will allow you to take close-up shots, which is what we'll need for documentation."

"And what exactly do you want me to photograph?"

"All of the tainted medical records, plus a few legitimate ones."

"That's probably a hundred pages in the first study alone."

"The proof is in the paper trail. If a patient didn't complete the study, like your friend Donald Sims, then I want a copy of everything BioloGen has in his chart."

"What happens once I hit my twenty-four image limit?"

"We're working on that."

"But no plan yet." Mackie shook his head as he lifted up the small box the size of soap. "And what about this?"

"You'll need unrestricted access to the storage room for the new drug application. That's the putty you'll use to duplicate the key."

"I'm sure you're working on a plan for me to do that as well?" Mackie didn't hide the sarcasm in his voice.

Aiken didn't miss a beat. "You'll need to be alone with the key for one minute. The putty contains ultra-fine silicone beads to replicate the impression within tenths of a millimeter. You'll need to clean the key, press it into the putty, and hold it there for thirty seconds. Both sides. Once you're done, put the putty back in the box. We'll make arrangements to pick up the impression and get the duplicate key back to you within twelve hours."

Mackie packed the items back into the larger shoebox and secured the lid. In the last two days, he had gone from a curious employee to a government informant. The transition didn't sit well with him. He opened the passenger door in the car.

Aiken said as Mackie stepped out of the Lincoln, "Hey, Doc, one more thing."

Mackie cradled the box of spy gear under his arm and turned to face the FBI agent. "What?"

"Be careful who you talk to at BioloGen," Aiken said. "As you've already seen, we can't get much information from a dead witness."

ℭHAPTER TWENTY-SEVEN

𝓗OFFMAN SAT IN the leather chair in his office, appreciative of the nighttime quiet of the NIH. He stared at his computer screen.

    Please enter password.

His door locked and the window shades closed, he knew he was the only employee in the building at this hour. Even the cleaning crew had completed their nocturnal tasks. Taking a sip of coffee, he glanced at the letter and typed in the seven-digit password. The computerized patient record paused for several seconds before a new screen appeared.

    Welcome Compton Drew. Please enter patient
    identification.

The dead man's name, combined with the earlier image of his bloodied body, nauseated Hoffman. He had shown Dirk the picture of Compton's body and a photocopy of his obituary. He'd requested an immediate evaluation of the envelope for fingerprints.

"You want handwriting analysis, too?" Dirk had asked.

"Whatever it takes to identify this guy," Hoffman said. "You got close-up pictures of his face?"

"And his car."

"How long until we know something?"

"About three days."

"Five hundred bucks if you get it to me in two."

"Seven-fifty."

"Deal."

The two men had parted ways at half past midnight. Once he saw the dark SUV drive off, Hoffman opened the thick envelope and read his instructions. He was to drive immediately to his office at the NIH and begin the final phase of the chart revisions. The specified chart changes seemed more extensive than before. In addition to altering certain test results, Hoffman would also erase some charts in their entirety. He knew from personal experience in running clinical trials, this assignment would wipe out months of painstaking research.

He now re-read the final paragraph of the letter in the package. His heart thundered with both the carrot of compensation and the stick of fear.

You have twenty-four hours to complete this assignment. Once you do, you will receive 50% of your final payment. Failure to comply with this deadline will be dealt with swiftly and decisively.

Hoffman's hands trembled. By this time tomorrow night, he would either be independently wealthy or he would be dead.

The letter also contained his new stolen CPR password. If he stayed at his desk all night, Hoffman expected to finish the chart changes before sunrise. With a little luck, he might even be able to take a short nap before his colleagues arrived for work in the morning. He began.

Within an hour, he'd altered seven patient charts. On one chart that read, *Patient complains of right knee pain*, the complaint disappeared a few seconds later.

Another patient reported feeling well, but a routine

analysis of her urine revealed evidence of abnormal protein. Hoffman recognized an early warning sign of possible kidney problems. In his own diabetic patients, he prescribed cocktails of medicines to control blood pressure and prevent kidney failure. In this patient's chart, he corrected the problem by deleting the abnormal labs. It didn't change her prognosis, but as far as the NIH records were concerned, the lab had never been drawn.

Ten other patients completely disappeared from the CPR system in the first hour. Researchers might remember their faces. The patients might have already received compensation for their participation. Some of them might even be scheduled for follow-up appointments, but all of the information gained from studying these ten patients no longer existed.

A part of Hoffman wanted to search through these patient charts and find a common theme or side-effect. His academic curiosity nagged at him before he erased the patient data, but he lacked the time to look. He soothed his guilty conscience by reminding himself that none of what he did actually impacted patients. The side effects had been caused by a medicine, not his actions. Others inflicted harm. He was simply altering the record keeping.

By 4:00 a.m., he could hardly keep his eyes open. He had changed over fifty charts with only a few remaining. He knew he should press on and finish the task. He buried his face in his hands and rubbed his temples.

And exhaustion claimed him.

* * *

The neighbors kept banging. "Shut up," he mumbled, but the banging continued. What the hell were they doing? Hammering nails into the wall?

He cracked his eyes open, expecting to see his bedroom. Instead, he saw a computer monitor.

The banging persisted.

"Shut up!" he shouted.

"Scottie? Are you okay? Unlock this door!"

What the hell was Yolanda doing here? He felt completely disoriented.

"Scottie, open this door right now!"

He sat up and realized something was drastically wrong. His mind started to clear. He registered the dark computer screen and the pages from last night's package, the latter now scattered across the floor like fallen leaves. He must have knocked over his cup because coffee-colored stains laced the pages. Looking down at himself, he saw the same jeans and t-shirt he'd worn to his midnight meeting. He glanced at his watch. Half-past seven.

One thought stood out in his mind above all others: if he didn't finish his task today, he would die.

"Scottie?"

"Just a second, Yolanda!"

He hurriedly gathered up the scattered pages. He knew he only had a few charts left to finish, but which ones? The anxiety blooming in his chest evaporated his lingering fatigue.

Shoving the pages into his top desk drawer, he tucked his t-shirt into his jeans and hurried to unlock the door.

Yolanda stared at him. "What the hell happened to you? I've been knocking on your door for five minutes." She stormed into his office and looked around. "What's going on in here?"

He swallowed, trying to get rid of the bad taste in his mouth. "It's nothing, Yolanda. I came in late last night to do some work and fell asleep at my desk. Why were you banging on my door?"

"Because you have a meeting in half an hour, and I need you to sign some papers before you leave."

"Cancel it."

"What?"

"Cancel the meeting." Hoffman grabbed the papers from her, returned to his desk, and began signing where indicated.

"I can't cancel the meeting. It's with the board of directors of the American Diabetes Association." She glared at him.

"Reschedule for after lunch."

"And cancel the fourth grade field trip? You are supposed to meet with *them* this afternoon and talk about working at the NIH."

"Take care of it, okay?" Hoffman handed the signed documents to her. "I've got to go home, shower, and then get back here. Plus, I need to finish up what I was working on. I don't have time for a bunch of nine and ten year old kids today. Find a replacement to give them a tour and tell the ADA board that something came up so we have to reschedule for after lunch. Any other questions?"

"Lots, but I won't waste my breath." She slammed the door on her way out.

Hoffman removed the pages from his desk drawer. Some of them had stuck together from the spilled coffee, resulting in partially smeared ink. As he began to organize them, he realized he couldn't recall which charts he'd completed and which ones he still needed to do.

He took a deep breath and slowly exhaled, using his self-taught relaxation techniques. Rechecking all of the charts might take hours. At that moment, he saw no other option. He had a fleeting thought of the KeyTracker disk, wishing he hadn't taken it home months ago.

The screen flashed a message.

```
Please enter password.
```

Flipping through the crumpled pages, he found the first page with the instructions. It seemed to have absorbed the majority of spilled coffee, with the seven-digit password now smeared. Hoffman squinted at the stained paper and typed in what he thought was the proper code.

    `Password incorrect. Please enter password.`

Not again.

He held up the paper to his desk lamp to read the password. He figured out the first six characters, but the last one was completely obscured. Was that a *3* or an *8*? Maybe it was an *S* or a *B*. Not trusting his memory, he recorded the password he had already entered before entering the new one. He couldn't afford to repeat his mistakes.

    `Password incorrect. Please enter password.`

"Come on," he moaned to the computer. His head ached from lack of sleep, and he needed to get home and shower. He tried another ending to the password, pressed *enter,* and waited. When he looked at the screen, he broke out into a cold sweat. He blinked and reread the message.

    `Password incorrect. CPR access now disabled`
    `from this computer. Please contact the`
    `Medical Records Department with questions.`

ℭHAPTER TWENTY-EIGHT

ℬY THE TIME he arrived at work that next morning, Mackie was already late for his first meeting. Sleep had evaded him the night before thanks to the FBI. Even as he scrambled to make up time while getting ready, he worried about finding the time to track down the key. Lost in thought as he stepped off the elevator, he almost bumped into Ms. Franks, who waited for him in the hallway. He tried to deflect his tardiness by asking her about his to-do list for the day. "What time do we need to send out the first round of Anginex advertisements?"

"Ten minutes ago, with the morning mail. If you'd been on time, Dr. McKay, you'd see that all I needed was your signature on a few pages to send them out," she said. "You're also expected in a strategy session in five minutes. Did you finish reviewing the ads?"

"The *Are you ready for a revolution* one?"

"Not Ms. Kiley's first choice."

Mackie shrugged out of his jacket as he walked to his office. Ms. Franks followed. "She delegated that decision to me," he said.

Mackie tossed his jacket on the corner chair and quickly scanned the proofs Ms. Franks had set out for him. This was the easy part, he thought. Not mentioning the name Anginex in the ads meant not having to bother with the fine print. This initial phase of marketing was all about buying good will for BioloGen. The more direct advertising would come later. After looking at the ads, he handed the proofs back to Ms. Franks. "Good to go." He breezed out of his office toward the conference room.

He'd hoped to interact with Dr. Martin at that meeting, but her assistant mentioned she was sequestered in her own office, sidelined with a stomach bug. Mackie tried to focus on the topic at hand. He did his job that morning, getting tasks done even as his heart and mind were elsewhere. By lunchtime, however, Mackie could hardly concentrate on work. He needed to get to Dr. Martin and secure the key. Under the auspices of needing to cross-check facts from the new drug application for his marketing team, Mackie reached Dr. Martin by phone. She encouraged him to come by soon as she anticipated leaving work early that afternoon.

Mackie pulled on his jacket and felt the soap bar-sized putty box in the pocket. He took the elevator to the second floor. When he stepped into the hallway, he heard Dr. Martin's voice as she spoke to someone on the phone from her office. He passed the single bathroom near the elevator, but he stopped short when he saw a light spilling into the hallway from the NDA war room.

As he drew closer, he noticed that someone had used a chair to prop open the usually locked door. Stepping into the room, he noted the same fourteen boxes lined neatly against the back wall with extra boxes positioned near the collapsible table and waiting to be filled. Stacks of papers surrounded the boxes. Spreadsheets and patient charts, mostly, but also copies of reference studies. On the table, Mackie also saw an open Mountain Dew can and a single key on a BioloGen keychain.

Time to change plans, Mackie thought as he walked to the

table and picked up the key.

"May I help you?"

Mackie turned around to face the unfamiliar voice. He saw the young college intern standing in the hallway. "You're working in here today?"

The intern look startled. "Yes, sir," he said, even though Mackie couldn't be more than ten years his senior. "I'm not used to seeing *you* down here, Dr. McKay."

Mackie made a decision on the fly. If he was to do what he needed to do, he couldn't wait for Dr. Martin's consent. "I'm double-checking some facts from the NDA. I didn't know someone else would be working in the room today."

The young man smiled. "I'm down here a lot, but it seems you have to have a medical degree to fully understand this stuff." He appeared enthralled with his small role in the introduction of a new drug to the FDA, and then to the market. "Dr. Martin has me collating the patient files from off-site locations—San Francisco and Houston, so far. The NIH files should arrive by the end of the week."

Mackie glanced at the piles of papers stacked across the floor. "All patient-related documents."

"Yes, sir."

"*Private* medical records?"

The intern lost his enthusiasm as confusion laced his answer. "As far as I know."

Mackie held up the key. "This the key to the room?"

"Dr. Martin's, actually. She usually escorts me to the room to unlock the door and take the key with her. But she's not feeling well today…" He reached for the key that Mackie held. "I should probably take that from you and return it to her now."

"You're Andrew, right?"

"Yes, sir."

"I'll take the key back to her."

192

˙y, I'm the only one right now that she's given

˩t it on the table while you stepped out of the
˩ sure Dr. Martin didn't have *that* in mind when she
˩usted it to you." Mackie's words honed a sharp edge, the
kind heard commonly in the surgical suites of his training. "If
she finds out about your apparent disregard for the security of
these documents, I doubt you'll have a chance to come in here
alone again."

"It wasn't like that," Andrew insisted.

"Be more careful next time." Mackie tucked the key in his
pocket. "How much longer are you planning to be in here?"

"Maybe ten minutes."

"I'll come back to lock up if Dr. Martin hasn't returned by
then."

Mackie strode down the hall toward the elevator. When
he saw that no one else was in the hallway, he ducked into the
lone restroom. His heart hammered as he locked the door.

He retrieved the putty box from his pocket then wiped
his hands on a bathroom paper towel. When he opened the
box, he saw a translucent block looking like a bar of soap. He
pried loose two alcohol pledgets affixed to the inside of box
and wiped both sides of the key, removing all the dust he
could see. He then placed the key onto the putty and pressed.
It sank into the block as if pressed into clay. Mackie held it
in place and counted to thirty. As he slowly freed the key to
make the impression on the other side, someone knocked on
the bathroom door.

Mackie jerked in surprise. He knocked the putty onto the
floor. They key fell into the sink. "Just a minute," he called out.

"Hurry, please," Dr. Martin implored.

Mackie froze, took a steadying breath, and focused on the
task at hand. Thirty more seconds.

Wiping the other side of the key with the second alcohol

swab, he pressed it into the putty adjacent to the first impression. He reached over and flushed the toilet with his free hand. Then, turned on the water, trying to buy time. He counted to thirty.

Mackie removed the key from the putty and snapped the lid onto the box. He slid the box into his pocket. Placing the key in his other pocket, he turned off the water and wiped the counter with a wad of paper towels. Once finished, he unlocked the bathroom door. Dr. Martin stood outside.

"Pardon me." She hurried into the rest room and shut the door behind her.

Mackie closed his eyes and focused on regaining his composure. In the time it took him to calm his nerves, he heard the toilet flush and the water run in the sink. Moments later, Dr. Martin emerged from the bathroom.

"I'm heading home," she said to Mackie. "This stomach bug's gotten the best of me. But didn't you need to see me about something in the NDA?"

"It can wait. But your intern wanted me to give this back to you," he said, holding the BioloGen keychain.

"What's it to?" she asked.

Mackie stared at her. "The key to the storage room?"

Dr. Martin shook her head. "Mine's back in my office."

Mackie stomach lurched. Had he made an impression of the wrong key? It looked exactly the same as the one she had used when Mackie first came into the war room with her, and it was the only one he'd seen on the counter. Could Andrew have mistaken that key for another one? He turned the keychain over and spotted a pinch of translucent putty stuck to the base of the key. His heart seemed to skip a beat as he asked, "Whose is this, then?"

"I'm not sure, but I'll hold on to it." Dr. Martin took the key and chain from him, seemingly unaware of the tell-tale bit of putty. "My office is open to you, Mackie. Let me know if you need access to those files."

She turned and shuffled back toward her office, leaving Mackie uncertain and alone as he stood in the hallway.

CHAPTER TWENTY-NINE

MACKIE SAT AT his desk two days later, waiting for the last person in his department to leave. He fiddled with the Dycam digital camera. The device, not much bigger than a glasses case, fit comfortably in his palm as he held it. When he turned the lens away, grooves in the black plastic shell guided the grip of his fingers. He had attached the lens and focused on random pages in his office, learning to pinch his elbows close to his chest to steady the image. The results were legible, even if the images he captured presented a grainy appearance.

Earlier that morning, when Mackie had retrieved the newly-cut keys to the storage room, Agent Ron Thibodaux had given him tips on optimizing the photo quality. Recognizing the risk of walking through BioloGen headquarters with a state-of-the-art digital camera and its twenty-four image limits, Agent Thibodaux also provided Mackie with a Sony Walkman Discman. The portable compact disc device looked exactly like the popular music player, but the FBI had stripped the insides of the factory-provided electronics and replaced them with a 3.5 inch disk drive. Thibodaux had demonstrated its use when he handed over the faux-music player to Mackie that morning. "Insert the floppy disk in the back," he said as he handed over a stack of plastic disks, "and plug the camera cord into where the headphones would go. It will automatically download the images for you."

He gave Mackie his final set of instructions. "We made six keys for you from the impression you provided us. Each key is slightly different from the rest," he told Mackie, explaining that the locksmith felt the truest impression was cut on the red key. "Once you get in, we need as much data as you can copy. Start with the first trial since we know the most about the B-AGX-23 patients. Those documents will establish problems with Anginex, which date back to the earliest trials. After that, you can photograph the Phase Two data. We're documenting a trend of illegal activity."

"You know that's hundreds of patient charts," Mackie said.

"No one said this would be easy, Dr. McKay." Thibodaux went on to explain that the FBI wanted to document all the charts for patients lost to follow up. Once Mackie had completed the night's work, he would take the discs and Discman home with him. Each morning until the job was done, Agent Thibodaux would meet with him to collect the copied data.

Mackie reviewed the instructions as he waited for all of the employees on the third floor to depart. He heard a noise outside his door and immediately hid the Dycam camera and Discman in his desk drawer.

Ms. Franks poked her head into the open door. "You're working late tonight."

"No choice. Nineteen days to go before we submit the NDA. I can't waste any time."

She pursed her lips in disgust as if she heard this before. "It doesn't change. There's always going to be another blockbuster drug in the pipeline. Another Anginex, maybe even better. Perhaps not as exciting as preventing cancer, but there will always be something, Dr. McKay." She pointed to a photo on his shelf of Mackie and Sarah on their honeymoon years ago. "What does your wife think of all this?"

"She understands," Mackie said, although Ms. Franks knew of their separation.

"Sure she does. Maybe for now. But you've only been on this job for six months. It's easy to come early and stay late when you're a bachelor, but you can't keep up this pace. You'll burn out."

"We'll see," Mackie said.

Ms. Franks started to say something else, but apparently thought better of it. "Don't stay at your desk all night." She walked away.

Mackie waited an additional ten minutes, pacing in his office then taking a tour of the third floor. Convinced that he was alone, and supposing his colleagues on the second floor had left, too, he returned to his office to slip on his jacket. He hid the Dycam in one pocket and the Discman in the other. He removed a stack of ten floppy disks and also placed them in his pocket. Mackie opened his top desk drawer and removed the red key. He walked to the elevator.

He estimated it would take him about half an hour to fill up the memory on the Dycam and probably another five minutes to set up and down load the images to the disks. Conservatively, he expected to put in five hours tonight and hopefully complete the B-AGX-23 trial. Even as his mind wandered to the logistics, his body focused on the present. His heart hammered against his chest as the elevator stopped on the second floor.

Mackie stepped into the hallway. Except for the overhead drone of the central heat, the carpeted halls remained silent. He walked forward, past the single restroom and toward the NDA storage room. The faint glow of the exit sign near the elevator illuminated his path. When he reached the locked door, he removed the red key from his pants pocket and placed it into the deadbolt. The key slid right in, but it failed to unlock the door.

Mackie jiggled it and tried again. Nothing happened.

Sweat slicked his palms as he mumbled, "Come on, dammit," but the lock never engaged.

He wiped his hands on his pants then removed the key, inserting it into the doorknob. Again, the door did not unlock. Mackie jerked out the key and shoved it back into his pocket. With only nineteen days left before submitting the NDA, he could not afford to be sidelined in this assignment with something as simple as getting into the room. He retraced his steps, boarding the elevator back to his office.

Mackie retrieved the five remaining keys from his desk drawer and tucked them into his pocket. He returned to the elevator. When he pushed the call button, the door did not immediately open. Not good. Either the elevator had reset on its own back to the ground floor, or someone had called it. Before he could run through the implications in his mind, a ping announced the elevator's arrival. He moved back as the doors opened. Out stepped a security guard.

"Evening, Doc," the burly security guard said. "Eager to get home?"

"Late night at the office," Mackie responded.

"We're just getting started, actually." The night guard wore a leather jacket and polyester pants with a gun and a night stick on his belt. To Mackie, he looked like a retired cop whose better days were behind him. The walkie-talkie on his belt crackled.

"You okay, Earl?" a voice asked through the static.

Earl unclipped the device from his belt. "Roger that. We got a late employee up here, is all." He turned to Mackie and extended his hand as he introduced himself.

Mackie shook it, wondering how he was going to negotiate this newest obstacle. Of course there would be nighttime security, but Mackie hadn't figured them into his plans when he'd considered the job before.

"It sure is nice to see some faces on the night shift," Earl said. "That's the ironic part of it, though. We usually don't see you guys, so when the motion sensor on the third floor went off, I figured all was okay but I had to come see for myself." He hitched his belt beneath his pot belly. "I'm just gonna walk the halls up here and double check."

Mackie settled on the truth to sell his lie. "Take your time. I'll be down on two for a few hours before making one last trip up here. It's gonna be a late one."

"Whatcha got there?" Earl pointed to the Discman poking out of his pocket.

Mackie moved onto the open elevator. "Just some music to keep me company."

Earl furrowed his brow. "One of those Walkman compact disc players, right?"

"Have a good night, Earl." Mackie pushed the button for the second floor. The doors closed.

He had to be more careful, Mackie thought as he stepped on the second floor and retraced his steps to the storage room. In the dim light of the exit sign, Mackie scrutinized each of the keys, trying to guess which one—if any—would open the door. Unable to tell any difference among the other five silver keys, he selected one at random and inserted it into the lock. It didn't slide in quite as easily as the red one had, and when he tried to turn it, nothing happened. Mackie repositioned it with the same results. One key excluded. He removed it from the lock and placed it in his back pocket, out of the way.

The second and third key had the same results. With two keys remaining, he began to plot his next move. If Dr. Martin had been right in that the key he copied was not hers, then he would have to return to his original plan to ask her outright to borrow her key to the room. She would probably say yes, but that request had its own risks. He wondered about bringing in a locksmith the next night under the guise of a colleague. Too risky with at least two security guards on site at night.

While he planned his next move, the lock engaged. Mackie was so preoccupied with his thoughts, he almost missed the success on his fourth try.

His pulse quickened. He twisted the key to re-lock the door, then retracted the deadbolt once more. The key worked. When he removed it and inserted the key into the doorknob, the door opened. Finally.

Placing the other keys with the first in his back pocket, Mackie stepped into the room. He shut the door and turned on the light. The room looked exactly as he had seen it earlier that week, minus the open Mountain Dew can and the abandoned key chain. More files from the table had been added to a fifteenth box, but the table still held stacks of documents waiting to be filed. The size of the task before him, and the time needed to complete it, was readily apparent to Mackie. Tonight, he opted to concentrate on photographing the charts from the B-AGX-23 trial. He committed himself to working for four hours before he measured the accomplishment.

Nineteen days until submitting the files to the FDA, he thought. Eighteen nights.

He focused on the first few boxes of data. Within an hour of beginning, he had established a cadence to his work. He began to quickly flip through files, checking the patient flow sheet first. If the patient had completed the trial, he replaced the chart and picked up the next one. Whenever he saw the words *Patient Lost to Follow Up* written on the flow sheet, he removed the chart and opened it on the carpeted floor. Removing each page in sequence, Mackie lined up the relevant documents. When he was ready to copy them, he adjusted the lens on the Dycam to line up with the specific page, trying to capture the entire page in one image. After finishing the chart, he would reassemble it and place it back where it belonged in the box. He used a surgeon's precision with the task, efficiently removing and replacing pages from the medical record until he filled up the memory of the digital camera.

Downloading the images proved even easier than he expected. The 3.5 inch disk easily slid into the back of the Sony Discman, but it took a careful inspection of the retrofitted device before Mackie identified the open slot for the disc drive. He then plugged a cable from the back of the Dycam to the headset jack on the Discman. The images automatically downloaded. Agent Thibodaux advised Mackie that while the download should be quick, he should wait at last five minutes before unplugging the device. With the original images downloaded and deleted, Mackie ejected the disc, marked it, and went back to work.

In the first three hours, he had completed photographing the five aberrant charts in the B-AGX-23 trial plus several apparently normal ones. Completing that, he moved on to the initial charts of the Phase Two trial. To speed the process along, Mackie didn't focus much on the records themselves, but he couldn't help but notice the repetitive theme of patient complaints. Many experienced nausea when taking Anginex. Some complained of muscle pain or even headache. Not unusual complaints for even a healthy patients taking a safe study drug. The more he photographed, though, the more he realized that the real answer to the Anginex concerns lay not in the patient's medical records but in the follow up interviews by the FBI.

By midnight, Mackie's mind felt numb and his knees ached from kneeling before the charts on the floor. He replaced the final chart back into the completed box and surveyed his progress. A stack of 3.5 disks sat on the table, each marked with a sequential number and the time he downloaded the images from the camera. He had completed twenty one charts in all but he looked at the rows of boxes yet to explore. He put his jacket back on and slipped the Dycam into his pocket. He then snapped a rubber band around the stack of discs and placed them in the other pocket. Once he was sure the room looked exactly as he had found it, he grabbed the Discman and turned off the light. As expected, the hallway was quiet when he opened the door.

Knowing his movements would be detected by the security detail downstairs, but gambling that Earl wouldn't report it, Mackie strode toward the elevator with a confidence he didn't feel and headed for the parking lot.

ℭHAPTER THIRTY

ℬY MID-WEEK, Hoffman felt remarkably well for a man who was supposed to be dead. He sat in a diner booth by himself, tapping his foot to the Christmas music overhead. A black turtleneck hugged his body, and his face held the wry smile of a man who had made a lot of money — and expected to make substantially more. He marveled at the events of the last few days.

Unable to regain access to CPR from his office, he had become resigned to his fate. Instead of reacting with fear, he became numb. He drove home that fateful morning to shower, but he didn't remember leaving the office. He met with the board of the American Diabetes Association, but he couldn't recall the details. After that interminable day, he returned home expecting to die. Rather than feeling fear that night, he only experienced disappointment: at squandering a once promising research career at the NIH, at the decisions he'd made during the last year, and at the certain and likely end to his life. He shuddered imagining what his mother would think of his actions if she were still alive. When he arrived home, he found a thin envelope that someone had slid under his front door. Written in familiar block letters was, *S. Hoffman.*

When he read the letter, he almost passed out. Inside he

found a note clipped to the paper, which read, *Your down payment.* The photocopy of a wire transfer to his bank account was for the amount of $2.5 million.

Someone else knows, he thought.

Someone with access to CPR must have spot-checked his work and overlooked the unfinished charts. He didn't know if the man with the deep voice had remote access to CPR or if another employee was involved. He had no way to find out, but at this point, he didn't care. His luck appeared to be changing as fast as his bank account.

That night, he celebrated his success by planning his next vacation. With a bottle of wine and the brochures for Belize, he thought about the balance of his payoff. Once the FDA approved Anginex, he would retire, leaving the NIH with his sterling reputation intact. He flipped through the glossy photographs of thatched beach huts and tanned sunbathers. Maybe he would start his retirement off the Central American coast. That night, as he fell asleep, he felt intoxicated by good wine and good luck.

Three days after his financial windfall, Hoffman still had a bounce in his step. He now waited at the diner for Dirk to deliver the photos, and hopefully, the true identity of the other man. Hoffman sipped his coffee and kept an eye on the front door. Several minutes later, Dirk arrived, his football-player's frame filling the doorway. His winter gloves looked like oven mitts, and he hid a leather attaché case under his arm. Hoffman waved the big man over.

"Let me tell you about those pictures," Dirk said as he slid into the booth. "I got an ID on the guy." He unsnapped the attaché and pulled out two unmarked file folders, plus the sealed envelope Hoffman had previously given to him. He slid the envelope and folders across the table. "The dude's name is Eddie Fackler."

The glossy photos showed clear views of the mustached

man in the stocking cap. Hoffman studied the pictures with the concentration of a stamp collector.

Dirk continued. "He left prints on the envelope, so it was easy to track him down."

"He's a known criminal?"

"Previous DUI." He reached across the table and opened one of the folders in front of Hoffman, pulling out a small stack of papers. "Looks like he's a rich kid from the suburbs. The night he was arrested, the police report says he blew three times the legal limit." Dirk chuckled. "Must've been more than a *few* beers."

Hoffman hung on Dirk's every word, waiting to see how all of this related to his present circumstances. "How'd he get to Washington?"

"I ain't sure about that," Dirk said.

"So the trail went cold?"

"Best I can tell he just fell off the radar."

Hoffman continued to grill Dirk for any scraps of information about Eddie Fackler, hungering for more. "What about the rental car from the other night?"

"Rented it with a fake ID and matching credit card. Paid for it in cash." Dirk leaned back in his booth and glanced at his watch.

"You hungry?" Hoffman asked

"Not really."

"I'm about to starve." Hoffman reached for a menu as he scanned the remaining pages in front of him. He looked across the table at Dirk. "This information is interesting, but I don't see the connection to me. Who's paying Eddie? Why all the secrecy? How did he get access to those pictures of the body."

"Not sure."

Hoffman became increasingly unsettled with the results of his investment in Dirk. He knew what Eddie Fackler was capable of, but once he knew who he was working for, he might have enough information to blackmail him if more threats came. Hoffman reached into his wallet for the balance of Dirk's payment. As he tucked the stack of bills under his outstretched palm and slid them across the table, he whispered to Dirk, "I need to know more about this guy. Where he lives. How he managed to contact me. Who's paying him."

Dirk accepted the bills and put them in his shirt pocket without even counting them. "It's gonna cost you extra."

Hoffman shooed the idea away with the back of his hand. "Whatever it takes." As Dirk extracted himself from the booth, Hoffman extended his menu. "You sure I can't interest you in a bite to eat?"

"I got another job." With that, Dirk left the restaurant.

Hoffman looked around for his waitress, but she was occupied with another table across the room. Diners continued to pour into the eatery and formed a line near the doorway for seating. He studied the menu. His appetite had returned mightily these last few days, and he considered either breakfast for dinner or the Hungry Man's Special. So engrossed was he with his dinner options, he didn't even look up as someone approached his table.

The person slid into the seat across from him. "Good evening, Doctor."

Hoffman's head snapped up, and he startled at the stocking cap and mustache of Eddie Fackler.

"Who just left?"

"No one," Hoffman stammered. "I mean...just a guy I work with."

"He doesn't look like the NIH type."

The menu trembled in Hoffman's hands. He set it on the table. "How'd you find me?"

Ignoring his questions, Eddie withdrew his trademark thin envelope from inside his jacket and placed it on the table. "Are you familiar with the journal, *The Medical Weekly*?"

Hoffman scoffed, emboldened by the crowds inside. "Are you kidding me? What doctor isn't?"

"Next month, a landmark study will be published about Anginex. Along with it will be an editorial response written by you."

Still unnerved by Eddie's presence, Hoffman blurted, "I've not submitted a manuscript to them in over a year."

"My colleagues have written a two-page supportive editorial that will be published under your name in *The Medical Weekly.*" He slid the sealed envelope across the table. "I suggest you review the references in the paper since you'll be fielding questions from the press about it. We expect you to be the public face of the NIH in support of this drug."

Hoffman slid the envelop back across the table, not even bothering to open it and inspect the contents. "Did you even stop to think that for a cancer drug, you might want to have a *cancer* specialist speaking on your behalf?" he snapped.

"Diabetic retinopathy," Eddie said.

"Excuse me?"

"The overgrowth of blood vessels in the back of the eye in patients with uncontrolled diabetes."

"I'm the lead diabetic researcher at the NIH, for Christ's sake. I know what retinopathy is," Hoffman shot back.

"I'm certain that you do. Your editorial will propose using Anginex for indications other than cancer prevention, such as preventing blood vessel overgrowth in patients with diabetes. Even though the drug is going to the FDA for a cancer prevention indication, my colleagues think that an expert opinion about other potential uses for Anginex will increase the market for the drug. Think of the profits."

Hoffman was stunned. "That's against FDA policy, and it's unethical. You can't market an FDA-approved drug for anything other than its government-approved indication."

Eddie didn't bother to hide his impatience. "The company

making Anginex won't be pushing for that new use, Dr. Hoffman. You will."

"And if I refuse to cooperate?"

Eddie laughed. "If the remaining $2.5 million isn't enough to motivate you, perhaps the fate of Compton Drew is."

Hoffman slumped in the restaurant booth as all of his confidence evaporated.

"You've got work left to do for Anginex," Eddie said. "You're still instrumental in getting our drug through the FDA."

Hoffman's heart sank. Two words came out of his mouth in a whisper. "Advisory committee?"

"Yep," Eddie answered. "When the new drug application is submitted to the FDA, we've made arrangements for you to take a seat on the FDA Advisory Committee that will review it. We expect unwavering support for Anginex to sway the other members of the committee. I trust your experience with hiding data in earlier drug trials will serve you well."

Hoffman couldn't come up with a single response. Eddie pushed himself out of the booth and headed for the door, leaving the thin envelope on the table.

CHAPTER THIRTY-ONE

MACKIE PULLED HIMSELF out of bed earlier than usual the next morning. He dressed quickly, grabbed his gear from the FBI, and drove to the arranged location. Exhaust billowed from the back of the Lincoln Town Car as it idled in the loading zone of a local elementary school. He recognized the silhouette of Agent Thibodaux in the driver's seat as he approached the car. Mackie opened the passenger door and slid in, escaping the late November chill.

"I photographed about two-hundred pages last night." He handed over the small stack of 3.5 inch disks fastened with a rubber band.

In exchange, Thibodaux gave Mackie an unopened box of identical discs. "Making progress."

"There're probably a thousand more pages to find."

"It's a big case, Doctor McKay. You're on pace." Thibodaux took a sip of coffee. Across the school yard, two members of the custodial staff walked toward the building. He turned his attention back to Mackie. "Have you uncovered any irregularities in the Phase Two studies?"

"Similar complaints, but not as many. Some joint pain. A few kidney issues. I think only a handful I've seen were listed as *Lost to Follow Up.*"

"Three of those patients who identified themselves as Phase Two participants have Alzheimer's dementia. One former study patient is missing."

Mackie gripped the box of discs in his hand. "How do you know this?"

"You're not the only informant."

"Is that patient dead?"

"We're looking into it. Guy was a bachelor."

Mackie thought of the Sims's burned out trailer. He thought of the man murdered in the front seat of his car. Of course this missing patient was dead. He knew what these guys were capable of. The images motivated him to continue, even as it made his hands tremble. He said, "I photographed a chart like that."

Thibodaux took another sip of his steaming drink. "No one was around for this guy to notice when he didn't arrive home. He missed an entire week of work before his boss called the police. No corpse yet, so we don't really know what happened. Your work last night in his chart—if that's the same guy—might help us locate him. We've got our crew in Cincinnati and a team in Washington working on this. You'll meet them before it's all over."

"In Washington?"

"That's the plan."

"And how do you propose I explain that? It's bad enough to be lugging all that equipment to and from work each day. Now you want me to find a way to leave town for a meeting with the FBI in Washington, D.C.?" For the first time since his work for the FBI started, he began to fear for his own safety.

"You're a smart guy, Doctor McKay. I'm sure you'll figure something out."

Mackie rubbed his eyes. "Back at it tonight."

"Same time tomorrow morning."

"Except in Pizza Hut parking lot."

Mackie crammed the box of discs into his jacket pocket. Once he stepped out of the car, Agent Thibodaux drove away. Mackie's head ached from lack of sleep. He needed a cup of coffee. With Sarah and Reagan coming for a visit in two weeks, he needed to push himself now. Sarah only knew fragments of his nighttime activities and even less about the patient deaths. Mackie looked forward to her input on his situation. He tried not to think of the legal implications of his involvement, but he knew those questions would have to be answered eventually. No longer a matter of *if*, simply a matter of *when*.

Mackie ate breakfast in his car and lunch at his desk. He attended meetings with his team that afternoon and contributed to discussions on the Anginex marketing plan. He spent his late afternoon on a conference call with BioloGen marketers in Los Angeles. All the while, his mind scrolled through the boxes of charts one floor below his office. He plotted his next move, considering the time it would take to photograph the remaining data. He mapped out an evening schedule and counted down the hours until he would have the building to himself once again.

By the end of the workday, Mackie's sixth cup of coffee sat in a half-empty mug on his desk. His mind hummed on adrenalin fumes, making him feel like a surgical resident once again. Most of the marketing employees had already left, but Mackie remained moored at his desk, finishing one of his projects. He closed his eyes for a moment. They hadn't been closed for more than a few minutes when he heard footsteps in the hallway approaching his office.

"No sleeping on the job, Dr. McKay," Karen Kiley said, mock indignation in her voice.

Mackie bolted upright in his chair. Unsure of how long he'd dozed, he rubbed his eyes and reached for the remaining coffee. "Late day for you today?"

"For both of us." She grinned at him as she sank into the chair in front of his desk, car keys in her hand and clad in her jacket. "Are you ready?"

"For the NDA submission? About as ready as I'm supposed to be, I guess."

"Good. You can come with me, then." She stood up and walked toward the door.

"Where are you going?"

"You mean where are *we* going?"

Mackie started to protest, searching for an excuse.

Karen cut him off with a good-natured laugh. "So far, I've convinced three others to join me, but with you in attendance we have four, which is more than enough to call it a business meeting and charge it to the company. Douglas, our college intern, Andrew, and now you. We're headed to happy hour."

Mackie tried to delay once more. He glanced at his jacket draped across the chair feet from where Karen stood. Of course, she was oblivious to the Dycam and Discman inside his jacket pockets. "You guys go on without out me. I have a few things to finish up."

Karen walked back over to his desk. "When I walked in you were sleeping—"

"Resting."

"Whatever. You just told me you were ready for the NDA submission."

Mackie shuffled some papers on his desk, looking for something to occupy his time. "The pre-launch marketing is done, but once we submit to the FDA…."

Karen stared at him, one hand on her hip as she waited for an explanation. "Bottom line, Mackie: I'm your boss. Marketing is my department. You've been working your ass off since we brought you on board. You're done for the day. If you've got leftover work, which I doubt, then come in early tomorrow. Or stay late. I don't care, but tonight, you're coming with me." She turned around once more and grabbed his jacket, preparing to hand it to him.

Mackie froze when she picked up his jacket.

"Damn, that's heavy. What're you carrying to work, rocks?" As she held the jacket, she lifted out the Discman.

Mackie reached across his desk. "I've got that."

"What the hell is this?" she asked. When she turned it over, her eyes lit up. "You've got a Sony Discman?"

His mouth felt dry. "Birthday gift. It's not working right now. I was going to take it by Radio Shack this evening on the way home to get them to look at it."

Karen ran her fingertip over the slick black device. "That's so cool. Once you get it fixed, I'd love to hear it. I understand the sound quality is so much better than cassettes." Seemingly satisfied with the explanation, she slipped the device back into his jacket pocket and handed it across the desk to Mackie. "I shouldn't be surprised that a surgeon is also a techno-geek."

"You have no idea." Mackie reached for the jacket, but Karen let her hand linger a moment longer than necessary before releasing it. He slipped it on. Mackie followed Karen out to her car. At least she let him drive himself. She revved her Jaguar and peeled out of the parking lot, an unspoken challenge to Mackie to try and keep up with her. By the time they reached the pub's parking lot, he saw Douglas Schofield and the intern, Andrew, standing outside the front doors to the pub. Mackie slipped the Discman and Dycam into his glove box before he joined them inside the restaurant.

Vaulted ceilings and slate-tile floor magnified the noise from the happy hour crowd. In spite of the chill of the late-November air, dozens of patrons spilled onto the back patio alight with Christmas decorations. Holiday music played overhead, raising the conversation a decibel level.

Douglas led them to a booth reserved for six, engrossed in a conversation with the host. He ordered a round of Christmas lagers for the table and three plates of appetizers. Conversation quickly turned to work matters.

Douglas said to Mackie, "Andy tells me you guys in marketing are ready for the NDA submission."

"We'd better be," Mackie said, soothing his nerves with a long pull of beer. "Once we submit the NDA, you'll be seeing ads for BioloGen in every major medical journal."

"How long before you recoup your research and development costs?" Andrew asked.

"About eighteen to twenty-four months," Mackie said.

Douglas clapped Andrew's shoulder, causing beer to slosh from his mug. "Told you so. BioloGen can get a billion dollars quicker than most."

"You guys have plans for the holiday?" Mackie asked.

"We're flying to London if we can find someone to care for my wife's horse." Douglas reached across the table and helped himself to a few appetizers.

"Chicago for me," Karen said. "At least for Thanksgiving. Once December hits, it'll be balls-to-the-wall until the NDA is signed, sealed, and delivered to the FDA."

Mackie sipped his beer, considering this. "Do you go with the boxes when BioloGen submits to the FDA?"

"It's more of a formality, really," Karen said. "Actually, it's a pain in the ass, if you ask me. I'm just another pretty face from BioloGen, making sure the NDA gets where it's supposed to."

Mackie took a bite of an appetizer, sensing an opportunity. "You should let me go for you."

"To Washington?"

"Why not? I know the drug about as well as anyone on the team by now."

Douglas popped a stuffed jalapeño in his mouth. "Good idea," he said with his mouth full. "It's not like she hasn't done a half dozen of these submissions before. I'm sure we could squeeze you into one of her low cut blouses and tight skirts, Mackie."

Karen brushed aside Douglas's remark. She took a sip of her drink and then slowly nodded. "It might work."

Mackie tried to mask his enthusiasm. "Sarah and Reagan are coming for the BioloGen Holiday party, then I won't see them until Christmas. I'll have all sorts of free time on my hands. Let me know when we're leaving and what I'm supposed to do when we get there."

"I've got to run it by Red. He makes a big deal about BioloGen's NDA submissions, but there's not much for you to actually do once you're there other than to be the visible presence for the marketing department. You'll do fine, even if you can't get into my skirt." She winked at Mackie.

Andrew nearly choked on his beer at the comment.

"Red wants to make sure the FDA sees the president of the company, the chief biomedical engineer, and the chief medical officer when we drop off the NDA," Douglas said. "So that means Red, Dr. Martin, and I will definitely be going. I don't think it would hurt to have a ne'er-do-well from marketing join us, too." He downed the rest of his beer. "Besides, the feds need to know that we stand to lose a lot of money if they don't grant approval for Anginex."

Karen said, "I doubt Red will mind, especially since we're all flying back to Washington early next year for the Advisory Committee hearing." She raised her glass. "Here's to a new year for BioloGen. Here's to Anginex!"

Mackie raised his beer mug. Here's to not getting caught, he thought as he toasted each of his colleagues.

* * *

Two days later, Mackie headed back to the storage room after he completed his work day. Having lost an entire night due to his impromptu happy hour engagement, he had redoubled his efforts. While still behind his intended pace, Mackie felt comfortable that he could finish photographing the charts in the time he had left, provided he had no further interruptions.

He didn't see another employee, including the security guards, on his trek down to the NDA war room. The first thing he noticed when he turned on the storage room light tonight was that the table had been completely cleared of documents. Andrew and Dr. Martin must have been busy today, he thought. Two additional file boxes sat against the back wall, marked with consecutive numbers. Mackie removed the Dycam, Discman, and box of plastic disks from his jacket and went to work. He located the last chart he'd documented and began to remove new charts to photograph.

Agent Thibodaux wanted a sampling of apparently legitimate charts, too. Mostly to establish a trend, the agent had said, but also to acknowledge that time and technology did not allow for a complete duplication of the BioloGen record. As had become his custom, Mackie photographed the first and last charts he saw each night as well as one legitimate chart each hour. Once he established a rhythm, the hours slipped by and the disks would stack up in the quiet room as he photographed charts and downloaded the results to the Discman. He had been working for at least three hours when he heard a knock on the door.

Mackie froze, not even allowing himself to exhale.

He surveyed the room. Three charts stacked near one file box, waiting to be photographed. The Discman sat on the table, cables extending from the jack. No resemblance to headphones. His jacket was still draped across the table as he gripped the Dycam. Mackie waited. The knocking sounded again, louder this time.

His heart slammed like a wrecking ball in his chest. If he waited, would the person go away? Did he even have a key? Weighing his options, Mackie made up his mind. "Just a second!" he yelled.

He grabbed his jacket from the table and put it on. Stuffing the Dycam in the inside pocket, he grabbed the Discman and slid it into the outside pocket, still visible to a casual observer. He wrapped the cable around the device, making sure a loop protruded from his pocket. Not perfect but passable. He made no attempt to conceal the disarrayed patient charts. He opened the door.

Rocking back and forth on his heels in the hallway, stood Earl. The night security guard's palm rested lightly on his holstered gun. "I sure didn't expect to see you here at this hour, Doc. Whatcha doing?"

"Evening, Earl." Mackie struggled for a calm he did not feel. "Been out here long?"

"Nope. Just knocked twice. Was making my routine midnight rounds when I saw the light under the door." Earl craned his neck to look beyond Mackie. "I got suspicious. Don't you work upstairs?"

Mackie managed a laugh. "I've got projects down here, too. You want to come in? Keep me company while I work?"

Earl stepped inside and looked around. "That's a lot of charts out. What kind of project are you working on?"

"All of this goes to Washington in a couple of weeks. I'm double-checking the charts to make sure they're in order."

Earl nodded, then rubbed his chin with a callused hand. "Forgive me for prying, but I thought this was a restricted area."

"Damn right, it is," Mackie agreed. "All this patient information and drug data...if it left the building, BioloGen could get in big trouble."

Earl looked suspicious. "What kind of trouble?"

"Financial trouble, mostly," Mackie said, winging it. "Do you know how much money it takes to research and develop a drug?"

"I dunno. Fifty or sixty million dollars."

"Try ten times that." Mackie could tell Earl was impressed.

"Six hundred million dollars? C'mon..."

"No kidding. It takes ten years and hundreds of millions of dollars to develop these drugs. If this information gets leaked to our competitors, we would all lose a lot of money. It's no wonder we pay top-notch security like you to keep this place under lock and key."

Earl smiled. "We do work hard."

"And you don't get paid half of what you're worth. Working at night like this, there's no telling what you might encounter."

"It *could* get dangerous."

"I don't know if I could do your job, Earl."

Squaring his shoulder, Earl hitched up his polyester pants and adjusted his belt. "It looks like you got plenty of work to do. I'd love to keep talking, but I need to make sure the rest of the building is secure."

"I've got more long nights ahead of me before I'm done," Mackie said.

"Suit yourself, Doc. I'll be here if you need me." Earl turned and walked down the second floor hallway.

Mackie closed the door and slumped against it. Several minutes passed before his hands stopped shaking enough for him to return to work.

CHAPTER THIRTY-TWO

SARAH COLLINS-MCKAY and their year-old daughter, Reagan, had flown to Cincinnati to spend the weekend with Mackie. Sarah objected to bringing Reagan at first, complaining that with such a short trip, Mackie wouldn't get to see much of her anyway. Add to that the need to get a babysitter for the BioloGen holiday party and Sarah was reluctant from the start. She pushed for letting Reagan stay in Nashville with her parents, arguing Mackie could catch up with his daughter when he was home for Christmas. Mackie refuted her argument point by point. For the first time in months, Sarah relented.

They spent the better part of that first afternoon outside, enjoying the crispness of a late Fall day as they ambled through Cincinnati's Ault park. Reagan slept beneath her blanket in the stroller while Mackie pushed it. In the distance, preschool kids squealed on the playground while parents sat around picnic tables and chatted. Mackie enjoyed their time together on neutral ground and he appreciated Sarah's input into his current situation.

As they circled the playground, she picked up on a theme they had discussed earlier. "So you're working on the biggest clinical trial data right now?"

"Phase Three."

"Which is thousands of patients spread across multiple testing sites, some taking Anginex, others taking a placebo."

"That's right." He gripped the handles of the stroller in response to her aggressive tone and maintained his pace. An errant soccer ball bounced across the grass and rolled toward them on the sidewalk. Mackie didn't miss a stride as he kicked it back toward the pick-up game.

"I still don't get it," Sarah said. "Anginex works to prevent cancer, so how do you know if your drug really works or if you've got a group of patients who wouldn't get cancer to begin with?"

Mackie steered the stroller toward a vacant park bench. "It's actually pretty simple. The first two drug trials told us that Anginex worked. To confirm those results, we took a large group of people at risk for cancer—based on their age, or family history, or other illnesses. Half of them took Anginex for several years. The other half only took a sugar pill—"

"The control group?"

"Correct. At the end of the study, we compared the two groups to see how many developed cancer."

Sarah stopped as Mackie took a seat on the bench. She didn't sit down. "That doesn't sound fair to the ones taking the placebo."

"And that's the point. You test a drug against a control group when you don't *know* if your study drug will work or not. That's the only way the trial is ethical."

"So what about when the study drug has more side effects than the placebo? *That's* considered ethical?"

He and Sarah had been through rounds like this before. Minds made up before the discussion began. Points and counter-points thrown like barbs at the other, tips sharpened and dipped in ridicule. Mackie recognized her desire to underscore the folly of his current job and the consequence of a bad decision. He tried to retain enough emotional distance to talk her back from the edge of a miserable weekend.

"Medical ethicists have debated the placebo question for years," he said, moving Reagan's stroller back and forth with his foot. "Most agree that if you don't know that a study drug is helpful, it's ethical to test it against a placebo in a clinical trial. That's the best way to get your answer. After all, for the patients enrolled, it's a voluntary study."

"Provided the study patient really knows what he's getting in to."

"Kind of like marriage," Mackie mumbled before he could stop himself.

If Sarah heard him, she ignored the jab. "I still don't get it."

Mackie tried a different approach. "Think of it this way. Let's say you cut yourself in two places working in the yard. Same kind of cut in every way, just different locations on your body. You want these cuts to heal as fast as you can, so you buy some antibiotic ointment and smear it on the wounds. One week later, your cuts have healed and no one even notices. Here's the question: how do you know that the antibiotic ointment even helped?"

Sarah considered this for a moment, putting on a professional expression of legal concentration Mackie recognized. "Next time that happens, you could refrain from using the medicine and see how long it takes to heal."

"Excellent point. Or try this: next time you cut yourself in two different places, put the ointment on only *one* cut and see if it heals faster than the one you didn't treat."

Sarah appeared to soften, going down the intellectual path Mackie had hoped she'd pursue. "Maybe simply having something moist on the cut helped it to heal."

"And with that question, you've just designed a clinical trial." Reagan stirred at the sound of Mackie's voice. He lowered his voice. "In these studies, BioloGen tries to minimize all contributing factors to the results. In your case, the healing arm. That way, the company can study the effect of just one factor. In the case of the cut, you could design an ointment that is exactly the same as the antibiotic but without the active ingredient. So you apply the real medicine to one study group, the dummy medicine to the control group, and you measure the length of time it takes each to heal. With enough patients enrolled, you'll have your answer by the end of the study."

"So for BioloGen, Anginex is like the *antibiotic ointment* except that it prevents cancer," she said, nodding her understanding.

When Reagan stirred again, Mackie pushed up from the park bench. They began walking back toward the car, Sarah now by his side. "Half of the patients in the BioloGen studies that I'm recording each night took a placebo—a sugar pill that looks, smells, and tastes like Anginex, but it lacks the active ingredient to prevent cancer. The rest took Anginex. The trouble we're up against is that the only patients who didn't complete the trial were taking Anginex. The FBI contends that if those taking Anginex had side effects, they were dropped from the study to make the side effects look similar to those taking placebo."

"Burying the side effects by dropping patients from the trial."

"Exactly," Mackie said as they reached the car. "This case hinges on findings that aren't there."

"What do you mean?"

Mackie unlocked the car door. "In all the charts I've photographed, there were no patients lost to follow up in the control group."

* * *

The détente in their relationship didn't last. Their conversation cooled again later that afternoon as the BioloGen

Christmas party approached. Sarah felt uncomfortable leaving Reagan for the evening with a babysitter she didn't know, and she insisted on providing the sitter with extra numbers where they could be reached. Mackie tried to avoid contentious topics, but he couldn't refrain from telling Sarah about his travel plans before Christmas. Even the wine and appetizers he'd set out on the kitchen counter couldn't soothe sore feelings.

"I may have a chance to go to Washington with the NDA next week," he said, following up by revealing that the FBI expected a meeting with him on their home turf.

"Is that a good idea?"

"I can finally wash my hands of this mess."

"And then what?" Sarah stood before the mirror, struggling to fasten her necklace.

Mackie walked over to help her, but she shrugged off his assistance.

"Are you supposed to live a life on the run? Waking up everyday, hoping that the people at BioloGen don't come knocking on your door when they find out you've been a snitch for the FBI? Did you even stop to consider that, once they find out what you've done, they're going to come after you like they went after Donnie Sims?"

Mackie took a sip of wine and measured his response. "I'm in too deep to back out now, Sarah."

"You should've thought of that before you agreed to help." She grabbed her own wine glass and gulped it down before slamming it down on the counter. The stem snapped. She met Mackie's gaze with a piercing one of her own. "Ten minutes with legal counsel could have radically changed your approach—"

"I tried to tell you earlier this fall."

"—but instead, you've jeopardized not only your own safety but that of our one remaining child!" Tears formed along the corner of her eyes. Sarah rubbed them out with the base of her palm, smearing her make-up. She stormed back to the bathroom mirror.

Mackie followed her. "All good points, but we need to behave tonight like nothing's wrong. I have to let this play out. I've got two or three more nights to finish photographing the charts, but I honestly don't think anyone suspects a thing right now."

"Except the night security guard." Sarah fixed her eyeliner. When she finished, she turned around to face Mackie. "I can't do this."

"The eyeliner?"

Sarah didn't even acknowledge the levity of his peace offering. "I'm sick of this, Cooper. You're asking me to spend an evening with colleagues you don't trust, many of whom are prime suspects in this entire scam."

"So what do you expect me to do, Sarah? Keeping my mouth shut would have been easy, but that doesn't change the fact that thousands of people could die from a side-effect that I now know about. I didn't sign up to be a whistle blower, but I have a chance to spotlight a promising drug with deadly side effects and turn it into a safe drug." He took a deep breath, then exhaled. "I don't see that I have much of a choice."

"Legally, I think the FBI could build a case without you as a witness."

"I've already provided them boxfulls of photographic evidence. Whether they would succeed with what they have and without more involvement from me is anyone's guess. But I still have to carry on as if everything's okay at work, which includes playing the part of dutiful employee at the Christmas party tonight."

Sarah walked back to the kitchen, removed a new wine glass from the cabinet, and refreshed her drink. "What happens if the charts from the Phase Three trial are normal? What if the problems only occurred in the first two phases of the study?"

"That's best case scenario for Anginex," Mackie said. "That means that BioloGen recognized there was problem, made a change, and fixed the drug. It still doesn't exonerate them from the death of patients in the earlier trials, but it can make a bad situation better."

Sarah tipped her glass to Mackie. "That's what I'm talking about. If the problem's fixed, then you don't have to say anything else about it, either to BioloGen or to the FBI. You finish your sabbatical, come home, and get back to your regular life. Case closed."

"The fact is, we can't be assured of any of that right now, which means we have to go to the party tonight and act as if everything is normal."

"With the company or with us?" she asked.

"Both."

"If you say so." She drained her wine glass.

* * *

When they drove up to the BioloGen headquarters, the first change Mackie noticed was the Christmas tree. With the hallway and office lights dimmed, the two-story Douglas fir situated in the great atrium of the building shimmered. Seemingly thousands of lights covered the festive fir, casting a warm glow onto the sidewalk as they approached the front door.

The smell of fresh pine and the orchestral sound of holiday music created a festive atmosphere when they entered the building. The fountain in the center of the room had been draped in Christmas garlands, which matched the huge fronds of the tree. A makeshift stage along one wall housed a dozen men and women of the orchestra, all dressed in formal black. Floral centerpieces and fine china decorated banquet tables situated around the room. The crystal glasses shimmered in the reflected light of candles on each table.

"Your company knows how to throw a party," Sarah said, craning her neck to inspect the top of the tree.

When he spied them walking through the front door, Douglas loped across the lobby. "Better late than never!" he bellowed above the din. He already appeared to be three drinks ahead of them with his black bow tie tilted and his shirttail partially untucked. He walked right through Sarah's personal space and gave her a bear hug. "Don't you look delicious?"

Mackie gave him a tolerant smile. Even from a foot away, he smelled the liquor on his friend's breath.

Douglas tipped up his empty cocktail glass for one more sip. "They make these damn drinks so small, you have to suck the ice to get a buzz. Who needs a drink?"

Mackie and Sarah followed their host to the bar. Men in tuxedos and women in evening gowns filled the foyer, giving the room a full but uncrowded feel. Mackie didn't recognize many of the faces, supposing they were either spouses of the employees or people who worked in other BioloGen departments. He did notice that most of the Anginex team had already arrived. Ms. Franks stood by the Christmas tree, a coiffed version of her daytime self, listening to the young intern, Andrew, give an animated explanation of something. Andrew gripped the hand of a young bombshell who looked barely old enough to legally drink. Mackie thought they could have walked into a high school prom and fit right in.

Mackie and Sarah ordered drinks and settled into their assigned seats. Douglas's wife joined them across the table, looking not much older than Andrew's date. Pescatelli sat at the table closest to the orchestra. Before the dessert course, he rose from his seat to address the crowd. "Merry Christmas to all of our employees at BioloGen Pharmaceuticals!" he began with a buoyancy uncharacteristic for him. On his tuxedo, he'd replaced the black bow tie with a diamond-studded bola.

Polished cowboy boots anchored his body. With his slick scalp and trimmed beard, he looked like the perfect combination of formal elegance and rugged masculinity. Like BioloGen itself, Mackie knew Pescatelli had carefully crafted the image.

"What a night to celebrate all that BioloGen has accomplished this year," Pescatelli began. "For the fiscal year, our humble company has increased sales by thirty-five percent."

With this announcement, Karen Kiley raised her glass from across the room and let out a whoop.

"In the last year, NuCor has maintained its position as the most prescribed cholesterol-lowering drug in the country," Pescatelli continued.

More polite applause rippled through the crowd.

Like a political candidate at a state fair, Pescatelli responded to the energy of the crowd. "In 1993 alone, the technology division of BioloGen has used ADAM to identify ninety-one new molecular compounds that we can develop into promising treatments, adding to hundreds more we have already discovered to treat an array of diseases. Some we've sold to start-up companies for further testing. Others we've tested ourselves. And we're leading the industry in new discoveries." Pescatelli raised his own champagne flute in a toast.

"Before I sit down, though, I would be remiss to not mention the next big thing in modern medicine. As you all know, in one week, a small group of us will travel to Washington to introduce the world to Anginex. We expect FDA approval early next year. As a token of BioloGen's appreciation for what each of you has done, I invite you to reach under your chair to find an envelope with your name on it. This is a small token of my appreciation for your hard work."

He stepped off the stage as the orchestra struck up a chorus of *Joy to the World*. Around Mackie, gasps of surprise and murmurs of excitement greeted the opening of individual envelopes.

Sarah leaned close to Mackie as he lifted the personalized envelope from under his chair. "What'd you get?"

Mackie ran his fingers under the envelope flap and pulled out a card with a BioloGen logo on it. "From our family to yours..." he read. When he opened the card, a slip of paper fluttered free. His smiled faded.

"What's wrong?" Sarah asked.

He handed her the slip of paper which read, 'Mackie, we need to talk. Come find me after dinner. -Red.'

* * *

The longer Mackie waited outside of Pescatelli's second floor office, the more anxious he became. His buzz from dinner was gone, replaced by a throbbing headache. Although it seemed much longer, Pescatelli arrived at his office a few minutes later. He looked grim. Mackie met his gaze, but Pescatelli ignored him until he unlocked the door.

"Come in and sit down," Pescatelli said.

When Mackie walked inside the office, he heard Douglas and Karen chatting in front of the large window that overlooked the lobby. Both turned as Pescatelli pushed open the door. Mackie paused when he saw them.

"Sit down," Pescatelli said again as he strode to his personal wet bar and poured himself a drink.

Mackie glanced around. The office looked exactly the same as it had when he last met with Pescatelli. On the shelf, Mackie saw an updated picture of Pescatelli in SCUBA gear standing beside a boat named *Aruba Diver.* In the corner, two easels displayed the poster-board proofs for the major Anginex ads.

"We know about your late nights at the office," Pescatelli began.

Mackie's heart stuttered. He chose not to respond, waiting for Pescatelli's next move.

"One of our security guards saw you in the building after

hours when it was obvious the office was supposed to be closed!" Pescatelli bellowed.

"Did you really think you could get away with this?" Douglas demanded, slurring his words.

Mackie winced. His mouth felt so dry, he couldn't even speak to defend himself.

Pescatelli took a step forward. "You know we have a strict rule against overtime."

At first, no one's expression changed. Then, Karen began to giggle. Douglas tried to suppress a laugh, but he ended up snorting, instead.

"What are you—?"

"Relax." A smile spread across Pescatelli's face. "Your dedication to the Anginex project goes above and beyond anything we expected when we hired you."

"You remember what we talked about at the bar last week?" Karen asked.

Disoriented from weeks of deception, Mackie couldn't judge the tone of his colleagues. He didn't hazard a guess at what Karen meant. "Remind me."

"You're a part of the BioloGen family." Pescatelli extended an envelope to Mackie. "We brought you up here to show our appreciation to your dedication so far."

Mackie reached out, but his usually steady hands shook.

"Enjoyed the wine?" Douglas snatched the envelope from Pescatelli's hand, ripped the seal, and pulled out a sheet of paper. He waved it in the air. "Congratulations. You now own a part of us."

Mackie steadied his hands enough to relieve Douglas of the sheet of paper. Across the top of it, under the BioloGen logo, he read a notification from the company's financial department. Mackie looked up. "Stock options?"

Pescatelli beamed. "Five years from now, those shares will make you a wealthy man."

"Is this a joke?" Mackie's voice wavered.

Pescatelli narrowed his eyes. "Do you want it to be?"

"Of course not. I just…didn't know what to expect."

Karen reached over and squeezed Mackie's arm. "You've earned a little financial security."

"And loyalty," Pescatelli interjected. "We take care of our own, Mackie, and over the last six months, you've shown that you will take care of us, too. Let's keep it that way." Pescatelli turned to open his office door. "One more thing I want to show you." He strode into the second floor hallway.

Mackie glanced at Karen, who gestured him to follow.

As they walked down the hall, Pescatelli said, "Those options are a pittance compared to what will be yours once we start selling prescriptions of Anginex. If you stay with us, you could make a fortune in the pharmaceutical industry." He stopped outside of the locked door to the NDA storage room.

Mackie heard the sound of Karen and Douglas's laughter in Pescatelli's office. A floor below, he could hear the orchestra playing familiar Christmas favorites. He also heard Pescatelli jingle a set of keys as he searched for the correct one. Mackie's heart hammered. He hoped Pescatelli couldn't hear it.

"Karen wants you to join Douglas, Dr. Martin, and me on the flight to D.C. for the submission, and I think it's a great idea." Pescatelli inserted the correct key into the lock as Mackie had done so many nights over the last few weeks. And as he expected to do two or three times more to finish his task. "You've seen this room before, as I recall," Pescatelli said. "Well, check it out now."

Pescatelli opened the unlocked door. When he turned on the lights, Mackie almost panicked. Pressure swelled inside his chest, choking off any verbal response to the vacant room.

The room was empty.

All of the boxes that contained the new drug application were gone.

$\mathscr{C}$HAPTER THIRTY-THREE

$\mathscr{M}$EREDITH BEUKELMAN AWOKE with a start as a bolt of pain shot through her right knee. The bedside clock cast its glow across her fiancé. 3:06 a.m. Christmas lights on her apartment balcony gave a red-green hew to the drawn curtains. She remained in bed. Waiting. The throbbing continued. Not again, she thought.

Meredith slipped out from the covers. She had to steady herself as she hobbled to the bathroom. She closed the door and groped for a towel to snug against the crack beneath the door. Her swollen right knee buckled when she squatted. Her hand shot against the wall with a *whump*. Meredith slumped against the bathroom door, holding her breath against the pain. Tim's rhythmic breathing continued from the bed, undisturbed. She pulled herself off the floor to turn on the light.

Even squinting against the glare, her face looked puffy. Meredith rubbed her eyes. She filled a cup on the counter with tap water then opened the cabinet drawer. From the back, behind her hair dryer, she eased out a box of tampons. She had stuffed a wad of cotton balls inside to mute the pill-rattle of a family-sized bottle of Advil. Behind that, she kept her monthly allotment of Anginex. Out of sight, out of mind, she thought as she removed a single Anginex pill from the plastic bottle. She set the pill on the counter next to the glass of water.

Meredith had no intentions of keeping secrets from Tim. He knew about Anginex, of course. Even encouraged her to take it. He just didn't know about her dependence on Advil. After a while, she had decided to stow the two medications together so she didn't have to entertain daily conversations about her health.

During last month's med-check visit with the clinical trail coordinator, Meredith had filled out the interval health questionnaire. She pointed out to the nurse the trouble she was having with her knee. The nurse typed her complaints into the computer and placed a soothing hand on Meredith's tender joint. She said she would let the doctor know, but encouraged Meredith to keep treating her symptoms. Someone would contact her if she need to stop taking Anginex.

Since then, no one at the trial center had contacted her.

Meredith and Tim had spent the week looking at cakes and considering caterers. They had already booked the band for the reception and met with the minister. The more wedding planning they could accomplish during her holiday break, the easier her final semester as school would be. Still, all of the walking that week had terrorized her knee. She kept a steady intake of pain killers recently and Tim had not seemed to notice. Easier that way.

She eased herself onto the closed lid of the toilet. With the vanity doubling as a make-shift pharmacy, Meredith unscrewed the cap and tapped out three Advil pills onto the counter top. The knee continued to throb, maybe even worse than it had yesterday. She tapped out one more. Raking all four pills into her palm, she dry-swallowed the anti-inflammatory cocktail.

She picked up the Anginex pill. Studied it. For a brief moment, she wondered if somehow this tiny lifesaver could be related to her present problems. Maybe. Maybe not. Either way, someone would let her know. Besides, in five hours she had a full day of wedding dresses to consider. She needed to get back to bed.

Meredith lifted the glass of water and took her Anginex.

*C*HAPTER THIRTY-FOUR

*F*ROM SCOTT HOFFMAN's seated position on the marble steps, the Jefferson Memorial looked more like an abandoned ruin than a national monument. Ice had already annexed the edges of the tidal basin, and the cherry blossom trees waved their skeletal branches in the breeze. Across the basin, a dog chased the few birds brave enough to venture out this morning. Not far away, a homeless man slept on the sidewalk, shrouded in a blanket. Hoffman jiggled his legs to keep warm. He wished he'd covered his head, and he wondered why this hand-off couldn't have taken place in an equally secluded but much warmer location. He couldn't leave now, though. Eddie's instructions had been clear. Jefferson Memorial. 7:00 a.m. Come alone. Wait on the steps for his arrival.

Hoffman hadn't slept for more than two hours at a time since Eddie's call. Every time his home phone rang, he flinched. Fear shackled him to familiar places.

Hoffman had considered asking a friend to shadow him, but felt reluctant to involve anyone else. He was an integral part of the team. Eddie needed him to make the plan work as much as Hoffman needed the money to get out of this God-forsaken business of pharmaceutical consulting. Hurt me, hurt the project, Hoffman rationalized. He assumed that left him room to bargain.

He heard Eddie's voice before he saw him.

"Let's go." Eddie wore his trademark stocking cap, a long coat with the collar flipped up, and boots. He emerged from behind the statue of Jefferson, then down onto the sidewalk. Hoffman followed, feeling the stiffness in his back and the groaning of his knees as he stumbled his way down the steps.

Eddie didn't look directly at him when he reached inside his coat and pulled out a thin envelope. "That's the final copy of the editorial you'll submit. You are now the expert on alternative usage for Anginex. My clients expect you'll memorize what they've written and commit the references in the article to memory."

A yellow labrador retriever across the basin sniffed around a nearby tree and then darted over to the two men, his tail wagging. Hoffman concentrated on the envelope, trying to ignore the wind biting his ears and the dog eagerly panting at his heels.

"Stupid mutt," Eddie said, kicking but missing the dog.

The lab seemed to enjoy the game and started running circles around the two men, his tail a barometer of his excitement.

"Is that it?" Hoffman asked.

"For the article. The rest of this is for your seat on the Advisory Committee." He produced a small package, thicker and heavier than the first. "These are financial disclosure statements and conflict-of-interest forms. They've already been filled out for you. Sign them and put them in the mail later this morning so we can finish the paper work."

"Did you disclose my involvement with Hepatazyme? If they know a woman died under my care in an earlier trial..."

Eddie kept walking. "Pertinent information is included. You'll be asked if you have any financial ties to BioloGen

Pharmaceuticals, and your answer is no. You'll be asked if you know of any conflict of interest that precludes you from making an objective decision about Anginex, and your response will be the same. The first closed-door committee meeting is next month."

Hoffman persisted. "If they find out about my previous experience, the entire approval of Anginex could be jeopardized."

"Let us worry about that."

"We're talking about a cure for cancer, Eddie, not a cold remedy!"

Eddie walked on in silence. The dog sprinted ahead of the two men and then doubled back, his breath misting the morning air.

Hoffman thought of the money. If he could shepherd Anginex through this final hurdle, $2.5 million would be deposited into his bank account on the day of approval, adding to the fortune already there from Hepatazyme. Retirement would not only be close, it would be comfortable. Besides, if the side effects from Anginex were as bad as predicted, surely someone else would discover the problem once the drug was approved.

He then imagined a parade of patients marching through his consciousness. One lady's arthritic hand patting his leg as she thanked him for visiting her in the hospital. Another patient's spouse sobbing in his arms when he informed her of her husband's kidney failure. He imagined holding the hands of dozens of patients during the clinical trial, then recalled his instructions to destroy their charts in the name of easing drug approvals. Even now, he didn't fully understand the study drug's problems, but he knew the side effects of Anginex would be amplified countless times as doctors began to prescribe it. If it ever came out that Hoffman knowingly approved a deadly drug, he would surely face criminal charges. He couldn't remain at the NIH. Retirement would be far away from the comforts of his home. It would be years before he could return, if ever.

He glanced over his shoulder, seeing the Jefferson Memorial in the distance. They had walked a quarter mile, maybe more. The dog ran ahead, circling the sleeping man in the blanket then darted near Eddie. "I can't do it," Hoffman finally said to Eddie's back as he kept walking. "There are too many problems with the drug."

Eddie stopped, close enough to step over the bundle of the homeless man, but turned around. Hoffman nearly bumped into him. Eddie's stocking cap was pulled down over his eyebrows. Frost covered his mustache. The lab stopped, too, and sat, his body vibrating with anticipation as he waited for Eddie to pull something else out of his jacket for a game of fetch.

It all happened fast. Hoffman didn't register Eddie's actions until after. Eddie never said a word. He unbuttoned his jacket. Removed another object.

Hoffman heard two staccato coughs. The dog yelped and sprinted away. Then, silence.

The breeze rustled nearby tree branches.

Hoffman stood speechless, paralyzed by fear. Beads of sweat prickled his neck. He tasted tufts of cotton. Stomach acid in the back of his mouth.

"You're next," Eddie warned, "if you don't finish the job we hired you to do."

Eddie walked away. Cold and alone on the sidewalk, Hoffman stared at the matted blanket while the blood of the homeless man created an ever-widening pool at his feet.

$\mathscr{C}$HAPTER THIRTY-FIVE

$\mathscr{M}$ACKIE ROSE EARLY and took the elevator down to the hotel lobby before sunrise. The chartered flight with the BioloGen executives had left Cincinnati after work and arrived in Washington, D.C. late the night before. Pescatelli and Douglas both had seemed effusive in their praise of the FDA and the possibilities of Anginex. Both bragged about their plans to meet with members of Congress early that morning before the actual submission of the new drug application. Mackie would meet them at nine o'clock in front of the hotel, when all of them would drive to the FDA together. That didn't leave him much time for his own meeting. He adjusted the cumbersome weight of his jacket, shifting the electronic devices that he was to return that morning. The small stack of disks bulged from his side pocket when he adjusted the gear. He removed them and slid them into the inside pocket. Better. As he stepped off the elevator, he checked a piece of paper with a street address on it. Fourteenth Street and G Street. Not far from their hotel. Lost in concentration, he almost ran into someone waiting to board.

"Good morning, Dr. McKay. Where are you going at this early hour?"

Mackie looked up, startled, nearly dropping the paper in his hand.

Dr. Rita Martin gracefully stepped out of Mackie's way. She wore a smile of contentment and exhaustion.

"I guess I'm not the only early riser in the group," Mackie said.

"It's good to finally be in Washington." Dr. Martin held a steaming cup of coffee in one hand while in her other she cupped something in her fist that Mackie couldn't see. The elevator door closed behind him.

Mackie couldn't answer her questions about his early morning destination. "Each FDA submission's a little different, I'm sure," Mackie said.

"One would think, but this is the first time I've forgotten to bring my checklist." She took a sip of her coffee. "I left it on my desk at home. The front desk is waiting on a fax from my husband."

"Any luck?" Mackie asked.

"Not yet. But he'll get it here before we deliver the NDA." She uncurled the fingers of her fist, revealing a handful of pills.

"What are you doing?" Mackie asked.

Dr. Martin jumped at the sound of his voice, almost spilling her coffee. "What's wrong?"

"Those pills..." Mackie didn't know what to say. He felt a prickle of sweat underneath his jacket. "It's just that...I guess I'm surprised to see you take so many."

Dr. Martin blushed as she rolled the three pills in her hand. "I asked my internist to prescribe NuCor years ago after I found out I needed to lower my cholesterol. Plus, a woman my age shouldn't neglect an aspirin a day." She placed both pills in her mouth and swallowed them with a sip of coffee. Picking up the last pill, she rolled it between her thumb and index finger. "My mother had breast cancer. Twice, actually.

She beat it the first time, but when it returned, there was little the doctors could do."

Mackie stared at the small blue pill in her hand. "But that's not even FDA approved yet."

"You know as much about this pill as anyone, Dr. McKay." She chuckled, oblivious to his distress. "Once you get past the first few doses, the nausea subsides and it's as safe as a placebo. I consider it one more way to help me beat the odds. I've just gotten a head start on the FDA."

She lifted the little pill and placed it in her mouth, using a long pull of her coffee to swallow her morning dose of Anginex.

* * *

Situated one block from the White House and across the street from the National Press Club, the coffee shop was a beacon for early morning commuters. It took Mackie less than twenty minutes to get there from his hotel. A large sign with the Starbucks logo hung on the front door, informing customers that the store would open to the public one hour later than usual today. Mackie walked into the Starbucks and saw FBI Agent Brian Aiken at a small table by the window.

Agent Ron Thibodaux stood behind the counter. "Can I get you some coffee?" he asked from the coffee bar, his jacket off and a green apron over his shirt and tie.

"What the hell kind of joke is this?" Mackie's voice echoed off the tile floors. The Dycam, the Discman, and the small stack of floppy disks weighed down his jacket pockets.

"Relax. We've got the building secured, and no one will be coming in for another hour. You should really try a latte—it's on us." Agent Aiken kept his seat at the table while Thibodaux prepared a mug of steaming coffee.

Mackie walked over to the table, locking eyes with Aiken. "Why doesn't the Chief Medical Officer of our company know about the problems with Anginex?"

Aiken didn't break eye contact with Mackie. "What are you talking about?"

"Dr. Rita Martin. Do you now who she is?"

"Of course."

Mackie continued to stand. "A few minutes ago, I discovered that she's been taking Anginex for almost a year. She's forgetting things a woman her age should remember. It's obvious now but no one else seems to notice. She's developing early signs of dementia because she's still taking Anginex!"

Aiken lowered his voice in response. "She doesn't know."

"You think?"

"In fact, most of the BioloGen employees don't know."

Agent Aiken stood. Mackie reflexively stepped back. Aiken walked past him and toward the counter. He brought two cups of coffee back to the table. Agent Thibodaux stayed behind the bar, keeping watch.

Aiken sat down once again. "Have a seat, Dr. McKay. We have a lot to talk about."

Mackie's frustration and confusion mounted. Ever since the FBI had contacted him, he'd assumed that all of the executives at BioloGen knew about the Anginex scam. He sat down and slumped back against the chair. "Who's in on the cover up?"

"We can confirm three other executive who know."

"Only three?" Mackie said. "It must be Red Pescatelli, Douglas Schofield, and Karen Kiley."

"Close." Aiken took a sip of his coffee. "Pescatelli, Schofield, and Leslie Franks."

"She's a secretary."

"A nice cover, isn't it?" Aiken blew on the steam wafting from his mug and took another sip.

"What about Karen Kiley?" Mackie asked.

"We're pretty sure she knows, but we can't confirm it yet."

"Did you get all this information from your other informant?" Mackie asked. Not getting an answer from Aiken, he said, "How did a handful of people get sick after taking Anginex and no one other than Red, Douglas, and maybe Karen know?"

"And Ms. Franks," Aiken added.

Mackie's stomach sank. "She's peered over my shoulder every day since I started my job there. She's got to know what I've been doing after hours with the patient charts."

"She doesn't appear to."

"How do you know all of this?" Mackie demanded, pounding his fist onto the table and causing coffee to slosh over the edge of their mugs. "How can you sit there and tell me what my secretary does and does not know about my work?"

Unmoved by Mackie's outburst, Aiken placed a napkin over the spill. "You're the only informant we have at BioloGen," he said. "I'm sure you want some answers about what we've found out."

"I think I'm entitled to them," Mackie shot back.

Agent Aiken slid a manila file folder across the table. "Take a look at this."

Mackie opened it and pulled out a sheaf of BioloGen documents. The first page contained miniature photos of Pescatelli, Douglas, and Ms. Franks lined up next to one another. A photo of Karen was positioned to one side with a question mark near it. Below them, situated like descendants in a family tree, were the photos of two other men. One appeared to be a serious man with a thin face, which bore the label *Scott Hoffman*. Mackie looked at the other one. "I know this guy." He pointed to the labeled photo of a man with dark curly hair and glasses.

"Hoffman?"

"No. Lampley. He's the one who tracked me down in Aruba."

Agent Aiken leaned forward. "Before I answer any questions, let me give you the full picture of what the FBI knows. Let's start with Bolten & Ferris Pharmaceuticals."

"What about them?" Mackie asked.

"They're the largest drug company in the world."

"Common knowledge."

"Forty-nine billion dollars in revenue last year. Seven blockbuster drugs on the market," Aiken said.

"Red Pescatelli has told me all of this. He used to work for them before he founded BioloGen."

"He still does."

Mackie scoffed. "That's ridiculous. He's the CEO of BioloGen."

"But as an employee of Bolten & Ferris." Aiken paused, letting the impact of his words hit Mackie. "President Clinton's push toward comprehensive health care reform has rattled the pharmaceutical companies. He's threatening their financial security. In response, larger companies like Bolten & Ferris are acquiring small biotech firms with promising drugs. In exchange for millions of dollars up front, the small companies give up the right to license and market their promising drugs. But it's a double win. Big Pharma sinks money into marketing new drugs that will reap huge profits. And they don't have to gamble research and development dollars because the potential drugs have already been vetted by the baby biotechs."

Pescatelli's dual role in BioloGen and Bolten & Ferris shocked Mackie, but Aiken's economic analysis of health care in America was not news to him. "The pharmaceutical industry is not the first sector of the economy to cannibalize younger companies through mergers and acquisitions."

Aiken kept his gaze on Mackie. "Like politics, Doc, success depends on name recognition. Take the drug Livoxx. The FDA approved it five years ago to treat arthritis pain. You could probably teach an MBA course on product development based on the experience of that drug. It was beautifully marketed."

"Livoxx was pulled from the market last year," Mackie said. "Also common knowledge."

"But not before the company raked in more than one-and-a-half billion dollars each year from it. Even if you concede it was a good drug, you still don't get those kind of sales because your medicine works. You get it because doctors have been educated to prescribe it, even over cheaper drugs that are equally effective. I'm sure you've heard there's a push in Congress to allow companies to advertise specifically to patients."

"Direct-to-consumer advertising," Mackie said.

"Can you image the revenue for pharmaceutical companies if those flood gates open?" Aiken took a sip of the remaining coffee in his mug and then pulled a photocopy of a newspaper article out of his satchel. "Look at this."

Mackie glanced at the article.

"That company pled guilty to illegal marketing practices this past year for something they didn't even do. You may have heard of the case. Large company buys small company, only to find out after the deal that their acquisition had broken the law by paying doctors to prescribe their drug."

"Again, old news," Mackie said. "Red Pescatelli's got a file folder full of articles like this. Companies cheat to gain market share. Some get caught. Most don't."

"Self-righteous of him, don't you think? Back in the eighties, Bolten & Ferris decided to out-smart the competition. Like every other company, they wanted profits if a drug became a blockbuster but immunity from prosecution if problems arose."

Mackie rubbed his eyes with the base of both hands. As Aiken's case against BioloGen grew, Mackie started to connect the clues. When he looked across the table at the FBI agent, he started to understand the implications of what he was being told. "So you're telling me that BioloGen is one of the companies financed by Bolten & Ferris?"

"Not one of them. BioloGen is the *only* company financed by Bolten & Ferris. Completely off the radar screen of regulators."

"How?"

"Initial investments from venture capitalists that are essentially untraceable to the parent company through a series of financial tricks and off-shore accounts. The top executives at the parent company garner a percentage of BioloGen's profits. So long as no one knows of the connection, they're exempt if problems arise with any of BioloGen's drugs."

"Like Anginex."

"Bingo. Bottom line: if problems arise with Anginex, Pescatelli takes the fall."

Mackie ran the edge of his thumb along the Dycam digital camera in his jacket pocket. "What about NuCor? ArthroDerm? Those are fantastic drugs, and from everything I've seen, some of the most effective drugs in their class."

Aiken nodded. "I'm sure those things have been great for patients. Those two gambles paid off. By all accounts, BioloGen is a legitimate drug company that happens to be financed by Bolten & Ferris Pharmaceuticals. It's been a huge financial windfall for everyone involved."

Mackie wrestled with the information Aiken continued to give him. "So why would a company even take the risk on a potentially dangerous medication like Anginex?"

"Greed," Aiken said, "and a chance to make more money. You know the financials better than I do. Within eighteen months, Anginex is expected to hit a billion dollars in sales. Your own marketing projections predict that three years after FDA approval, Anginex will be the most prescribed drug on the market. For ostensibly good reasons, too, as you can appreciate better than most. BioloGen developed a drug that can spare people from their worst nightmare. Could have spared you and Sarah untold heartache with your son. They developed a way to prevent cancer."

Mackie felt the familiar anxiety crest inside his chest, pressing on his lungs, constricting his breathing. Thoughts of his son's suffering remained powerful and probably always would. That the FBI could tap into that emotion, and exploit it, aggravated Mackie. In his most truthful moments, he readily admitted to himself that escaping those feelings was one of the main reasons he'd left Nashville. Was he that transparent to everyone else?

Aiken continued. "With so many people taking Anginex, there were bound to be some problems. I doubt the executives at Bolten & Ferris could have predicted the fallout from the unanticipated side effects of dementia. Their response to that information only underscores their belief in the profits of the drug."

Mackie remembered his own excitement as his sabbatical had begun. On a mission to beat cancer, he'd sensed the same excitement among the other members of the Anginex team. Almost everyone he worked with felt that Anginex could revolutionize the pharmaceutical industry, paving the way for more research on disease prevention. He also knew that most members of his marketing team felt that BioloGen was a different kind of pharmaceutical company, ready to prove that developing medicine to prevent disease could be profitable. He could only imagine the crestfallen looks on their faces when they learned what he was hearing now.

Mackie reached for the page with the family tree of photographs and held it up. "Tell me how Hoffman and Lampley fit it."

Agent Aiken cracked his knuckles as he answered. "Years ago, back in the early phase of Anginex testing, Bolten & Ferris sent Jason Lampley to BioloGen as a research assistant for the B-AGX-23 study. He was the only link between the BioloGen executives and the patients in the study."

The realization hit Mackie as he heard the story. Since there was no way an FBI agent could have gotten access to the confidential patient data of a pharmaceutical study, the FBI must have gotten to Lampley like they'd gotten to Mackie. But how? "So Lampley rigged the study results," Mackie concluded.

"At Pescatelli's urging. If a patient had a bad drug reaction, Lampley was instructed to drop the patient from the study."

"Did Jason Lampley kill the fifth patient from that trial? The one I couldn't track down?"

"He didn't pull the trigger," Aiken said. "Lampley identified an independent contractor hired by Pescatelli to do BioloGen's dirty work. His name is Eddie Fackler."

Mackie couldn't fit all of the pieces together. "That makes no sense. If Lampley changed the study results, why would he even approach me in Aruba?"

"For revenge."

"Against whom? I'd never laid eyes on the guy before that trip."

"Revenge against Bolten & Ferris. Lampley has also worked with them at the National Institutes of Health on a drug called Hepatazyme. He was a research assistant with the Division of Endocrinology. He worked with the lead diabetic researcher, Dr. Scott Hoffman."

Mackie studied his picture on the line-up again. "That name sounds familiar."

"It should. He was the public face for Hepatazyme, which is Bolten & Ferris's newest drug. He's a well-known and well-paid consultant for the pharmaceutical industry."

"How'd Lampley help him?"

"He hid a few issues with Hepatazyme, including a death on the NIH campus."

"My God."

"It worked. That drug sailed through FDA approval

because of his behind-the-scenes help. He kept his involvement with Hepatazyme to himself. His silence so impressed his bosses at Bolten & Ferris, they recommended him for a job at BioloGen—"

"To influence the Phase One clinical trial," Mackie said in astonishment. "How deep is Bolten & Ferris's influence?"

"They have their fingertips on every step of the drug development process."

Agent Thibodaux abruptly bolted from behind the coffee counter and ran to the front door. Aiken stood up, his chair scraping across the tile floor as he did. Mackie whirled around in his chair. An elderly woman cupped her hands around her eyes and peered through the front door.

"I'm sorry, ma'am," Agent Thibodaux said through the glass door. "We're closed for another thirty minutes." He gestured to the sign on the front door.

She looked at her watch, stepped back from the front door, and flipped up her middle finger at the FBI agent before walking away. Thibodaux returned to the coffee counter.

Mackie turned back around. "Are we safe here?"

Aiken sat back down. "Don't worry about it. We've got the building surrounded and the shop to ourselves for another twenty minutes."

Mackie took a sip of his coffee, now tepid and bitter. "What caused Lampley to turn his back on Bolten & Ferris and start working for the FBI?"

"Lampley claims he got screwed out of money. He was supposed to be paid for shepherding Hepatazyme through the clinical trial process. Once it won FDA approval, he was promised a lump sum payout that never happened."

"Not anything?"

"Not one cent. Or so he says. He thought he could get revenge on Pescatelli by raising doubts about Anginex. Lampley set out on his own first before he came to us. Knowing that BioloGen would play a major role in the ASCO conference this past summer, he flew down to try and poach a BioloGen employee. Turns out, you were ripe for the picking, and you were the only one in Aruba who wouldn't recognize him."

"Douglas could have identified him."

Aiken shrugged. "I guess he was willing to take that chance to stir up some trouble."

"So he contacted the FBI?"

"He called us from Aruba." Aiken smiled. "We had a head-start on our investigation before you even touched back down on American soil. Which brings us back full circle to you."

Mackie pulled the Dycam out of his coat pocket and set it on the table. "Lampley left after the B-AGX-23 trial. Who's been altering charts since then?"

"Probably Leslie Franks. Maybe Karen Kiley, if she's actually involved." Aiken reached across the table to collect the digital camera, then looked at his watch. "Time to wrap up."

Mackie removed the Discman and downloading cable from this other pocket and placed them on the table, too. He raked his fingers through his hair, trying to soothe his aching head. He thought about the implications of this information. He also thought about how lucky he'd been to not be caught in the second floor storage room by anyone other than the security guard, Earl. It could have just as easily been one of his colleagues. "You know that we're turning in the new drug application for Anginex later today."

Aiken collected the Discman from the table then stood. "It's not going to be easy, Doc. Since Bolten & Ferris have Dr. Hoffman in their pocket, they probably also have a physician at the FDA on the payroll, too. Someone to influence the Advisory Committee that will consider Anginex. Our plan is to build an air-tight case against BioloGen using this information," he held the photographic devices in each hand, as if Mackie needed a visual demonstration. "We'll take it to a Grand Jury, hope to get an indictment. We expect the press will eventually pick up on this, too, which will provide another wave of pressure on these companies."

"You *expect?*" Mackie's voice startled Agent Thibodaux behind the counter. "You're telling me that for the last month I've busted my ass copying charts and sneaking around my office, but you guys don't even have a final plan on how to use this information!"

"It's more complicated than that," Aiken said. "Your cooperation has been invaluable. When you testify before the Grand Jury—"

"Why wait?" Mackie vibrated with tension. "Let's take this to the press right now. Call CNN. Get it on the morning news cycle."

Aiken shook his head. "It's too soon. We need you to verify what you've seen and what you've copied. With your cooperation, this can be an air-tight case. I want the evidence to be overwhelming when the story breaks."

Mackie's legs ached when he finally stood for the first time since this early morning encounter began. "Who else knows I'm involved in the case?"

"The two of us," Aiken said, gesturing to Agent Thibodaux, "plus our support team."

"What about Lampley and Hoffman?"

"We don't reveal our sources."

"But you sure as hell didn't have a problem telling *me* about *them.*"

"We've arranged for you to meet with a federal prosecutor about your testimony." He handed Mackie a business card. "This is the best way to get in touch with me."

Without saying another word, Mackie snatched the business card from Aiken and shoved it into his pocket. He turned, walked out the front door of Starbucks, and felt the bite of fresh, cold air.

*C*HAPTER THIRTY-SIX

*M*ACKIE HEADED BACK to his hotel. The street lights guided him. As he strode down the sidewalk, he paid little attention to the magnificence of the White House backlit against the dawn. He pressed on, his head down as the cold air seared his lungs. Soon, he would meet his colleagues in the hotel lobby to leave for the FDA submission; before they flew out at the end of the day, he was supposed to talk to the Department of Justice lawyers about his cooperation. But Mackie had other plans. He just wasn't sure how to make them happen. Not yet, anyway.

He stepped into the nearly empty lobby he had left only one hour ago.

"Good morning, sir," a young hotel attendant said from the front desk.

Mackie pulled a ten-dollar bill out of his wallet and approached the desk. "Could I get a roll of quarters?"

"Of course." The young female clerk with an eyebrow piercing exchanged his money while Mackie glanced around him. "Is there anything else I can help you with?"

"Do you have a business center or some other work station with a phone book?" he asked.

"We've got a pay phone down the hall."

"I need a phone book."

"Yes, sir. You'll find those in the Business Center, along with a photo copier and fax machine." She smiled, crinkling her pierced eyebrow. "It's down the hall and opens at eight o'clock."

Mackie glanced around again at the empty lobby. He lowered his voice and leaned against the front desk. "I was hoping I could get in there now."

"Yes, sir. I understand," she said with a nervous smile, "but it's only an hour."

Mackie tried a different approach. "You ever stay up all night and write a term paper?"

"Excuse me?"

"When you were in school, did you ever pull an all-nighter to finish a project?"

When she laughed, he spotted a retainer on her top teeth. She probably wasn't even out of high school yet, Mackie thought, but she was his best hope of getting out of the pinch he was in between his company and the federal government.

"There was this one time in my World History class last year. God! It was awful. So we had this twenty-page paper that had to be double-spaced and referenced—no long block quotes, either—and I started, like, the week before it was due. Still didn't get finished until early that morning."

"That's exactly what I'm talking about," Mackie said.

"It was bad. I got a C-plus on the paper, which I considered a win, seeing as I didn't even remember a thing about the topic."

"Right." Mackie nodded, politely biding his time while glancing over his shoulder. "I work for this drug company, and we're turning in a really big paper today—"

"It never ends, does it?" the desk clerk said. "The papers, I mean. You graduate from high school and think you're done with all that bullshit..." She stopped, obviously remembering where she was. "Sorry. All that stuff. The next thing you know, you've got a job that requires even more paperwork. It's ridiculous."

"So listen, I've got this project due and I need to check some things in the phone book before we turn it in. I wonder if you could make an exception just this one time and let me in before it opens."

She giggled again. "My boss would be, like, so pissed if she knew I was doing this. She doesn't get in until eight, though." She gave a conspiratorial glance around her and said in a softer voice, "Promise me you'll be done by seven-thirty and I'll let you in."

"Promise."

She put a *Be Right Back* sign on the counter and stepped around to the narrow hallway that led to the Business Center. Mackie followed her to a small alcove with a glass door clearly marked with its hours of operation. Outside the room, he saw a single pay phone. As predicted, no phone books anywhere near it. Beyond the glass, Mackie saw two copy machines, a row of desks with push-button phones, and a small shelf lined with what appeared to be local phone books.

"Remember, seven-thirty." She unlocked the doors and flipped on the lights. "I'll come get you if you're not done."

"Deal," Mackie said.

When she left, he walked over to the shelves and ran his fingers across the spine of the phone books. Northern Virginia. Southern Maryland. Washington, D.C. He pulled the Metro D.C. book and found the first address without much trouble. It was the second address, though, that eluded him at first. He didn't suspect he would find the second one in the D.C. phone book, but he checked just in case. Not locating it, he pulled another off the shelf for Southern Maryland. After a moment of thumbing through the pages, he found what he was looking for.

Mackie glanced at each work station. A small cup of sharpened pencils waited to be used but no signs of scrap paper. He thought of ripping the page from the book, but he couldn't bring himself to deface the directory or leave a trail. Walking over to the fax machine at the far side of the room, he removed a single white sheet from the paper tray. He wrote down the address in Washington. Once he finished, he added the address and phone number of the location in Maryland.

Mackie re-shelved the phone books then double checked his tracks. Other than a missing sheet of copy paper and a dulled pencil, no one would know that he'd been here. He walked to the glass door and turned off the light to the business center.

Mackie gripped the piece of paper. He pulled out the roll of quarters from his pocket and stepped to the pay phone, dialing the long distance number from memory. He fed a handful of quarters into the phone. At this hour, he was uncertain as to whether he would catch his friend at home. By the third ring, Mackie assumed he would have to try and call the work number, instead. Right before he disconnected the call, someone picked up on the other end.

Mackie could tell immediately that he'd awakened his friend, but at this point, he didn't care. "Tom, listen, I need a favor?"

Tom Philips cursed under his breath with a sleep-filled voice. "What the hell, Mackie? You're calling me at seven-thirty on my one weekday off in the last month."

"Sorry about that," Mackie said. "I'm in trouble, and I need your help."

He explained what he needed, and how Tom could get it. Mackie then thanked his friend. As he was arranging a time to call him back later that afternoon, he heard a familiar voice.

"How was your run, Mackie?"

Surprised, Mackie hung up on Tom. He gripped the plastic

receiver as he slowly turned around.

Pescatelli had spotted him. He approached Mackie, a cup of water in his hand, wearing sweat-stained shorts and a white t-shirt with the BioloGen logo on it. "The kid at the front desk saw my shirt and said someone who worked for a drug company was finishing up on some stuff in the Business Center down here. Whatcha working on?"

Mackie locked eye contact with Pescatelli, trying hard not to bring attention to his nervousness. "Calling home."

Pescatelli gestured to the paper in Mackie's hand. "What's that?"

"Nothing much," Mackie said, "Just looking up the contact info of a friend of mine in the area."

"Someone you know from med school?"

"Yep." Mackie folded the paper and slipped it inside his jacket pocket. He kept his hand on the pages to calm himself down. "Seems like a cold morning for a run."

"It's invigorating." Pescatelli slurped the last of the water in his cup. "You ready for today?"

"The NDA submission?"

"Is there anything else going on today?"

Mackie smiled. "Sightseeing."

"No time for that," Pescatelli said. "This is one of the highlights of my job, Mackie. Submitting an NDA has none of the pomp and fanfare that goes along with the public launch of a drug, but to me it's like watching your son leave for his first day of school—" He paused awkwardly, realizing his obvious slip in front of Mackie. "Son. Daughter. Whatever. Point is, you know you've done everything you can do to get them ready. Now it's time to send them off and wish them well. The NDA, that is."

Mackie did nothing to relieve Pescatelli of his awkward comment. "So I'll see you in the lobby at nine?"

"You got it." Pescatelli walked back to the front desk to

refill his water cup, leaving Mackie wondering how much luck he would need to accomplish all of his tasks today.

* * *

At precisely nine o'clock, the driver of the black Suburban pulled away from the hotel. With traffic, it took the four BioloGen employees almost an hour to drive to the FDA campus. Pescatelli passed the time in the car with a running monologue, mostly reliving old drug launches and telling stories about the mishaps of other companies. Douglas chimed in, leaving Mackie and Dr. Martin as passive observers for most of the ride. Mackie wouldn't have had it any other way. He listened with feigned interest to Pescatelli's bravado in recounting Congressmen he'd wooed and senators he'd bribed to accomplish his pharmaceutical agenda.

When they arrived at the FDA's Center for Biologic Evaluation and Research, Pescatelli stepped out of the car and stretched. He poked his head back through the open car door and looked at Mackie and Dr. Martin in the backseat. "Who's ready to change the world today?" he said with a thinly disguised mania in his voice.

Dr. Martin gave an appreciative smile and said to Mackie, "He says that every time we come up here."

"Yes, Rita, but this time's different," Pescatelli said.

An older man with glasses and a limp walked over to the car. He wore an FDA badge around his neck and a starched dress shirt. "Early, I see. I wasn't expecting you for another half hour," the elderly man said.

Pescatelli gripped the man's hand. "We've got a carload of Anginex data for you guys to review."

A small crew of FDA employees trailed the older man. They began to unload boxes of data onto handcarts. "All in good time, Mr. Pescatelli. We're not going to take a day longer than we have to."

Pescatelli and Douglas led the way into the building to certify their data drop-off. Mackie and Dr. Martin followed behind. "One of these days, I predict we're going to arrive with a stack of computer disks rather than boxes full of stored data," Dr. Matin said as they walked down the heated hallway. "There's even been talk of electronic submissions to the FDA, either through electronic mail or some other means," she said. "But don't expect that in my lifetime."

"Technology's changing faster than you think," Mackie said.

"Not for an old woman like me." She rubbed her eyes and replaced her glasses. "Even if they go to electronic submissions, it wouldn't change our timetable. We still have to gather all of the basic scientific and clinical trial data and organize the information from other sites that have run trials on our drugs. Can you imagine trying to copy all of that data into electronic format?"

Mackie winced. "Not an easy task."

"Nor a quick one. And not something to cut corners on, either. The FDA would much rather have us complete the process with an air-tight case for approval than to have to send back portions of the NDA for further explanation and review."

They stopped near the end of the hallway. Red and Douglas entered a small office, leaving the two to talk outside. Mackie welcomed the diversion. "When's the last time BioloGen had to do that?"

"Not once," Dr. Martin said. "Red sees it as a personal affront if parts of the NDA get sent back. He also takes great pride in sticking to a deadline once we set it. Which is why he hates having to rely on other sites to complete the data acquisition and analysis. Loss of control, I guess, is what fuels his frustration."

"And loss of direct oversight of the drug," Mackie said.

Dr. Martin gave him a look of uncertainty. "What do you mean?"

"If BioloGen has a group of doctors testing the drug in California or Cleveland or even at the NIH, I can imagine Red get's nervous about possible side effects." Mackie waited for a response.

As if reading from a well-vetted and company-approved script, Dr. Martin said, "We don't see that as a problem at BioloGen."

"Side effects?"

"Or loss of quality control at our sister sites. The drug will either perform well in clinical trials, or it won't. Our job is to vigorously test it to make it as safe as possible." She peered over the top edge of her glasses. "Do you think I would take it if I had any concerns?"

Mackie side-stepped the answer. "Livoxx was pulled from the market after FDA approval due to unexpected side effects," he said.

"True, but it later came out that the company knew about those dangerous problems long before they made it this far." She reached out and patted Mackie's arm. "It's normal to be anxious after all your hard work, Mackie."

It took another hour for the paperwork to be processed. By the time the four BioloGen employees stepped out into the noontime sun, Pescatelli seemed positively ebullient. "If it's good enough for the government, then it's good enough for us. We can celebrate tonight, but right now I've got a one o'clock meeting up on Capitol Hill."

Mackie followed Pescatelli back to the waiting Suburban. "What time do you want us back at the hotel to leave for the airport?"

"I'd like to have wheels up at four o'clock. Four-thirty at the latest," Pescatelli said. "Let's plan on leaving the hotel at three." The driver opened the back door to the car. Pescatelli climbed in first.

Mackie paused at the curb. "You guys go ahead. I'm going to grab a cab and catch up with a buddy from med school. Time permitting, I may even do some sightseeing."

Pescatelli waved his hand at Mackie's announcement. "Do what you want. You know how to get back?"

Mackie nodded and stepped back onto the sidewalk.

"Don't be late." Pescatelli slammed the back door to the Suburban. The vehicle pulled into traffic and headed back to Washington, D.C., leaving Mackie less than three hours to finish the job he'd been recruited to do by the FBI.

*C*HAPTER THIRTY-SEVEN

*F*ROM THE BACK of his cab, Mackie watched the Maryland neighborhood turn from urban to suburban in a matter of blocks. The cabbie parked in front of a row of well-kept brownstones with swept sidewalks. He squinted out the back window and then down again at the sheet of paper in his hand, double checking the address. The neighborhood resembled a suburban ghost town. He saw no one. Although it was the middle of the work week, his earlier phone call told him that he would not find this townhouse empty. Mackie handed the cabbie a twenty dollar bill. "Give me five minutes."

From the sidewalk, the brownstone looked perfectly serene. As he climbed the steps, though, he noted the chipped paint on the wrought iron railing and a few patches of moss along the cracks of the steps. He knocked on the front door.

At first, nothing happened. Then, he heard the rattle of a security chain and a deadbolt disengage. The front door opened, revealing a wiry man with thinning hair. His skin had the pallor of an overcast sky. "Can I help you?"

"Dr. Scott Hoffman?"

"Who are you?"

Mackie extended his hand. "I work with BioloGen Pharmaceuticals. I'd like to ask you some questions about an investigational drug of ours known as Anginex."

Hoffman's already hollow cheeks sagged without the support of a smile. "What you are doing here?"

"Are you familiar with Anginex?"

Hoffman scoffed. "I see thousands of patients a year at the NIH taking untold number of drugs. I can't possibly keep up with all of them."

Mackie stood several steps back from the cracked front door, but even from his vantage point he saw Hoffman's nostrils flare. He appeared to be willing himself to stay calm with deliberate breathing exercises.

Mackie pressed on. "Someone at BioloGen mentioned your name in connection with Anginex. Specifically, we're tracking unreported side effects of the drug and finding out what others may have known about those problems." When Hoffman didn't respond, he said, "I was led to believe that you participated in the confirmatory Phase Three studies at the NIH of Anginex."

"That's ridiculous," Hoffman mumbled. His nostrils picked up their pace, keeping time with his breathing.

"Were you aware that patients have developed significant problems from taking the drug? Problems with their kidneys and their memory?" Mackie asked.

Hoffman opened the door a little wider. "I'm an endocrinologist. Unless your company's drug is a diabetes drug—and I'm certain it's not—there is no possible way I would have interacted with it."

The cabbie honked his horn. When Mackie turned around to see what he wanted, the cabbie tapped his finger against his wrist. He was running out of time. Mackie nodded, then faced Hoffman once more. "Dr. Hoffman, let me ask you one more thing, one physician to another. Did you change any data for our study drug, Anginex? Did you alter the patient outcomes like you did with Hepatazyme?"

Hoffman stiffened. "Get the hell off my property."

"I just needed to—"

The door slammed shut in his face. Mackie heard the deadbolt engage, driving home the answer to his question.

Mackie descended the stairs and climbed back into the cab. He didn't know if Hoffman would notify anyone of his visit, but Mackie had one more stop to make before it was his turn to make a call. He knew he wouldn't make his meeting with the DOJ. They would track him down in Cincinnati, of course, unless Mackie could give them something, or someone else, to pursue. He unfolded the sheet of paper from his pocket and read the address to the cabbie for his next destination.

* * *

The cab passed the Capitol building on Independence Avenue and pulled to the curb halfway between First and Second Streets. Mackie stepped to the sidewalk. Before him stood the enormous columned building of the Library of Congress. Off to his left, beneath a cloudless blue sky, rose the rotunda of the Capitol. Pescatelli's inside right now, he thought. Even though he knew there was virtually no way he would run into his boss on the sidewalks of downtown Washington, Mackie's heart sped up as he considered a chance encounter. He didn't linger long on the thought, though. He double-checked the address on his crumbled sheet of paper and headed into the James Madison Building of the Library of Congress.

It took longer than Mackie had hoped to obtain a library card, and by the time he made it to the Newspaper and Current Periodical Reading Room, he had less than an hour before he was supposed to be back at the hotel. With the staff's assistance, Mackie quickly identified the recent unbound issues of *The Washington Post* and began his search. Honing in on the terms *Scott Hoffman* and *National Institutes of Health*,

Mackie found more than a dozen citations in the newspapers. Scanning the article's titles, Mackie found references to Dr. Hoffman testifying before a Congressional committee regarding funding for the NIH. Another article highlighted Hoffman's involvement in a local fund raiser for the American Diabetes Association. Mackie continued to run his fingers down the listings. Bingo! Just as Agent Aiken had mentioned earlier that morning, Scott Hoffman had garnered a front-page article in a Sunday edition of *The Washington Post* less than one year ago in reference to Hepatazyme. From the title alone Mackie could tell that Hoffman was hailed as a 'medical hero' for his dedication to testing new advances in diabetes management.

Mackie memorized the citation and had the same staff member help him locate the actual paper, still unbound and easy to read. Mackie placed the year-old periodical on a table in the reading room. He scanned the article, finding references to Bolten & Ferris Pharmaceuticals and predictions of a new era of treatment success with Hepatazyme. The article tried to maintain a dispassionate tone, but even the journalist's objectivity seemed to fray as he praised the local doctor's heroic research. Mackie returned to the beginning of the article, and starting with the reporter's name, he carefully absorbed the information. Finally, Mackie turned to the editorial page of the thick Sunday edition of the *Post*, searching for contact information. Satisfied he had memorized what he needed, Mackie returned the paper to the staff member and headed back outside.

He needed a pay phone. Mindful that his time was running out, he set out at a brisk pace toward the Capitol along Independence Avenue. The farther he walked, the closer he came to his hotel, but he knew he would ultimately have to hail a cab to make it back in time. He mentally wrestled with the implications of his next move. He knew that with the dozens of disks of photographed documents, the FBI had most of the inside information to proceed with the case. Agent Aiken had said that Mackie's job would not be complete, though, until he testified against BioloGen. Mackie saw two obvious options. He could continue to deceive his colleagues by staying at the company until an indictment was brought against BioloGen; or he could resign now and endure the inevitable questions that leaving Cincinnati would bring. Either way, his colleagues would ultimately identify him as the mole inside the company. If what he'd seen so far was true, that meant Mackie would never truly be sure he and his family were safe.

Mackie considered his third option once more. The same option he'd been working on since his early morning meeting at Starbucks with the FBI. Not a perfect solution, but if done correctly, Mackie might be able to feign ignorance during the fallout this plan would bring. He could stay at the company and act as surprised as everyone else when the accusations finally came. In order for the plan to work, he would have to place complete trust in a man he'd never met. And he would have to hope that Tom Philips had found the missing piece of the puzzle.

Mackie finally found a pay phone along the sidewalk as he neared the National Mall. Reaching into his pocket for more change, he first called Tom. His friend in Cincinnati answered on the second ring.

"So why all the secrecy in having me look up an article on one of the country's best selling drugs?" Tom asked.

Mackie pressed the handset to his ear. "What'd you find?"

"Interesting stuff," Tom said. "But it's all part of the public record." He described the handful of case reports he'd found in the medical library, describing a rare but potentially fatal side effect of Hepatazyme. They all detailed liver problems. "The most interesting part of the reports, though, is not the side effects themselves. It's that the only problems with

Hepatazyme have been reported after the FDA approved the drug. Nothing that I could find happened before that."

Not a smoking gun, Mackie knew, but taken together, it might be enough to attract the interest of the right people. He thanked Tom again and disconnected the line by pressing his finger to the receiver as he held the plastic handset. The line went dead.

A flag in front of the Capitol's rotunda snapped in the winter breeze. A quiet and serene image of democracy, hiding the inner workings of deceit and deception by men cut from the same cloth as Red Pescatelli. Mackie knew Red would dump huge sums of money into certain Congressional re-election coffers in exchange for protection for the pharmaceutical industry. How many more drugs like Hepatazyme and Anginex lurked out there? Mackie wondered. How many killer combinations of drugs being polished for a presentation to the FDA? How many more people would die before someone blew the whistle on the few tainted drugs that slipped though the regulatory process? Mackie couldn't stop all of them, but he could stop at least one, which might be enough to bring reforms to an industry blinded by its own greed.

He'd made up his mind and completely committed himself to the plan. He reached into his jacket pocket, grabbing the quarters but brushing up against the hard plastic that had been there all day. Earlier forgotten but now reminding him of what he was about to do. He lifted his finger off the receiver. When he heard the dial tone, Mackie inserted a quarter and punched in the numbers from memory. A woman answered the phone.

"Bill Baldwin, please," Mackie said.

The pleasant sounding woman asked, "May I tell him who's calling?"

Mackie hesitated. Bill Baldwin wouldn't have a clue who he was, but Mackie needed him to be intrigued enough to take the call. "It's a friend of Scott Hoffman's from the pharmaceutical industry."

The woman sounded skeptical, but said, "Hold, please."

Mackie scanned the few pedestrians along the sidewalk while he waited. He thought of the potential deaths if Anginex received FDA approval. He thought about Donnie Sims, wasting away in Louisville for years until meeting with Mackie, then ending up dead twenty-four hours later. He also thought about the promise of the drug if only the underlying issues would be addressed by the company. Anticipation dried his mouth. A man answered the phone.

"Bill Baldwin, Washington Post. How can I help you?"

Mackie cleared his throat to speak. He introduced himself as an executive in the pharmaceutical industry before saying, "I read your article from last year about Scott Hoffman at the NIH."

The reporter sounded pleasant but hurried. "Thank you," he said, even though no compliment had been offered. "Is there something I can help you with?"

Mackie took a deep, steadying breath. He removed the last of the hard plastic stacks of floppy disks that he'd held back from the FBI that morning. His one ticket out of this predicament, along with circumstantial evidence that he would explain. Evidence supported by Aruban hotel registers and photocopied medical articles. Evidence photographed and downloaded in digital images on the discs. Mackie had already decided that if Bill Baldwin asked for proof, he would leave the rubber-banded stack at the front desk of the hotel, wrapped and marked for him to pick up. Not perfect, he thought, but probably good enough.

Mackie tried to swallow against a dry throat. "I have some valuable inside information and documented proof of criminal activities in the pharmaceutical industry, some of which directly involves Dr. Scott Hoffman."

CHAPTER THIRTY-EIGHT

HOFFMAN ROSE EARLY the next morning and drove to work, hoping to review his ghostwritten editorial in the seclusion of his office. He didn't bother to close the office door. He intended to memorize the article and make it his own. He also needed to look up the references cited in the piece. When the press called him for a response, he would be an expert on Anginex. After *The Medical Weekly* published his comments, every doctor in the country would have access to it. Most researchers craved that kind of national exposure. For Hoffman, the pending publication only nauseated him.

He spent an hour at his desk without interruptions, the ticking of his watch his only companion. He scrutinized the editorial in front of him, taking notes as he read and thumbing through some of the citations in his personal file of clipped articles. Of course he would know many of these references, since the person who wrote the article cited other studies well known to the community of diabetic researchers. As was his tendency when writing, Hoffman lined a series of annotated cards on his desk so he could see at a glance his train of thought. He was so engrossed with his work, he didn't hear the knock on the door. Another knock, louder this time. Hoffman's head snapped up.

Yolanda stood in the doorway, smiling at her boss. She wore sweat pants and black sneakers, clearly not dressed for a day at the office. "What's with you and these early mornings?"

Hoffman returned to his work. "What are you doing here?"

"You need to get away from the office for a while. Take some time off for the holidays. Maybe leave some of that grumpiness behind when you come back." She came over to his desk. "Whatcha working on?"

"An editorial for *The Medical Weekly.*"

"Impressive." She folded her arms. "You've been so strung out lately, I didn't know you had the energy to write one."

He tried to ignore his secretary but she stepped closer, leaning across his desk to take a look. He bristled. "Do you mind?"

"Who typed it?

"What?"

"As long as I've worked for you, Scottie, I've typed all of your manuscripts. Don't tell me you've gone and taught yourself how to type." She smacked her gum as she spoke.

"I'm trying to work here, okay? Is there anything I can do for you, or are you just here to annoy me?"

"I came in to pick up some work for the weekend and thought I might as well see how you're doing. There was a message on my answering machine when I got here." She placed a yellow sticky note on his desk that contained a phone number. "I wrote it down for you."

Hoffman paid it only a casual glance. "Who's that from?"

"Bill Baldwin."

"Who?"

"C'mon. Don't pretend like you don't remember that man who last year called you a medical hero on the front page of *The Post.*"

Hoffman grunted. "What's he want?"

"A quote from you, I'm sure. He didn't say in his message.

Only said that he wanted you to call him."

Hoffman unstuck the yellow tab from his desk and pressed it to the handset on his phone. "I'll call him later. Anything else?"

"You want me to order you some food before I leave?"

"I'm not hungry."

"Suit yourself." She turned and walked out of his office, still smacking her gum.

Hoffman returned his attention to the editorial. The text reviewed the landmark trial that proved that Anginex prevented cancer. It then went on to propose alternative uses for the drug. Overall it was well written and clearly referenced. In only two pages of text, the ghostwriter had included twelve references to scientific articles that supported alternative uses of Anginex. Some of the references pointed to animal studies in which researchers used angiogenesis inhibitors for treating cancer. Hoffman would need to make a trip to the medical library to look those up. Other references cited more familiar territory in which different compounds had been used to treat diabetic complications with excessive blood vessel growth. Those he knew by heart.

Hoffman's name appeared at the top of the article as the lone author, which meant the media would be calling him for questions about Anginex. Bill Baldwin must have received an advanced copy of the editorial, he thought. He glanced at the sticky note on his handset, debating whether to call the reporter now. Even though Baldwin had given him nothing but good press in the past, Hoffman wanted to be as knowledgeable as possible about the references before speaking to the reporter. But then again, was there any reason to think that Baldwin would grill him on something as small as a two-page editorial?

"What the hell," he said as he picked up the phone.

Yolanda poked her head back through the office door. "You need me?"

"Just talking to myself," Hoffman said.

"All the more reason for you to get out of here and take a vacation." She disappeared from sight.

Hoffman dialed the number. The phone rang three times on the other end before he heard a vaguely familiar voice answered. "Hello, Bill Baldwin."

"Bill, it's Scott Hoffman from the NIH. Got your message."

Yolanda returned once more with a look of anticipation on her face. She stood at the office door. When Hoffman glanced in her direction, she mouthed the words, "Can I listen?"

Hoffman shook his head and pantomimed for her to shut the door. "Sorry, Bill, what'd you say?"

"Thank's for calling back, Doc."

"No worries." Hoffman said. "I assume you're calling about the Anginex editorial."

Silence on the other end of the line. "What editorial?"

"The one about angiogenesis inhibitors. The one that's coming out in *The Medical Weekly* in response to the landmark clinical trial of Anginex."

"Interesting. But I was actually calling to get a statement from you about something different."

Hoffman scratched the stubble on his chin. "Okay. About what?"

Bill Baldwin said, "I received a call from a drug company insider, who claims to have first-hand knowledge of illegal activities in certain clinical trials."

Hoffman froze. His mind raced, thinking of the BioloGen employee who'd come to his door yesterday. Surely that guy hadn't called the press.

Baldwin continued. "This insider mentioned you as possibly having some useful information for this story, especially in regards to your previous involvement with Hepatazyme. Of course, I'm trying to verify or refute his allegations, and I was hoping you might be able to answer some questions."

The next several seconds crawled by in slow motion. Hoffman couldn't stop hyperventilating. Even when he leaned back in his chair, he felt the room spinning out of control. The last thing he remembered before losing consciousness was his office door flying open and Yolanda screaming for someone to call 9-1-1.

* * *

The team of FBI agents sat around a conference room in downtown Washington, D.C., cups of coffee and classified papers littering the table. Five men, all still clad in suit jackets, listened to Agent Thibodaux tell his story. A woman in a business suit sat on the edge of the table, swinging one leg while he talked.

"So there I am yesterday, standing behind the counter at Starbucks in my green apron, and this woman walks up and presses her nose against the window." Thibodaux did his best to imitate the elderly woman he'd seen yesterday, but a man of his size and strength had little feminine skill. The mere sight of his imitation had his colleagues doubled over in laughter.

"He's probably the only Starbucks employee to wear a side arm while working," said Agent Aiken.

"So," Thibodaux said, "we have six agents surrounding this building and this little old lady manages to make her way to the front door. I'm thinking, what the hell are we teaching these guys about securing a location?"

The other members of the FBI's Pharmaceutical Task Force laughed. While Thibodaux continued his tale, a secretary quietly walked into the meeting and whispered into Aiken's ear, "You have a phone call about the Anginex case."

Aiken didn't even look at her when he said, "Take a message. I'll call back when we're done in here."

She stepped out of the conference room to deliver the

message, but in less than a minute she returned to Aiken's side. "The caller said he'll wait."

"What?"

"Until your meeting is over," she whispered. "He said he'll hold the line."

Aiken mumbled an obscenity as he stood.

Thibodaux didn't miss a beat, whipping his colleagues into fits of laughter as Aiken left the room.

Minutes later, Agent Aiken returned. The other agents immediately sobered when they saw his expression.

"What's up?" Thibodaux asked his partner.

"That was Bill Baldwin calling from *The Post* about Anginex," Aiken said. "We've had a leak."

* * *

When Hoffman regained consciousness, he saw a bright light behind his eyelids. He heard the clink of metal-on-metal, which reminded him of his surgery rotation during medical school. Several people spoke around him in muffled voices. A monitor beeped in the background with metronomic precision. He tried to lift his head, but it was pinned against a hard surface. Even the slightest movement caused his skull to explode with pain. The heart monitor sped up.

"He's starting to wake up," a woman said.

A man asked, "More Versed?"

"No, I'm about done here," she said.

Hoffman felt pressure on his scalp. It wasn't painful, but it felt as if someone was gently tugging on his hair. His mind began to clear. He tried to open his eyes, but the bright light assaulted his senses. When he breathed in to speak, he smelled the antiseptic odors of a hospital and the stale, acrid smell of old cigarette smoke on fabric. He felt a callused hand rub against his arms. "Relax, Scottie. She's almost done," Yolanda said.

Even when he tried to relax, he couldn't. A fog obscured his memory. He remembered Yolanda talking to him. A heartbeat later, he recalled the entire conversation. A reporter from *The Washington Post* had called about illegal activity at the NIH. Oh, my God, he thought. Someone knows!

He arched his back with all his strength, but his head wouldn't move. Adrenaline surged through his pinned body. The beeping monitor doubled its pace. His mind screamed for him to flee.

"Easy there, Dr. Hoffman," the surgeon said. "I'm almost done. Just one more...there!" Her voice smiled. "Even with a shaved scalp, you'll barely notice the scar."

"I nath ta weeve white mwow," Hoffman blurted in an unfamiliar voice. The only response he heard was laughter.

"That's still the Versed and Fentanyl talking," the surgeon said. "It'll wear off soon. I'll be back in a few minutes with a scrip for pain meds, but you're not ready to leave yet. Curtis is going to give you a little more medicine while he dresses your wound, okay?"

Before he could respond, he felt a cool liquid rush through the veins in his right arm. The palpable panic in his mind faded, replaced by peacefulness. When he tried to open his eyes, the bright light remained, but it didn't bother him like before. He felt mildly nauseated. Instead of worrying about his escape, he began to dream about his final destination.

* * *

Hoffman's head ached. Yolanda had driven him home from the hospital in his Ford Probe, stopping by the pharmacy on the way to pick up his pain medicines. In between waves of nausea and fits of pain, his mind passed though fleeting moments of clarity in which he was quite surprised to see Yolanda's nurturing side. While he staggered to the leather chair in his den, she rummaged though his kitchen to make sure he had enough to eat for the next several days. When his forehead felt feverish, she brought him a cool washcloth. She placed two Percocets and a glass of water next to his chair, and she promised to call later to check up on him.

"I'm clearing your schedule until further notice." She then insisted that he stay home and rest.

The pain medicine helped, but it did not take away the pressure in his head. When he tried to look at the wound in the mirror, all he saw were his sunken eyes and a gauze bandage taped to the back of his head. The top of his ear was purple. It sickened Hoffman to even look at it, so he closed his eyes while washing his hands. He would worry about changing the bandage tomorrow.

He awoke the next morning and stared at the ceiling. The reality of his situation stole the calm of the dawn. Somehow, the press had found out about the dark side of his pharmaceutical consulting at the NIH, and he suspected the man who'd come to his house a few days earlier was to blame. He must have told Baldwin about illegal activities. Hoffman knew he'd covered his trail of deception. He wondered if Baldwin had also learned of the deaths of Compton Drew and Delores Gonzales.

His heart beat faster just thinking about it, which made his head wound throb. He now felt certain that the press would eventually discover his involvement with Anginex. He also knew he didn't have the fortitude to deny the allegations. Remarkably, he still possessed enough shame to not be able to withstand the public scrutiny that was sure to come. Once Eddie found out about the press leak, he would come looking for him to fix the problem. The thought of being implicated in the leak made Hoffman's stomach cramp.

As he replayed the events of the last twenty-four hours, certain themes emerged. People knew about his data tampering at the NIH. He was being blackmailed to complete more pharmaceutical fraud. His health had suffered as a result of his poor judgement.

Replacing the intensity of his dreams was the more uncomfortable urgency of self-preservation. Hung over from the pain medications and motivated by fear, Hoffman saw only one sure way out of this mess.

While brushing his teeth, he crafted the broad ideas of his plan. In the shower, he solved the question of what to do with his substantial possessions. He had millions invested in the stock market, and it amounted to a notable portion of the portfolio he had accumulated over the years. Toweling dry, he made a final decision about a destination.

He walked back into his room. Standing in boxer shorts and knee-high socks, he pulled out his travel bag from the closet and set it on his bed. No sooner had he begun to pack than the phone rang. Hoffman stared at the handset. The phone continued to ring. If he planned to make a clean break from his past, he needed to start now. He turned his back to the phone and continued to pack. Finally, the answering machine picked up. He pulled out knit shirts and tossed them on the bed while he heard his own recorded voice asking the caller to leave a message. He waited for the beep.

"Scottie, pick up. I know you're there," Yolanda said.

Hoffman stood at his chest of drawers, pulling out socks and underwear.

Yolanda continued, "Your phone at the office has been ringing off the hook with well wishers. But that reporter called back—"

Hoffman paused and listened.

"—twice, saying he needed to finish a phone conversation with you. Said something about a new study that's coming out. He asked me if I could give him your home phone number."

"No!" Hoffman yelled at the answering machine. He darted

for the phone and picked up the handset. "No, Yolanda. Do *not* give him my number."

"Scottie? Why didn't you answer the phone? Have you taken your medicine this morning? It might take the edge off."

"Don't give him my phone number," Hoffman said. "And don't call him back. I'll take care of it later." He glanced at the clock's glowing red numbers. Twelve more hours, he thought. That's all he needed. Just twelve more hours.

"You're the boss, Scottie. I'll call you back if there are any more problems. Answer your phone next time. And take your meds."

Hoffman hung up the phone and accelerated his packing.

Baldwin wouldn't leave him alone. Hoffman wondered what information the reporter had so far and when he would publish the results of his investigative probing. He could imagine the headlines. NIH Researcher Influenced by Big Pharma. Or something even worse. Government-Sponsored Pharmaceutical Cover-Up.

There would be plenty of questions once the article was published. Colleagues would talk around the water cooler and gossip at lunch meetings. Yolanda would have more questions than anyone, especially since she'd witnessed his erratic behavior since last summer. A part of him felt guilty for running, but it beat leaving the office in handcuffs and answering questions in a courtroom.

It took him another half hour to pack his bag. Except for the one he wore, he left behind thousands of dollars in wool suits and dress shirts. Satisfied that he had all he would need, he walked downstairs into his study.

Although his ex-wife used to tease him about his compulsions, Hoffman's finances had been meticulously organized years ago. He could find all of the information on his accounts at a moment's notice. He had two bank accounts in Washington, in addition to his stock portfolio. He kept the papers for his pharmaceutical consulting account in a separate folder. He allowed himself a smile when he looked at his latest statement. The fruits of his labor—and a comfortable amount to take into retirement.

He placed the account numbers and withdrawal information into a single folder and put it in his bag. He took his checkbook and grabbed the stack of bills on his desk. No sense leaving town with bad credit, he thought.

He checked his coat pocket to make sure his passport was in place. Reassured that it was, he walked to the front door of his townhouse. The cab would arrive at any moment.

On his way to the door, Dr. Scott Hoffman, wearing a wool suit and a soggy head bandage, grabbed his sunglasses and the glossy brochures of Belize.

𝒞HAPTER THIRTY-NINE

Early January 1994

"𝒯HERE HE IS!" Karen Kiley said as she walked into Mackie's office without knocking. "Back from the battles of Washington and ready to start the new year right. Congratulations on your first NDA submission."

Mackie leaned back in his chair with the desk between the two of them. "It was anticlimactic, like you said it would be."

He had taken a week off to spend time with his family and repair his relationship with his wife. The time spent in Nashville paid dividends. Sarah and Reagan had packed their bags and moved to the rental house in Ohio, preparing for a winter in Cincinnati. With his family settling in at home, Mackie began to wonder what kind of reception he would get once he returned to the office. When he looked around him that morning, he saw almost everything differently. Every glance and gesture seemed ripe for interpretation, but apparently no one else saw it that way. Members of the Anginex team greeted him with renewed energy from their own holiday break. Whenever anyone saw him, all they seemed to want to talk about was his trip to Washington as he'd helped to escort the NDA.

Karen perched on the edge of his desk and grinned. "My holidays seemed to be one climax after another. I drank enough champagne in Chicago to pickle my liver and wound up sleeping through some of the best bowl games on New Years Day." She held one hand behind her back, out of Mackie's view, and smiled invitingly at him. "Aren't you the least bit interested in what I'm holding behind my back."

"My Christmas present?"

"Close." She extended her arms with a dramatic flare to reveal a magazine with a glossy white cover and the words *The Medical Weekly* printed across the top. "Check it out."

At first glance, it looked exactly like all of the other editions of the medical journal that Mackie had read for years. With a second look, though, he realized this was *the* edition BioloGen had been waiting for. He took the periodical from her and flipped it over. The entire back cover had a metallic blue background with the familiar BioloGen's logo prominently displayed in the lower corner. Above it, in large script, he read the ad as if seeing it for the first time: 'Are you ready for a revolution?'

Mackie couldn't help but smile, impressed at seeing his handiwork on the back cover of a magazine. "Where'd you get it?"

"The same place every other subscribing doctor in the United States will get it. I found it in the morning mail. But that's not even the best part." She reached across his desk and stole the magazine from him. She flipped to the table of contents and placed her finger near the top of the page. "Right there."

Published as the lead article in this issue was the largest and most recent study from the NIH that proved Anginex worked. He scanned the table of contents. His gaze snagged on a familiar name at the bottom of the page.

Karen must have noticed. "Thought you'd be more excited,"

she said.

Mackie fought to maintain his smile. "This looks great."

"Keep that copy, then. I've got a dozen more. I'll see you at lunch. Hank's planned a blow out celebration for all of us." She turned and left his office.

As Mackie looked at the journal again, anticipation and uncertainty churned in his stomach. He had not heard a word from Bill Baldwin since leaving the small stack of floppy disks at the front desk in the hotel. Surely this published data would at least corroborate some of his accusations. What Baldwin would do with this information, though, was less clear.

Mackie thumbed through *The Medical Weekly* until he reached the editorial section. Bold headlines proclaimed the potential of Anginex for new uses, written by the wiry endocrinologist from the NIH, Dr. Scott Hoffman.

* * *

In typical BioloGen fashion, the company spared no expense on the celebratory lunch. A tablecloth covered the conference room table on the third floor, with an ostentatious floral centerpiece befitting a country club. A local celebrity chef had prepared individual plates for the Anginex team members, complete with a celebratory New Year's theme. Pescatelli stood near the front of the room, greeting employees as they arrived. He had dressed down for the occasion in jeans and boat shoes, looking to Mackie like the Devil in denim.

Members of Team Anginex milled around the table, engaged in the excited chatter of big events. When it appeared that everyone had arrived, Pescatelli tapped a fork against his cocktail glass to garner everyone's attention. "First of all," he began, "let me congratulate all of you on your hard work. When I flew to Washington with Drs. Martin, Schofield, and McKay, we had one of the most promising NDA submissions in BioloGen history. To be able to submit a compound to the FDA that can prevent one of mankind's worst medical fears..." He paused, making deliberate eye contact with those standing around the table. "It's more than a dream come true for me."

Mackie sipped on a drink and maintained his silence. Clearly he was not the only one today who feigned ignorance about the lethal side effects of Anginex.

Pescatelli continued. "As the current issue of *The Medical Weekly* arrives in mailboxes around the country this week, word will spread about Anginex. Just this morning, I received a call from producers at Larry King Live and NBC Nightly News looking to schedule interviews about Anginex. Newspaper reporters have called by the dozens to get quotes for their stories. Later this afternoon, we will have a press conference downstairs about the drug. I encourage each of you to join us for the festivities."

As Pescatelli was speaking, Mackie saw Ms. Franks through the glass walls of the center conference room. She strode across the hallway with something pressed between her thumb and forefinger. She stepped into the room, quietly slipping the piece of paper from her hand into Pescatelli's. Had Mackie not been standing so close, he likely would have missed Pescatelli's reaction. A look of concern flashed across his face like a lightening bolt as he read the note. By the time he looked back at the Anginex team, he'd replaced the look with a broad smile. He lifted his cocktail glass. "A toast. To the people who make Anginex. May you market it so thoroughly that it becomes more common than aspirin and more consumed than vitamins. Cheers!"

The members of the Anginex team collectively raised their glasses and toasted their success.

"If you'll excuse me," Pescatelli said at last, "I need to return a phone call."

Mackie didn't see a trace of concern or even the slightest doubt on his boss's face as he turned and strode out of the room.

* * *

Pescatelli paced behind his desk with a cocktail glass in hand, crunching cubes of ice between his teeth. He waited. In the time it took him to return the phone call from Ms. Franks's message, his good humor had evaporated, leaving behind the residue of a foul mood that clung to him like a wet shirt. He stared at the lobby from his office window, watching workers prepare the building for the afternoon's press conference. A knock sounded on the door. "Come in!" he barked.

Ms. Franks quietly entered the room and shut the door behind her. "What happened?"

"There's a problem with Anginex," Pescatelli said, still staring out into the lobby. "Someone from *The Washington Post* knows what's going on."

"I should hope so," she said. "We're getting more publicity calls now than when you announced those results in Aruba."

"Don't be an idiot," Pescatelli said with his back still turned to Ms. Franks.

She gave a nervous laugh. "We must not be talking about the same thing."

Pescatelli whirled around and slammed his glass on the desk. Cubes of ice scattered to the floor. "Do you have the slightest idea what is going on?"

Ms. Franks looked away from Pescatelli's rage.

Before she could answer, he spoke again. "The New York office just called. Someone has leaked the full Anginex story— side effects, cover-up, all of it—to *The Washington Post*. They think the leak came from Cincinnati."

Ms. Franks didn't even have to be told what to do. She stepped out of Pescatelli's path, crossing behind his desk and reached into the deep desk drawer to his right. She pulled out the AT&T Videophone 2500 and adjusted the two inch screen. It took a few more minutes for her to set up the conference call. While she worked on it, Pescatelli's mind rifled through the potential sources of the leak and came to the same conclusion. No matter how he analyzed the situation, he felt certain that Mackie must be involved. He had no idea how Mackie had discovered the cover-up or how he'd investigated his suspicions. One thing was certain in Pescatelli's mind, though. This was a problem that would not go away unless he fixed it himself.

The Videophone alerted him to the caller waiting on the other end of the line. Pescatelli sat in his office chair, scooting forward to the phone so that the camera embedded in the device would capture his image. On the screen, he saw a conference table with a man in a tie clasping his hands as he leaned toward the camera. Two others flanked the suited man, but the narrowed focus of the camera limited Pescatelli's view of them. Having worked with this team before, however, Pescatelli knew he would first speak to the CEO of Bolten & Ferris Pharmaceuticals. Only after the big boss had vented his frustration would the Chief Financial Officer and the lawyer from risk management offer their opinions.

"You alone, Red?" the CEO asked without any introductions or small talk.

"Leslie Franks is in here, too," Pescatelli said.

"Get her out, then we'll start."

Ms. Franks nodded and slipped out of the room without a word.

"She's gone," Pescatelli said. "Tell me what the hell's going on."

The CEO leaned toward the camera and raised his voice, as if this would make him more intelligible to his colleague six hundred miles away. "I got a call from a source at *The*

Washington Post. They're working on a story from an unnamed industry insider about Anginex. We're not leaving this room until we have a clear understanding of the worst-case scenario based on this leak and what we are going to do about it."

The gangly Chief Financial Officer seated next to his boss reached for the video phone and adjusted the screen. "Here's the worst case scenario. First of all, convincing evidence is released that implicates BioloGen Pharmaceuticals in an Anginex cover-up. Next, the reporter discovers investments into BioloGen that skirted government regulators and are ultimately traced back to Bolten & Ferris Pharmaceuticals. Finally, the public blames Bolten & Ferris for the problems with Anginex, taking down two companies instead of one."

The CFO adjusted his glasses as he glanced at a notepad in front of him. "When that happens, our stock takes an irreversible hit. We'd likely file for bankruptcy protection and open ourselves up to a hostile take-over bid from one of our competitors." He took off his glasses and sat back in his chair, almost out of view of the Videophone camera. "That's your worst-case scenario for the company."

The lawyer from risk management swiveled the Videophone in his direction. "That fails to consider that we already have over a billion dollars earmarked for settlements for existing drugs on the market."

Pescatelli held his position at his desk, training his eye on the video screen. "Which means BioloGen could use that money to pay ten million bucks to each of the families affected in the Anginex clinical trials. No wrong is admitted in the settlement, of course, and we'd still be sitting on almost a billion dollars ready for the next legal threat. Our reputation may take a small hit, but the public has a short memory for things like this."

The lawyer shook his head, which to Pescatelli seemed jerky and robotic on the pixelated Videophone screen. "I say your worse case scenario is that Anginex gets FDA approval," the lawyer said. "That happens and you're going to have thousands of people at risk for drug-induced dementia. Once people connect the dots, you're looking at a class action lawsuit and some big-ass fines from the federal government. Especially if we have to ultimately pull Anginex off the market."

The video screen moved with a swift jerk to the CEO. "I don't buy it. Projected revenues from Anginex are in the billions a few years from now. Pull off a quarter of those profits as hush-money and you can shut anybody up with an out-of-court settlement."

Pescatelli shifted in his seat. Once he realized that his boss and his legal counsel had not offered any new arguments to answer his immediate concerns, he said, "Right now, I don't give a shit about downstream revenue. Screw the legal bills. I want to know what the hell I'm supposed to do over the next forty-eight hours to keep a lid on this leak!" He slammed his fist on the desk, jarring the Videophone from its location.

No one said a word after Pescatelli's tirade. The CEO centered the video camera on himself and ran the flat-side of his palm across his tie. He looked at the lawyer next to him and asked, "What about taking out the reporter?"

"Do you want a legal opinion on that?"

"I want some ideas on how to clean up this mess."

Answering an absurd question with a straight face, the lawyer said, "Taking him out is too risky, especially for a reporter that high-profile."

"A publicity counter-offensive?" the Chief Financial Officer offered.

"We've got a marketing team working around the clock on Anginex's image," Pescatelli said. "We would obviously use them to rebuff any bad press. Here's what I need to hear from you. Do I have the authority to plug the leak if I find it?"

Silence from the conference room in New York. Pescatelli

heard a pen scratching on paper. One of the men cleared his throat. The CEO glanced to his right, presumably at something scribbled on a notepad. Finally, he said to Pescatelli though the grainy distance of the Videophone, "You've already taken care of threats to Anginex in earlier trials. If you find that this leak is coming from within BioloGen, by all means, do whatever it takes to stop it."

Pescatelli pushed back from his desk. "I'll call you with the results." He then disconnected the conference call. Reaching for the other phone on his desk, he dialed the next number from memory. When Eddie answered on the second ring, Pescatelli simply said, "We've got an emergency situation in Cincinnati. I need you in my office as soon as you can get here."

CHAPTER FORTY

MACKIE APPROACHED KAREN after lunch. She had been practically manic during the catered meal, telling jokes and laughing at almost anything she heard. She acted like she'd just won the lottery. Based on her report of the anticipated revenue from Anginex, she may have been right. Mackie waited until everyone else had drifted out of the conference room to return to their jobs before approaching her. "Can I have a quick word?" he asked.

Karen winked at him. "You bet. Some place more private?"

Mackie ignored the comment. "I've got a question about all of the publicity for Anginex."

"You and everyone else." She dropped her napkin on her dessert plate and walked toward her office. Mackie followed her. "We've been getting non-stop calls from the press," she said, "asking for interviews and looking for quotes."

Mackie tried to gauge her mood, wondering about her exact role in the Anginex scam. He recalled the FBI's flow chart with Karen's picture off to the side of the family tree of suspects and the large question mark beside her image. The more Mackie considered the dynamics of the office, the more he felt sure she must be involved. Finally, when they walked into her corner office, he said what he'd come to say. "I got a call this morning from *The Washington Post*."

Karen raised her eyebrows. "What's a reporter calling you for?"

"I was hoping you could tell me." He steadied his hands as he spoke, falling back into the skills of self-control in crisis management that had been drilled into him during his surgical training. "This guy called with questions about Anginex."

"What'd you tell him?"

"I gave him the number for our press coordinator. I thought it was weird that someone called me directly. Is that common?"

Karen shrugged. "Who the hell knows? All those questions should go directly to our company spokesman, anyway. Every reporter knows that." Karen sat down in her office chair and leaned back. "There've been a ton of calls today. I think everyone's a bit overwhelmed right now. I've got some calls to return myself."

The intercom on her phone beeped, then Ms. Frank's voice came on. "Mr. Pescatelli needs you in his office."

Karen pointed to the phone. "See what I mean? Once you submit an NDA, the work just increases." She turned toward the intercom. "Tell him I'll be there in a minute."

"He's in no mood to wait today," Ms. Franks said. "He and Dr. Schofield are already waiting for you."

Karen gave Mackie a weary smile. "You, too, could have this responsibility some day. I'll catch up with you later."

Mackie stepped out of her office and turned down the hallway toward his own. He'd just initiated the end game for his remaining days at BioloGen.

* * *

Tim Styles stood at the entrance threshold to the intensive care unit, waiting for visiting hours to begin. Green and gold streamers hung from the unit clerk's desk. Behind the pulled curtain to Meredith's room, two sets of tennis shoes covered in blue booties moved at a workman's pace. Not frenzied. Not emergent. One small reassurance, Tim thought, on an otherwise frantic New Year's day.

Two nurses emerged from Meredith's room. One spotted Tim and waved him over.

He resisted the urge to sprint across the polished linoleum.

The nurse ushered Tim to one side of the bed as she began adjusting IV lines on the other side.

"How's she now?" Tim asked.

"The dialysis seems to have helped. She's still suffering from uremia—"

"The coma?"

"Right. But the doctor is encouraged she'll wake up, young as she is."

Tim took Meredith's hand, careful not to dislodge the IV. On one side of the bed, a machine the size of a dishwasher received the plastic tube from Meredith's mouth, freezing her lips in a surprised expression. Her chest rose and fell with the hiss of the ventilator. On the other side of the bed, another machine received lines of blood that snaked from plastic tubing in her arm. The nurse adjusted two round discs, which circulated the blood like a reel-to-reel tape recorder. Tim reached out and placed a finger on the plastic strips taping Meredith's eyelids shut.

"The eyes tend to dry out if we don't do that," the nurse observed.

Tim sniffled. "Any idea what…"

The nurse stopped her task. She placed her warm hand on Tim's arm. "We're almost certain it's not an infection. As hard as it is to admit this, sometimes we never find out."

Tim tried to pinch back a tear. He blinked three times. Then, he looked up and made direct eye contact with the nurse. "What's your best guess, though?"

The nurse never hesitated. "Kidney failure this rapid? I'd blame a medication."

* * *

Pescatelli stood in the corner of his office, waiting for Karen to arrive. An easel stood behind him, with photographs on it of all the BioloGen's employees arranged on a sheet of poster board. Ms. Franks paced in front of the bookshelves while Douglas sat behind Pescatelli's desk, picking at his fingernails.

Karen burst through the door. "Sorry I'm late."

Douglas looked up from studying his hand. "Good afternoon to you, too, Princess."

"What's up?"

"Let's get started," Pescatelli said. "The Bolten & Ferris CEO called me during lunch. Someone has leaked inside information regarding the BioloGen-Bolten connection and the falsified Anginex data."

Douglas dismissed the claim. "That's impossible."

Pescatelli continued. "A reporter from *The Washington Post* named Bill Baldwin is calling around for information. Apparently, he has internal documents to support the claims. I want to find out who's had access to what when it comes to Anginex."

"I think he's already contacted Mackie," Karen said. "He just told me that a reporter from *The Post* called him today, asking some questions about the NDA."

"And...?" Douglas asked.

"And he referred him to the BioloGen press coordinator."

"That's my boy," Douglas said. "Honest and well trained."

"Like you know about either one of those traits," Karen responded.

"Let's focus," Pescatelli said. He pointed to individual pictures on the poster board, putting either a black circle over their name or a big red X. "If the leak is coming from Cincinnati, I want to narrow down our list of possible sources. I think we can rule out most of our local pharmaceutical reps."

Douglas straightened in the desk chair, leaning forward on the desk. "Why?"

"They don't have access to any information that we don't give them." Pescatelli placed a big red mark over the individual photographs of the pharmaceutical reps. "What about the engineers?"

"First of all, ex-ing out the drug detailers seems premature," Douglas said. "Second of all, the engineers can do wonders with ADAM, but I doubt any of them could tell a difference between a trial publication and a pin-up."

Pescatelli didn't change his marks over the pharmaceutical reps, but he marked out several pictures of Douglas's engineering team.

The group continued to scrutinize each employee's picture. Fifteen minutes later, only seven pictures remained unmarked. Three of those people stood with Pescatelli in his office.

"It was Ms. Kiley, in the storage room, with the candlestick," Douglas said.

"Shut up," Karen said.

"As for the three of you in this room, you aren't stupid enough to leak company information," Pescatelli said. "You have nothing to gain from it and everything to lose." He marked a red X over the names of Karen Kiley, Douglas Schofield, and Leslie Franks. "That leaves four additional people from our office: Earl, the inside night security guard; Andrew, the intern who had unrestricted access to the NDA; Rita Martin; and Mackie McKay."

Karen shook her head. "I would narrow it down to only two. Can you honestly see Dr. Martin pulling the plug on what is probably her greatest contribution to medicine?"

"She's got one of the only keys," Ms. Franks pointed out.

"But no motive," Karen said. "Before today, I would have said to keep Mackie on the short list, too, but in addition to coming forward with being contacted by *The Post*, he's been under Ms. Franks' eye the whole time he's been here. He's had no time to do it."

"He's been working long hours," Ms. Franks said.

"He's a Type A personality who's been on the job for six months," Karen countered. "And he's got a personal stake in seeing Anginex make it to market."

"He doesn't have a motive," Douglas agreed.

"For once, Douglas is right," Karen said. "I don't see it."

"What about the night security guard?" Pescatelli asked.

"He's dumb as a bowl of nuts," Douglas said. "Think about it. That guy spends more time sleeping on the job than snooping around the building. If we didn't have additional perimeter security, Earl would be in over his head. Besides, I don't think he would even know what valuable documents look like."

"Earl is unreliable," Karen said. "I used to work late before other NDA submissions, and the only time I saw him was when he'd sit on his ass at the security desk, relying on the motion detectors to do his job."

"If he had a key, it could be plausible," Ms. Franks commented, "but I think he's more of an opportunist than an instigator. Maybe if he found a stack of incriminating documents sitting on his desk he might send them to a newspaper, but those kind of documents aren't lying around."

"And the intern, Andrew?" Pescatelli asked.

"Same thing," Ms. Franks said. "He's a bright kid, but you have to know what you're looking for in the NDA to have any useful information. We're talking about patients that were dropped from the study due to side effects."

"The dog that didn't bark," Douglas said. Turning to Karen, he said, "That's Sherlock Holmes, sweetheart."

"I've made sure that you could not tell just by looking at the charts what was missing," Ms. Franks concluded. "You would have to follow up with each patient to know there was a problem."

"Andrew knows the organization of the NDA as well as

anyone," Karen said. "But Ms. Franks is right. I don't think he has any idea what it all means. When I've been around him, he's either thanking me for including him in the Anginex project or staring at my cleavage."

"How's that different from the rest of us?" Douglas asked.

"He's not a sexist pig," Karen shot back.

"Give him time, my dear. He's still young." Douglas rubbed his chin and studied the poster board again. "So from our end, it looks like Rita Martin is the most likely candidate."

Pescatelli cracked his knuckles. "Can I act on that information?"

"For Christ's sake, Red, she's almost old enough to be your grandmother," Karen said.

"And smart enough to know what information to leak," Pescatelli said.

"We don't even know where the leak is coming from," Karen said.

"Listen up!" Pescatelli said, raising his voice. "If this information about Anginex goes public, we are going to lose a hell of a lot of money and quite possibly this entire operation." He jabbed a finger at the poster board. "That means all of these people could be out of a job, because one asshole leaked information to the press. When we identify who is responsible, I will contain the situation, even if it's Rita Martin. I don't give a shit if she's Ghandi's grandmother. And if it's Mackie, I'll personally nail his ass to the wall."

The room fell silent.

"What about the other clinical trial sites?" Douglas asked. "San Francisco? Houston? What about our guy in Bethesda?"

Pescatelli composed himself before he spoke. "We're working on that."

"And the research assistant who worked here on B-AGX-23? Lampley was his name? What ever happened to him?" Douglas asked.

"I said, we're working on it." Pescatelli turned toward the easel. "Karen, you talk to Andrew since you hired him. Leslie, you speak to Dr. Martin. Douglas, you deal with Earl. Stay late if you have to. Call me immediately if you identify the source of the leak."

"And Mackie?" Douglas asked.

Pescatelli didn't hesitate. "I'll take care of him."

CHAPTER FORTY-ONE

PESCATELLI STOOD ALONE in the middle of his office, waiting for a return phone call. He continued to stare at the activities in the lobby when the phone rang. He took the call on speaker phone. "Yeah?"

"I'm at the airport, Mr. Pescatelli, about to get a rental car," Eddie said.

"It's about damn time."

"Where do you need me?"

"My secretary dropped off a small gym bag at the lockers near baggage claim," Pescatelli said, giving him the relevant information and the location of the key. "Inside you'll find everything you need to identify the two employees."

"Addresses?"

"A picture of each of them is inside. An old black female and a young white male. It's not complicated. Once you've gotten the bag and the car, drive to the location listed inside. The rest of what you need will be there. Come see me once you've gotten it. At that time, I'll tell you which one is the target." Pescatelli walked to his wet bar and refreshed his drink. "Where are we with the other locations?"

"I spoke to our contacts in San Francisco," Eddie said, his voice crackling through the speaker on the phone. "Houston, too. Neither one claims to be the source of the leak, but they're looking into it."

"What about Bethesda?"

"Our guys's been off work for the last few days. I called his house, but I got his answering machine. His secretary thinks he may have gone out of town."

Pescatelli marched over to the phone, barely concealing his anger when he spoke. "When you're done in Cincinnati, I want you to deal with Scott Hoffman. Finish the job." He picked up the handset and slammed it back into its cradle. He yelled, "Leslie!"

His office door opened almost immediately. Leslie Franks stepped inside from her temporary desk right outside Pescatelli's office. "Yes?"

"Cancel the press conference for this afternoon. I want the entire Anginex team in the third floor conference room in half an hour. No exceptions," he said. "It's time to plug the leak."

* * *

Mackie walked back to his office from the break room. His mind raced as he planned his next steps that afternoon. He hardly noticed his colleagues. When he reached the marketing section of the third floor, Ms. Frank's stepped out of his office. She held something in her hand.

"I've been looking for you," she said. "Mr. Pescatelli has called another meeting for the Anginex team in the conference room. He's waiting for you so he can get started."

"What for?"

"I just deliver the messages, Dr. McKay," she said with a shrug. "Let's go."

He followed her to the conference room, his mind now fully alert. Even before he reached the meeting, he saw Pescatelli pacing in the front of the room. The chatter among Team Anginex revealed a combination of curiosity and frustration.

Mackie made his way to the back of the room. He declined to take any of the open seats.

Pescatelli surveyed the crowd before speaking. His eyes looked puffy from worry and fatigue. His shoulders seemed to sag under the weight of what he was about to say. Karen sat to Pescatelli's right, her hair scraped back into a ponytail. She sipped from a large cup of coffee as she stared at the table. Dr. Martin sat on the other side of Pescatelli, her glasses perched atop her head and her hands folded in her lap.

Pescatelli began. "During lunch, I received a call from a reporter, asking me to comment on anonymous claims that Anginex has been associated with some unreported bad outcomes." A murmur rippled through his small audience. "It should come as no surprise to any of you that we categorically deny these rumors. We all know the dedication required to produce a new drug and the tremendous resources needed to bring that drug to market. Not just financial resources, either, which are considerable, but the resources of your time and talents."

He shifted his weight as he spoke, keeping his voice under control. "I want you all to hear me say—although you should already know this—that BioloGen is committed to producing pharmaceuticals that set the industry standard for safety and efficacy. We will do whatever it takes to investigate these unfounded rumors about Anginex, working with the FDA to do the same."

Without saying another word, he turned his back on Team Anginex and strode out of the room.

Comments rippled through the team, a din of whispers like conversations in a concert hall after a virtuoso performance. With no other announcements, though, members of the team departed the conference room in groups of twos and threes, heading for their desks. Some had already started projecting ways to spin the news.

Dr. Martin remained seated at the table. She looked both betrayed and confused. Ms. Franks hurried out of the room with a stack of documents tucked under her arm. Karen walked over to Mackie, holding his car keys.

"What are you doing with those?" Mackie asked her.

"You must have dropped them," she said. "Ms. Franks handed them to me a second ago, right before Red spoke." Rather than giving them back to him, she said, "I've got some news of my own."

Mackie waited for her to continue, glancing at his keys in her hand. "Okay..."

"Hold on." She gave a deferential smile to Dr. Martin as she shuffled from the room, her head still down as she walked. A moment later, Karen said, "There's no easy way to tell you this." She paused, swallowed, then started again. "Red is considering pulling Anginex from FDA consideration. Not for good, mind you, but temporarily. Until these accusations blow over."

"But he just said—"

"I know, I know," Karen interrupted him. "This is a hard thing for him to do. It's a combination of his own pride and BioloGen's reputation that has prevented him from saying anything before now. He wants to reassure his employees that his company won't fold or abandon them at the first sign of a problem, but pulling back now gives us a chance to re-submit in the future."

"When's that going to happen?"

"We'll make the announcement tomorrow." She looked over Mackie's shoulder through the glass walls of the conference room, clearly distracted. "We'll deny the allegations, of course, and claim that they're a distraction to the company. I'm not worried about the spin on his decision. Just making it is the hard part."

Mackie stood in stunned silence. His ploy had worked.

Karen reached out to Mackie and lightly placed a hand on his arm. She bit her bottom lip, appearing to suppress a tear, and simply said, "Red wants to tell you himself. Now. In his office."

Mackie's heart rate surged. "You coming with me?"

"I'll catch up with you right after he talks to you." She turned at the doorway. "I'll leave your keys on your desk." She stepped from the center conference room, leaving Mackie alone.

* * *

The walk down the hallway to Pescatelli's office seemed even longer. Mackie paused outside the door. He heard movement inside the office. Not the excited movements spawned by major accomplishments but the heavy footsteps of frustration. In spite of that, Mackie steeled himself to receive the news. He knocked.

A voice came from behind the door, getting louder, "I thought I told you to—" Pescatelli swung the door open but stopped in mid-sentence when he saw Mackie. He only said, "You're early."

"Karen said you wanted to see me."

"Not yet."

"I'll come back."

"Don't. Let's get this over with." Pescatelli left the door open and returned to his desk.

Mackie stepped into the office. Most things looked as they had before, but an empty leather chair had been moved in front of Pescatelli's desk. One cocktail glass sat in front of Pescatelli. Mackie heard ice rattling against another one behind him. He turned toward the sound. Holding a bottle of liquor in one hand and a near empty glass in the other, a young man with a weathered face stared out the window, ignoring Mackie's presence.

"This is the promising young employee I've been telling you about," Pescatelli said to the man in the corner of the room. "Mackie, this is Eddie Fackler."

The man turned to peer at Mackie through hollowed eyes. Moisture from his drink glistened on his mustache. He wore an overcoat that seemed heavier than the weather required. Eddie set the glass down on the corner of the desk and nodded to Pescatelli. "Thanks for the drink." Turning to Mackie, Eddie smiled. "Maybe we'll run into each other again soon." He walked back into the hallway, closing the door behind him.

"Who's he?" Mackie asked.

"An old friend."

Mackie walked to the leather chair in front of the desk. He remained standing and steadied himself against it. Pescatelli now stood in front of the window, staring into the lobby. Mackie waited for him to say something, but more than a minute passed in silence. The only sound he heard was his boss' breathing.

Finally, Mackie asked, "What kind of problems with Anginex did that reporter ask you about?"

Pescatelli kept his back turned to Mackie. "You ought to know."

"I know a reporter called me this morning."

"And…"

"And nothing. I referred him to the right people who could answer his questions."

Pescatelli continued to pace his breathing, staring through his window overlooking the lobby the whole time. Trying to hold on. Or hold back.

"It's no secret Anginex had problems in the initial trials," Mackie said. "We talked about this, Red. More people than expected dropped out of the Phase One study—"

"Which you blamed on amyloid deposits."

"Which was a known risk with this class of drugs."

Mackie measured his own breathing. He had tried to raise this same idea with his boss last summer but never got that far in the conversation. "What I said was that other drugs like Anginex had problems like that."

"We never would have submitted the NDA if we knew Anginex was responsible for those five deaths," Pescatelli said.

"Five?" Mackie placed a steadying hand against the back of the chair. He had scoured the charts from the Phase One trial. Knew virtually every detail. Still, he could only track down four deaths. The fifth patient death—a murder—he'd heard about from the FBI.

"Our new drug application was completely transparent on those early...concerns."

"Since we're working with the FDA," Mackie said, "we should have nothing to worry about."

"We?"

"You hired me to help BioloGen launch the drug."

For the first time since this conversation began, Pescatelli turned to face Mackie. "I hired you to use your medical experience and your personal tragedy to lend additional credibility to Anginex."

"Credibility, Red? Or plausibility? Were you hoping answers from me would gloss over questions others might have?"

This was not the conversation Mackie had envisioned. Unless he measured his words, his days at BioloGen might be shorter than he expected. He pressed on.

"It's naive to expect that I wouldn't follow up on concerns I found," Mackie said. "But you'd have to be a fool to think the FDA would turn a blind eye, too."

"Who else have you been talking to?"

"The problems with Anginex are no secret."

"Was it in Washington? Is that when you leaked this story?"

Mackie balled his fists. It helped mute the tremble. How

much did Pescatelli *really* know? "Why did you ask me to come to your office? Are you firing me?"

"If it were only that easy."

Both men locked gazes across the desk. Pescatelli rocked back and forth on his heels. Mackie pressed against the chair. Neither spoke until Mackie finally said, "Are you going to pull the NDA?"

Pescatelli scoffed. "Who the hell told you that?"

"Karen said you wanted to tell me yourself."

Pescatelli gave a sarcastic laugh. "Not a chance."

Mackie's mouth turned bone-dry. He'd been set up. "You know you've got a problem with Anginex that needs to be addressed."

Pescatelli placed both palms on the desk, no longer rocking. He leaned toward Mackie. His shoulders tensed as he lowered his voice. "I've got a problem with assholes who can't keep their mouths shut."

Sweat slicked Mackie's palms. He considered what to say next. This entire conversation could have been avoided if he had either ignored the leads in Aruba or been more persistent with his concerns from the beginning. He should have told Pescatelli the results of his first trip to Louisville. Explained what had happened to Donnie Sims. If he had told him that there was a mistake somewhere along the way, maybe Pescatelli would have listened. Now, he tried to push all of that from his mind and focus on what he was about to say.

"Anginex has a deadly flaw and you know it. It's not just the death of *four* patients in the Phase Once study—maybe others not reported in the data. Dozens more died throughout the remaining clinical trials."

"And you know this because..."

"Because I did what you asked me to, Red."

"I asked you to market the hell out of a drug that's going to change the way we think about cancer."

"I told you the more I knew about the drug, the better I could sell it. Of course I know there's a problem with Anginex. You do too. But it's a problem that can be fixed. Until it is, though, Anginex has to be pulled from FDA consideration."

"Don't be an idiot," Pescatelli said. "Once you submit a new drug application to the FDA, you can't just take it back. What the hell do you want me to do? Call the FDA and say, 'Sorry guys. Our bad. Can we have a do-over'?"

Pescatelli had Mackie pinned in. He couldn't deny what he knew. Or how he knew it. "In the Phase Two study, ten more patients died after taking Anginex. Another twenty-one patients didn't finish the trial. In the Phase Three studies, the rate of confusion reported by those in the control group was *twice* that of those in the treatment group. To me, it looks like someone actually changed the assignments of the patients taking Anginex to make it look as if they'd been in the control group all along." Emboldened by the momentum of the truth, Mackie pressed on. "No one's going to question you if your patients taking placebo have the same rate of side effects as those taking the study drug. In fact, it makes your study drug look that much safer."

Pescatelli crossed his arms. "So what do you expect me to do about that, Sherlock?"

"I told you. Pull the drug from FDA consideration."

Pescatelli threw his head back and laughed. "That's ridiculous."

Mackie stood firm behind the chair. "If a million people take the drug in the first year, at least ten thousand people could be affected."

"And if I refuse?"

"You'll be exposed. And BioloGen will fold."

"And you'll be dead."

Pescatelli moved so quickly Mackie hardly had time to react. Red lunged across the desk at Mackie. Missed him. He grabbed an empty cocktail glass. Mackie ducked as Pescatelli hurled the glass across the room. It hit the bookshelf and shattered, knocking over books and breaking picture frames. "Did you leak the Anginex information to the press?"

"This has nothing to do with me." Mackie pressed against the back of the leather chair in front of Pescatelli's desk. "There's a flaw in the design of the drug."

"We've pampered you from the time you joined the company, and this is how you repay us? By trying to blackmail me? By going to the press with your bullshit story of tainted drugs?"

"Pull the drug, Freddie."

Pescatelli straightened his shirt, appearing to compose himself. He locked his gaze onto Mackie as he placed one hand on his desk. Then, bending at the waist, he reached into the drawer. He broke eye contact long enough to not have to grope for what he wanted in the drawer. Mackie stepped back toward the office door.

Pescatelli looked back up. "You're in over your head," he said, pointing the barrel of a gun straight at Mackie's chest.

CHAPTER FORTY-TWO

PESCATELLI CAME AROUND the desk, never wavering in holding the gun. He closed the gap between them with a few steps. Mackie didn't move. Both men stood staring at each other, alone in his office, until Pescatelli finally said, "You think you know what's wrong with Anginex? Show me."

"There's nothing to see," Mackie said, trying to maintain his composure with a gun inches from his chest. "It could be as simple as an impurity in the final product. Douglas would know."

Pescatelli lowered the gun slightly, then grabbed Mackie's shoulder. He pushed him back. When Mackie stumbled, Pescatelli closed the gap between them. He jerked Mackie around and pressed his weapon against the small of Mackie's back. "We're going to the basement. Once we get off the elevator, you're going to show me exactly how it is that you supposedly uncovered a problem with Anginex."

He reached around to open the office door then shoved Mackie into the hallway. As before, no one else was in sight. Pescatelli marched Mackie to the bank of elevators. Taking a key with his free hand, he inserted it into the only slot available below the elevator call button. Engraved red letters below the lock said *For Emergency Use Only*. Moments after turning the key, the elevator arrived.

Pescatelli forced Mackie onto the empty car and inserted his emergency key into the panel near the door. Overriding all other call requests, Pescatelli pushed the button for the basement.

Mackie's mind searched through the possibilities of his escape. He had little choice but to cooperate, but what Pescatelli was asking of him couldn't be achieved. Mackie had not been in the basement of the building since his first month on the job. He knew that the basement contained a tremendous storage room that connected the molecular libraries to ADAM using the sliding track of EVE's crane. Even knowing the layout of ADAM, though, Mackie didn't know where to begin looking for answers or for proof.

The elevator doors opened and Pescatelli pushed Mackie into the hallway. The generator rumbled above them, the sound muted by the low ceiling. Pescatelli turned to his left and swiped his card in the security reader at the storage room door. Behind him, Mackie heard the elevator door close.

When Pescatelli opened the storage room, the noise from the generator became louder. Mackie glanced down the hallway toward ADAM. He didn't have an access code to break free and run toward the room. Even if he did, Mackie doubted he could overpower his boss. Pescatelli still trained his gun on Mackie.

Pescatelli opened his mouth to speak, but he didn't get the words out. An explosion rocked the building. Mackie felt the vibration that rocked the building. Then, the generator stopped as the hallway plunged into darkness.

* * *

Eddie Fackler sat in his rental car by the entrance to the BioloGen headquarters. From there he could see the edge of the building and the trunk of the intended car. Hedges around the outside generator obscured the parking lot as well as the rest of the vehicle. Not that it mattered. He could see what he needed to in order to ensure that the job was done.

Only one car had come through the gates in the last few minutes. No one had left.

Eddie smiled as he glanced at his watch. He would wait as long as necessary for confirmation.

The force of the explosion shocked even him.

Although he had tested the device multiple times, Eddie had never had the opportunity to actually wire a car bomb before today. The concept was simple and made easier by the model of the car. All he needed to detonate the bomb was for someone to turn the key to start the engine. Even though he didn't actually see him get into the car, he assumed the young hot-shot Pescatelli had introduced him to had tried to flee. He'd obviously underestimated the effect the gasoline would have on the explosion, though, because even from the edge of the property, he felt the concussive impact of the explosion. His car windows rattled. Flames shot out from the side of the building, causing a second explosion from the power generator. No way the building would quickly recover from that, even if the emergency generator was spared.

Mr. Pescatelli said he wanted to plug the leak, Eddie thought as he started his car. From what he could see through the smoke and debris, he had delivered more than a plug. He'd given his boss at least one decisive kill.

* * *

Mackie didn't know what had exploded. Horns blared overhead, alerting the BioloGen engineers to a power failure. The noise echoed off the walls and floors, sounding like a staccato cry for help. A red light flashed above the elevator door. Mackie didn't hesitate. He lunged forward, slamming into Pescatelli with a linebacker's intensity and knocking him to the floor.

"Son of a bitch," Pescatelli yelled just before his head slammed against the concrete.

Mackie pushed up from the floor, groping for anything he could use to defend himself. He heard Pescatelli struggling to get up, too. Mackie kicked him in the gut, finding unexpected pleasure in the sound of Pescatelli's scream.

The lights along the floor flickered. Mackie heard the emergency generator groan to life. One emergency light flashed in the basement. Like watching a dancer in a strobe light, Mackie saw Pescatelli's jerking movements on the floor, first writhing in pain and then, several beats later, reaching for something.

Mackie spotted Pescatelli's gun. He bolted, deciding to head deeper into the basement storage vaults.

"You're a dead man!" Pescatelli yelled.

Mackie ducked behind one of the storage closets, pressing his body between the cool metal exterior and the concrete wall. As he reached out to feel his way, his hand bumped against a metal box with a joystick protruding from it. He immediately recalled his first week at work, and he realized that he now gripped the manual controls for EVE.

Without another warning, Pescatelli fired the gun. Mackie heard metal dent and glass shatter. Pescatelli fired again.

Mackie reached for the control panel. Two large buttons flanked the joystick. He pushed the green one, engaging the gears of the crane overhead. He looked up. With each flash of the strobe light, EVE moved closer. Mackie cranked down on the joystick. EVE's arm reached into the storage room directly below it, extracting a glass container the size of Mackie's car. Ten thousand test tubes sparked under the strobe light. Any one of those molecules in those test tubes might contain the next miracle cure for a disease.

At that moment, though, Mackie only cared that they might save his own life.

Pescatelli looked as the crane moved overhead, and then he turned and fired three shots in rapid succession at Mackie. Glass exploded above Mackie's head and rained down on him. A bullet ricocheted off the wall beside him. A fourth shot ripped through his left upper arm. Mackie screamed as the pain seared up his entire shoulder. Blood splattered his face and his shirt. He reached out and slammed his good hand against the red button and ducked below the metal box.

EVE's metal jaws opened. The enormous container in its grasp dropped, causing an explosion that resembled a wrecking ball smashing through a window. Thousands of glass shards from test tubes shot across the room, some coming to rest at Mackie's feet.

Then, the room became silent. The horn stopped blaring, although the emergency lights continued to flash. Mackie listened for any sound from Pescatelli. He heard nothing.

He stepped out from behind the storage closet. In the center of the walkway, Mackie saw the remains of the glass test-tube container amidst a slick sheen of spilled molecules. Trickles of blood swirled in the molecular soup, fed by the gaping wound in Pescatelli's head.

𝒞HAPTER FORTY-THREE

Summer 1994

𝒜LMOST SIX MONTHS had passed since the debacle at BioloGen finally ended. Mackie had moved back home to Nashville with Sarah and Reagan. For the last few weeks, he felt as if he'd never left. The Chairman in the Department of Surgery had welcomed him back without reservation. Apparently satisfied that the sabbatical had worked, he began scheduling Mackie surgical cases and clinic patients. On this particular morning, Mackie was walking out of the room of his last clinic patient of the morning when his nurse stopped him in the hallway.

"There's a person in the lobby who says he needs to speak to you," the nurse said.

"A patient?"

"He didn't say."

Mackie kept walking toward his office. "Tell him I'll see him after lunch."

The nurse hesitated. "The man said he'd prefer to see you now. He said he was an old friend from Washington, D.C."

Mackie paused. Only a few people he knew would travel that far to visit him, and none could be classified as an old friend. He set his chart on the counter and walked toward the clinic lobby. As soon as he stepped through the door, a man looked up from reading what appeared to be that day's edition of *The Washington Post*. "Dr. McKay," he said. "You're a hard man to track down."

Mackie turned to see Agent Brian Aiken as the only man sitting in the waiting room. "I'm in the phone book," Mackie said.

"Interesting article in *The Washington Post* in January," Agent Aiken said. "You do know some could construe the information provided for that article as interfering with an FBI investigation."

Mackie nodded. "I saw that, too." Measuring his response, he said, "The paper later reported that Dr. Scott Hoffman disappeared shortly after that story broke. Have you tracked him down, too?"

"We don't comment on active investigations." Aiken shifted in his chair. "I was hoping that you might have some information that would help us find the source of that newspaper leak."

Mackie shrugged. "I'm not sure what you want me to say. The drug application was pulled from FDA consideration. BioloGen was vilified in the press for three months before the media frenzy died down. And the guy you identified as a key player in the drug scam hasn't even been found yet."

"Karen Kiley died in a car bomb intended for you," Aiken said.

Mackie paused, still stung by the memory. "I don't think there is more that I can add that hasn't already been investigated by the press."

Agent Aiken folded his newspaper and stood. He handed Mackie a business card. "I can see you're a busy man, Doc, so I won't keep you. My direct number is on there. Call me if you think of any more information that might aid us in our investigation."

Mackie watched Aiken walk out of the front door and into the parking lot. He placed Aiken's business card in the breast pocket of his scrubs and returned to his clinic. Sarah would be meeting him downstairs soon. Taking time for a meal together was only one part of their reconciliation ritual. Plus, he didn't want work hanging over his head while they ate. Mackie turned from the waiting room and back to the hospital. He had medical records to finish working on before going to lunch.

* * *

July in Belize looked about like January with bright sunshine, blue skies and warm, clear water. Tourists laughed with one another off the side of the boat, their masked faces bobbing up and down in the water with the gently moving surf. Scott Hoffman sat in the captain's chair, reapplying sunscreen. Even seven months after arriving on the island, he still had a tendency to burn.

He glanced at the depth finder on his boat and then called out to the snorkelers. "There's a school of fish coming on the starboard side of the boat that you guys should check out." When the tourists dove under for a look, Hoffman sat back in his chair and closed his eyes. He never thought retirement would be so much fun.

He had bought a boat a month after arriving on the island of Caye Caulker, Belize. He had originally planned on taking tourists to view the manatees. At fifty bucks a person, though, he didn't have many takers. Even when he lowered his price to twenty-five dollars, the tourists came but the manatees hid from the boats.

After two months, he abandoned the manatee business and got into custom snorkeling tours. The money was better, the coral reefs didn't move, and he didn't have to do much work. The ideal retirement.

At the end of each day, he docked his boat at The Sand Box Bar and Grill. Today, he planned on enjoying another late afternoon meal of conch fritters and beer before he took in the island sunset. Late afternoons were his chance to catch up on current events in America and throughout the world. Although newspapers were scarce in Caye Caulker, the satellite dishes at the bar usually kept him current. He walked into the open-air restaurant, still clad in his trademark tacky t-shirt and straw hat from the boat.

"Hey, buddy," the Sand Box's owner said as Hoffman walked inside. He shifted a plate of food to one side to shake Hoffman's hand, then reached into his pocket and handed Hoffman a folded piece of paper. "I got a message for you."

"About what?"

"Probably some tourist wanting to book a date with you." The owner offered him a taste from a basket of appetizers.

Hoffman popped two conch fritters into his mouth. "What time did he call?" he asked with his mouth full.

"Almost half an hour ago. He said not to bother calling him back. He'd just catch up with you later."

Hoffman glanced over his shoulder, estimating he had at least thirty minutes before sunset. "I'll have a drink and give him a call," he said.

"Suit yourself."

Hoffman walked to the bar and reached over the counter for the phone. A half dozen tourists and a few regulars already had a head start on Happy Hour. Hoffman didn't try to strike up a conversation with any of them. He glanced at the phone number on the folded paper. Odd to get a call from a local number, he thought. Just as quickly he reasoned that maybe someone at a local hotel wanted a last-minute booking. He dialed the number and waited. It took a moment for the line to connect. At first, the background noise prevented him from hearing the person on the other end of the line.

"Hello?" Scott Hoffman said. "This is Caye Caulker Tours. What can I do for you?"

"So glad you called back," a voice said, deep and resonant with malice. "Nice shirt."

Hoffman jerked up his head, looking over both shoulders. It wasn't until he looked to his right that he saw him. At the other end of the bar, gripping the handset of another phone, sat a smiling Eddie Fackler.

ℭHAPTER FORTY-FOUR

Present Day

ℳACKIE TURNED THE disk over in his hand once more. He could just ignore it. Go back to his teaching cases. His dog. His quiet evenings at home. What could the FBI *really* do after all this time? But deep inside, Mackie knew that Aiken wouldn't forget. He would continue to remind Mackie, in one subtle way or another.

He fingered the plastic disk once more. Glanced at Bill Baldwin's obituary. Stared at Special Agent Brian Aiken's card.

A hell of a gamble to ignore it all.

Mackie reached for the phone.

~THE END~